CAROOM'S RAID

David C. Brown

CAROOM'S RAID

by

David C. Brown

The adventures of a modern man plunged into an alternate-history parallel world of Civil War era technology, slavery, drugs, and competing colonial empires.

David C. Brown

International Standard Book Nr: 978-0-9997994-1-3
Library of Congress Control Nr:
1 2 3 4 5 6 7 8 9 0

Cover Design: Mark R. Hayes
Editing: Molly S. Brown
www.DavidCBrownAuthor.com

Previously Published Works:
Concrete Girl
Serendipity Hollow
Gap Hollow
Sandlick Hollow
The Trashman's Daughter
Donnelly's War
Boilermaker
Nitro Wild

♠ Scott Depot, WV ♠

Chapter 1

"Did you recover the safe?"

Amy Caroom was referring to the safe from the Orleans Queen, a riverboat that she had destroyed.

"Have you seen it?" Rex Knight asked. He had salvaged the vault from the wreckage on his return from collecting the winter sloe nuts crop at Panther Creek. "It's a monstrosity. A heavy cubical iron box fashioned from layers of riveted iron plates. It's about the size of a large whiskey barrel with a round, flush-fitting, iron door."

"Is the door about thirty centimeters in diameter with a brass dial combination lock?"

"Yes and it's very heavy. Six of us were required to move the thing. It must weigh three-hundred kilograms," Rex said. "No one knows the combination."

"I'm familiar with them. My father had several of those Hittite safes," Amy said. "The door has six steel rods inside that lock it. No one has ever opened one without the combination."

"It can't be drilled?" He asked. She shook her head.

If he were still on Earth, he'd open it. All he'd need was a plasma arc. Alas, he wasn't. His modern world had vanished, gone without a moment's warning. It was the strangest thing. On that fateful day, he had been surveying, staking out the driveway to reach a new house site on a ridge overlooking Charleston. The complication was

1

laying out the new drive to bypass a large sandstone boulder the property owner wanted left undisturbed. He was beside the rock when the cold blackness struck.

The boulder was still there when he regained consciousness. It looked the same. The topography of the ridge and valley looked the same. The city had vanished. Now, a forest of massive old oak and chestnut trees blanketed the ridge and river valley. He had no idea on what had occurred. Judging by the scorched twisted remains of his Topcon total station, that he had survived was the wonder. Later he had learned the inhabitants called the Earth like planet Erden.

He had been fortunate in that the inhabitants where he rematerialized were Wapiti. They were an amalgamation of the aboriginal tribes, Clovis, fugitives like Rex, Prussian adventurers, and even a few Ichneumons. The diversity provided cover for him. He looked like a large Prussian. The Wapiti spoke a lingua franca of the indigenous Clovis language, English, and German that he was able to understand. It also meant other Earthlings in the past had been teleported and survived. And like him, they had realized bemoaning about the irreversible event was futile and had set about making a life for themselves in this alien world.

"Put the safe in my lab," Amy said, snapping his thoughts back to the matter at hand. "I'll work on opening it while you finish with the nut processing."

Amy was smart, but he doubted even a mathematical prodigy could reason out the safe's combination of five two-digit numbers. Rex had heard the nonsense that she was a witch. Maybe she planned to use magic on the safe. For sure, nothing else available in this primitive world was apt to open it.

"You're serious," he said, his skepticism escaping.

"Be nice, or I may not tell you what's in the safe," she said, smiling. She certainly acted confident as they waited for the Mischief to complete its docking maneuvers at Smithtown.

"Okay, it can rust in your lab as well as at the council office. I'll have the iron monstrosity left at your place."

Besides, he thought, maybe the challenge would help her put behind the Orleans Queen fiasco. The yellowing blue bruises and brown scabs on her face and arms offered grim verification that the beautiful woman's curiosity could eclipse her common sense. Three days earlier, at River Point, Amy had boarded her father's docked steamboat. She did that despite knowing he was offering a 10,000 D-mark reward for her head. She had wanted to inspect the condensate pump, see if it had failed as she had predicted. Instead, the crew had seized her. The Wapiti and Rex had rescued her, but their effort had resulted in several deaths that he suspected weighed on her conscience.

"What's this plan you wanted to discuss?" Rex asked as they watched the Mischief crew load the safe into a wagon. He feared he knew, but on the off chance she had found a supplier of metal working machines in Prussia, he asked.

The lack of manufacturing and heavy industry made the Wapiti businesses and development dependent on Prussian and Ichneumon industries for machines, metal tools, chemicals, and finance. The local blacksmith forges were inadequate for the maintenance needs of the developing steam age, mining, and timbering. Other than wood, salt, whiskey, and soap, most consumer goods came from foreign manufacturers, even gunpowder. Amy wanted to change that dependency. Otherwise, foreign interests, like her despicable father, would in the end control the Wapiti's land and wealth.

Their disagreement wasn't about the need for a local heavy machine shop or Amy's ability to make a success of the enterprise. Her design of a much-improved battery to power the proposed dot-dash wire that Rex knew as a telegraph proved the inquisitive woman brimmed with energy and ideas. Any machine shop run by her would be a success. The concern was with her plans for obtaining the equipment.

"Are we still partners?" Amy asked.

Talk about a loaded question. Rex nodded.

"Good, after you deliver the cargo at Delta, take me to Orleans. I'm going to collect the shop tools, lathes, drills, and that obsolete milling machine my dear father promised me in exchange for not contesting the boiler patent."

Ah Christ, Rex thought, *how can such an intelligent person be so blind?*

"It's about a bit more than collecting on a promise. Let's not forget Cinnabar's cocaine operation. We all know how that turned out."

Rex couldn't understand the man's loathing for his daughter. Then again, he didn't understand the misogynist mindset. Regardless, he couldn't allow her again to disregard the danger the man's animosity represented to her safety.

"What about the dead-or-alive reward? What more proof do you need to understand that your father had always intended for you not to return from Panther Creek? Now you want to confront him on his home turf?"

"I'm not asking. I'm taking the equipment. So are you going to help, Herr Knight, or do I need to find another mercenary?"

She ought to be more tactful to the man who had just saved her from her Orleans Queen foolishness, but Amy had seen what Rex had accomplished in Panther Creek. And she had listened to the Wapitis talking about his exploits in the Donnelly war. He was a man inclined to audacious actions, if he thought the goal worthwhile. Clearly, he had no appreciation for how scarce this heavy metalworking equipment was outside of Prussia. Amy didn't yet know how she would pull off her raid, but she hoped it didn't wreck their developing relationship. She liked the man.

"Well that's what you'll need," Rex said, "Plus an army. Be sensible, woman. No piece of iron is worth dying over. You're the smartest person I've ever known. You have to know it would be suicidal to sail into Orleans Bay and demand the machinery."

"It's no crazier than you and that girl attacking the Salt Furnace stockade."

"That was a thought out action, not some heedless attack," he said, knowing it had indeed been reckless. "You'd be operating blind with no idea of what to expect in Orleans. Not to mention the problem of loading heavy machines. I figure a milling machine would be a barge load by itself. Hell, you'd need a crane to lift it. You think Purnell's men are going to provide machines to help you steal their boss's equipment and iron?"

"We'll think of something," she said, trying a smile to soften his dark look. "Those machines will make the Smithtown Boat yard into a serious competitor to Purnell's yard. It's worth the risk. Please consider it."

"You're mad. Show them where to put the safe. I have to deliver the cargo to Salt Furnace." He was exasperated with her, turned, and jogged back to the Mischief without so much as a goodbye, only, "I have bills to pay."

Well, her smile hadn't worked, but he hadn't absolutely refused and his comments about the milling machine weight seemed encouraging. At least he had been thinking about Orleans. But first, she needed to open the Orleans Queen's safe. The Wapiti crew, along with Rex, hoped it contained gold and silver they could divide among themselves.

The Orleans Machine Works where Amy had worked used a Hittite safe for storing design drawings and other important papers. She knew the combination of that safe and the combination of the Hittite in her father's office. That knowledge was thanks to the Prussian crew that delivered her father's new safe, requesting her help on the setup of the safe.

Those Hittite safe combinations used five sets of numbers between zero and ninety-nine. The combination on the Orleans machine shop's Hittite was 12-34-67-5-91. Amy learned the company used 12-34-67-5-99 as the factory combination on all those models of their safes. As technician had explained, the company expected the customer to change the factory's test combination with their own secret combination. He had then shown her and Purnell's office manager the tedious process of changing the combination.

As Amy expected, her father didn't trust any of them. Instead, after sending everyone else away, Purnell told her to change the last number to 75 as he watched the process. He then told her that he'd finish the task later. A month later, she had a chance to check the safe's combination and learned the combination was unchanged. She hoped the Orleans Queen's captain had been as lazy.

"Well, Hokee, let's see if I have the magic," Amy said. She dialed in Hittite's factory combination, 12-34-67-5-99. That combination didn't work and she started from 0 and worked towards 99. An hour later of turning the brass dial, warming her feet on Hokee, and two cups of tea, the safe door opened on 12-34-67-5-89.

Winter would freeze the upper Erie River and stop boat traffic above the junction of the Erie with the Great Western River. To beat the ice, the Mischief was not stopping at dark, as was the custom of boats traveling on the river and riding the center of the river to take advantage of the fastest currents. Rex's goal was to reach the mouth of the Erie River at Port Delta in six days, sell his cargo of winter sloe nuts to the Atlantic Tobacco Company, and return to Smithtown before the river froze over.

However, Rex wasn't optimistic his schedule would survive. Amy had demanded to go with them. He could hardy refuse her request, after she had opened the Orleans Queen safe. That feat, along with her destruction of Purnell's steamboat, had renewed the gossip that she was a witch, one that knew powerful magic.

After his not explainable experience of switching worlds, Rex wasn't so dismissive of magic, but in these cases, he believed brainpower accounted for her success. Which was why he couldn't understand her insistence on that suicide mission into Orleans. He had been clear that allowing her to ride along to Port Delta didn't change the fact they were not going to Orleans.

"We'll see," had been Amy's response.

The little side wheeler tug was pushing four of those wooden barges used to ship coal. Rex had enclosed two of them to protect the 1,600 cases of the bagged nuts from the weather. The other two barges in the string he had filled with coal to save money and avoid having to stop for boiler fuel. To lend a commercial air to the boat, the crew had removed the brass cannon and stored it out of sight in the coal bin. To explain their presence to curious onlookers, he had hung large banners "Panther Creek Nut Company" on the both sides of the enclosed barges. He figured advertising never hurt. The crew had also fixed a small room in the port barge for Amy, the lone female aboard.

The Mischief made a brief stop at the Ichneumon army's fort at Hickory Ridge to deliver a gift for the Ichneumon garrison commander, General Mehta, a case of the salted winter sloe nuts and a case of Simpson's aged whiskey. Rex wanted to glean the latest intelligence about conditions down the Erie River and the attitude of the Ichneumon Empire towards Wapiti traders. The general welcomed him.

"I heard the Orleans Queen was sunk above Panther Creek. What was that about?" General Mehta asked while nipping the end of a cigar after finishing a second bag of nuts. "By the way, those nuts are excellent. Be sure to give the Port Delta commander a case. General Bezdek loves winter sloe nuts."

They were standing alone on the fort's wall overlooking the dock area. Rain was threatening, but the general didn't seem concerned about getting wet. Rex reckoned the Ichneumon commander was more concerned about others overhearing their conversation. He was glad to discover the cannon he was leaning against was unloaded. War apparently wasn't imminent.

"Purnell's thugs had kidnapped several Wapitis. They were fleeing us when the Orleans Queen boiler exploded." Rex switched sides with the general to avoid his cigar smoke.

"That section of the river around River Point is very hazardous. How many boats have been sunk, four?"

"Well Amy is always saying boilers are dangerous."

"Ah, the Caroom girl, such a beautiful woman," General Mehta said. The old soldier gave Rex a knowing look, before adding. "I heard her father was offering a ten thousand D-mark reward for her capture. Was she on that boat? What happened to her?"

"She's here, on the Mischief." The news caused the general to shake his head.

"Do you happen to know a bandit called Apophis?" Rex asked as he felt the first raindrop.

"I've seen him. Was he involved?"

He nodded, but didn't elaborate.

"Then you already know he's a murderous bastard. The rumor is that he is also a cannibal." Rex's doubtfulness must have shown, for the general added. "At least four Ichneumon traders have told me that and the man is missing his left ear. He's one of those big blond Prussians. He looks a lot like you. Feel free to kill him."

The general then cautioned Rex to avoid Bone Valley, explaining General Bezdek had severely reprimanded the fort's commander for allowing a group of Wapiti to steal Herr Purnell's property, slaves.

"That garrison hates all the Wapiti and might use your boat for a target. Your bigger personal concern should be Prince Cherukuru. I've heard he intends to offer a fifty thousand D-mark reward for your head."

"Fifty thousand!" The news stunned him for a moment. "Do we have a problem?" Rex asked, wishing he had his revolver. The fort's gate guard had it. He hoped he had judged the general's character correct.

"Not with me," the commander said. "After all, you salvaged my son's career, maybe even saved his life. But the lower Erie River is full of evil bastards, so a Rex Knight should be careful. The larger worry is war."

"The Wapitis aren't planning to attack anyone."

Could the Ichneumons plan to attack River Point? He was starting to feel exposed in a fort with hundreds of Ichneumon soldiers.

"I'm referring to the Prussian plan to seize control of the Erie River," General Mehta said. He blew out a cloud of smoke. "These local Clovis cigars aren't bad." He offered one to Rex who declined.

"As to the coming war," the general continued while pocketing the cigar, "As long as the Ichneumon army holds the fort at Delta, it will control access to the Erie River and the middle of the continent commerce. The Prussians can't allow that if they hope to expand their eastern coastal territories westward, so there'll be another war."

"Maybe so, but how can your emperor hope to hold the land since the Clovis, Wapitis, Prussians, and mutts like me, outnumber the Ichneumons twenty to one. And for sure, this land doesn't need more turmoil. I'm not, nor are the Wapitis interested in more war. What about the Erie River neutrality treaty?"

"The construction of our forts along the Erie made that accord irrelevant." General Mehta appeared amused by Rex's concern. "Look friend, the Prussian emperor hasn't shared his plans with me, but I expect hostilities within a year. You should focus on the business opportunities."

"Conflict might be good for undertakers and cemeteries, but not my business. I best get back."

"One more thing," the general said. "You and I both know fate is a fickle creature in war. I propose we each pick a password to authenticate our communications. If we need to contact the other, the password will help ensure the request for a meeting is legitimate."

"You think it might come to that?" The general nodded. "It can't be a complicated code."

"I agree, but we just need to use it one time, to arrange a meeting. I'll sign Ares," the general said.

"Okay, I'll sign, Indira," Rex answered. They shook hands and parted.

Chapter 2

The Mischief's crew thought the general's news that the Bone Valley garrison harbored hostile intent toward Wapiti traders, a good reason to stay in the middle of the river and steamed on.

"That's a dismal-looking place, and those solders look unwelcoming," Amy said. Unlike other small settlements they had passed, where people waved, the soldiers and workers just stared as they steamed past.

"He also told me to. . ." Rex said, before remembering too late, who his audience was.

"What? What did he say?" She looked concerned. He didn't want her to think it involved her.

"The general said there was a rumor that you weren't the only one with a wanted poster," he hedged. They were on the bench in front of the pilot house with Hokee under the bench.

"Purnell put a reward on your head! Why?" Amy asked.

"Not Purnell, the Ichneumon prince, and hold your voice down. I don't want everyone to know," Rex said, looking to see who was near enough to hear.

"Prince Cherukuru, that disgusting creature, you should have shot it."

"And leave those women in Bone Valley?" The Wapiti had ransomed the Ichneumon prince for their women held at the cruel saline works and a two-million D-marks payment.

"Well there was that," Amy said. "So what's your head worth?"

"Mehta heard fifty thousand."

"There is a fifty thousand D-mark reward out for you?" The amount make her gasp, but she added, "You can't go to Delta. There're Ichneumon soldiers everywhere."

"My business is with the tobacco company, not the Ichneumon army. No one in Port Delta knows me. We'll be in and out before anyone's the wiser."

"So it's okay for you to go into your enemy stronghold with a fifty thousand D-mark reward on your head, but it's stupid for me to go into Orleans with a ten thousand D-mark reward."

"No one knows me in Port Delta. Everyone knows you and the Mischief in Orleans. Besides I have no choice, I have to deliver the winter sloe and collect the money." She shook her head, not agreeing.

Rex changed the subject. "The general told me Apophis had a missing ear. That marauder from the Orleans Queen crew that you shot on the riverbank was a missing an ear. Was he Apophis?"

"We're not finished on the other matter," she said. "But to answer your question, I never thought so. The man, though a Prussian, wasn't near as large as the man I saw cranking up the front ramp, who I thought was Apophis."

Rex was aware the Ichneumons like to cut off body parts as punishment, so perhaps a thug missing an ear wasn't that unusual of a sight down the Erie River.

"I'll bet Captain Dalporto knows Apophis," Amy added.

Rex agreed. He planned to flag down and board the Clovis Belle when they met it on the Erie River. Captain Dalporto should be well along on his return trip from Port Delta to River Point. Rex was anxious for news after Amy's discovery in the safe and General Mehta's warning. She found thirty-six thousand D-marks in somewhat sodden paper currency and a letter, still legible, from Purnell to the captain. It ordered him while in Wapiti territory, to find or commission a drawing of Rex Knight. Also, he wanted the captain to learn if the Wapiti military leader had any other distinguishing marks, scars, and tattoos that would help identify him. Apparently, the Ichneumon prince couldn't remember what Rex looked like well enough to describe him to an artist.

"A reward poster without a face isn't effective. I'll go by the name, Friedrich Burgdorf. I'll be safe." She didn't agreed, but said no more on the subject.

The morning the Mischief arrived at the confluence of the Great Western and the Erie promised to be one of those clear, cool, autumn days that reminded Rex of football. He was relaxing on the front deck bench under the pilothouse stairs, enjoying the sunrise, and watching the approaching waterfront of Westport when Amy emerged from her small room on the port barge.

The crew that loaded the wood cases of bagged winter sloe nuts at Salt Furnace, at his instructions, had left a three-by-four-meter space inside the outer wall of stacked cases. With the tarps that covered the loaded barge, Amy had a small room for her bedding and some privacy. Pleased with the room, she had commented, more than once, on the pleasant scent of the beeswax used to seal the cases.

No slovenly hag disguise today. Instead, Amy wore a set of those yellow buckskin pants and vest favored by the Wapitis with a gray cotton tee shirt. The outfit showed her delightful figure to advantage. Rex wondered if she got cold at night and realized that scoundrel, Hokee, was in all probability warming her bed, the lucky mutt. Captain Malik yelled for him.

13

"Westport is a bit lawless, but its markets have fresh bison," the captain said, as Amy greeted them. "I'd like to make a brief stop and get a half side. I'm tired of salt pork and eel."

From the pilothouse, they could see the ramshackle collection of market stalls behind the wharfs. Unlike Hickory Ridge's market, horses of all sizes and shapes seem to be the leading commodity for sale. Other than a three small skiffs, there were no riverboats docked. The Mischief was the lone steamboat in the area. The two barges with cut stone blocks by the new wooden wharf at the fort construction site meant the Ichneumon engineers had a steam-powered boat.

"Okay, we'll stop for a short period," Rex said, "Send Kyle. I want you to stay with the ship and post a guard. I'm going to inspect the fort construction project."

She wanted to know what he planned for a disguise.

"I'm a retired Prussian feldwebel working for the Wapiti Council. Call me Friedrich Burgdorf." Amy studied him for a moment and then nodded in agreement.

"It might work," Amy said. "But you're gambling the reward offer isn't yet public and the tobacco men are unaware of it."

"Captain Dalporto will know if the reward has been posted. With the Prussian navy in the Port Delta harbor, the Ichneumon garrison ought to be concentrated on that threat, not some Wapiti farmers selling nuts. Besides they don't know what I look like."

"It'll still be dicey. Don't underestimate my father." After a moment's pause to glance at him, checking to see if he disagreed with her caution, which he didn't, she added, "There are no steamboats, I wonder where they are. Maybe the engineers have them busy hauling rock. Anyways, below Westport, as you can see, the river is huge."

"It looks more like a lake than a river," he agreed. "Malik should now make good time."

"The river's a bit treacherous, with all its meandering loops that leave sandbars and large submerged trees where you'd least expect them. If Captain Malik and Kyle don't ground us on a sandbar, we'll be in Port Delta in a few days."

Rex had just walked off the wharf into the market area when two men stopped him. The older one, with a full beard and long braided hair, reminded him of one of those mountain men he'd read about in history. The man wore a filthy buckskin outfit and reeked of horse, tobacco, and serious BO. The other man, more Rex's age, reminded him of a thinner Herr Jacobs, the Roanoke merchant. He was dressed in clean but worn gray coveralls. Both men had a revolver in a belt holster.

Whoever they were, the men had the best handguns this world offered, not the usual ball-and-cap revolvers common along the river. The revolver was the latest 9x19 mm model from Walters Arms, same sidearm as Rex had in his shoulder rig.

"Who owns that steam boat?" the younger man demanded.

"What business is that of yours?" Rex asked, bristling at the man's aggressive demeanor. Did the strangers represented a threat? Neither man approached his height or strong physique, but both were well armed and looked like men who knew how to use a revolver and knife. Prevailing in a dustup wasn't his concern. Attracting the attention of the local authorities was. Amy joined him.

"Ah, where are my manners? I'm Jerome Durer and this is my partner, Frank Siemen," the younger man said. "I want to buy that river steam boat you just disembarked from."

"What are you offering?" Amy asked before Rex could respond. Durer appeared startled that an old hag would ask such a question, let alone with a vigorous cultured voice.

"You are?" Jerome asked taking a second look at her that alarmed Rex. The thin man struck him as an opportunist who would know about rewards.

"She's our scullery maid. Pay her no attention," Rex said, before she could respond. He figured in her desire to learn what another businessman thought her invention was worth, she had forgotten she was a wanted person, in disguise, and in hostile territory.

"The scullery . . ." a startled Amy said. She looked chagrined.

"No call to be nasty to the lady," the mountain man said in a gravelly voice. He stepped beside Amy, who edged closer to Rex.

Wait until she got a whiff of her rescuer, Rex thought.

"Frank, behave. Who owns the, ah . . .," Jerome said, pausing to study the boat's bow for the name, before adding, "The Mischief. Is it the Panther Creek Nut Company?"

"Before I answer any of your questions, why are you interested in that decrepit riverboat?" Rex asked. He heard a snort that might have been a stifled laugh from Amy.

"You haven't heard about the gold strike? Gold been discovered in the Great Western mountains and I need a way to move my mining machinery."

"I doubt the Mischief would be of much help," Rex said. "Its old boiler can barely push my cargo down the Erie. No way could it push a load against the upper Great Western current."

"Perhaps, but I'd like to talk with the owner. I'm sure the captain can answer my questions." He made to step by Rex and Amy.

Two more armed and rough-looking bearded men joined Frank. The older man asked Jerome if there was a problem.

"There will be if this guy tries to stop me from talking with the captain."

Kyle, who was on his way to buy the side of bison, joined the group. Two Ichneumon soldiers patrolling the market area walked over, attracted by their group. A half dozen armed men gathered by the wharf was a bit out of the ordinary, even in lawless Westport.

"What's going on here, Herr Durer?" the sergeant asked. The Ichneumon private with the sergeant studied Rex before turning his attention on Amy. Rex was not happy to hear the soldiers knew Durer.

"Nothing, we're just talking about boats," the thin man answered. Rex wasn't the only one who didn't want the soldiers involved in his dealings.

"Good, keep it that way," the sergeant said. "You know the rules, no large gatherings without the commander's approval." The Ichneumon soldier looked at Frank, sniffed and shook his head, before turning his attention to Kyle. "Are you a Wapiti?"

Kyle nodded.

"Is that a Wapiti boat?" Jerome asked. His question had the Ichneumons' interest.

Kyle wasn't sure how he should answer and stalled.

"It's owned by the Panther Creek Nut Company. And Jerome, it's not for sale," Rex said.

"I still need to speak with the captain. Severing the gold miners would be a far more lucrative business, than hauling nuts."

"Herr Durer, will you first remind the captain that he needs to check with Colonel Savarin?" the Ichneumon sergeant asked. Durer nodded and the soldiers walked off.

"You might be right, but the captain only stopped for a fresh side of bison," Rex said after waiting for the soldiers to get out of hearing. "After he delivers my cargo, he can contract his services with whoever he desires. I'll tell him about your interest."

"Lord, your ignorance is pathetic," Jerome said. "The garrison commander will seize the boat when he learns about it. He's desperate to complete his fort and that requires hauling cut rock from down the river. Why'd you think there are no steamboats at Westport? The damn Ichneumons commandeer them, or the ones that could have fled."

"Then we need to go," Rex said.

"Too late, pal, he'll just send word to the Saukko at the quarry to intercept the Mischief."

"What's the Saukko?" Kyle asked.

"An Ichneumon warship that patrols the Erie for pirates and enforces the colonel's orders," Jerome said. "Where are you guys from?"

"Seems to me that you'll have the same problem," Rex said.

"Unlike you, I have an understanding with the colonel. Besides, you don't need a steamboat. Float your damn barges down the river. Boys, let's go find the captain." Jerome stepped around Rex and headed to the ramp.

"You don't need my help," Frank said. "There's nothing but Wapitis onboard. I'll take missy to First Choice for a whiskey." He grabbed Amy's arm and jerked her toward the bar, startling a squawk from her.

A quick simple stop for meat was morphing into a life-threatening crisis. Rex didn't even like bison meat. It reminded him of that tough, dry, grass-fed beef his mother liked to serve. At least the Ichneumon soldiers had left. Amy and he didn't need their attention, and he'd bet, Jerome didn't either.

"Kyle, skip the bison," Rex said, turning to see if Amy needed rescued.

Malik's yell for help grabbed their attention. Jerome and his aggressive henchmen had the captain crowded against the Mischief's stern. A rock swam better than the captain did. Rex feared a boat jacking was underway. Then he realized Frank was now dragging an unwilling Amy toward the bar. He could hear her threatening mayhem if the goof didn't release her.

"Kyle, go help Malik. I'll deal with Frank," Rex said, as a curse ripped the air and a gray burr charged by.

Amy had taken matters into her own hands. She had pulled her boot knife and sliced the man's hand to loosen his grip. The enraged mountain man had knocked her down and was pulling a hatchet from his belt when Hokee arrived. The wolf had the man's hand when Rex smashed his fist into Frank's face. A second blow to the man's gut sent the man to his knees with a grunt and the hatchet flying. Amy was screaming at Hokee to stop. The wolf was trying to reach Frank's throat.

"We need out have here," Amy said getting to her feet while holding Hokee. "I'll untie the barges."

Hokee and she were already back to the wharf by the time Rex relieved Frank of his revolver and ran to the Mischief. Amy was at the landlines holding the boat to the wharf when they heard blowing whistles. The two soldiers had reappeared.

"That whore tried to murder me," a blood-spattered Frank, on his knees, screamed, catching the soldiers' attention. "He's helping her." The mountain man pointed towards Rex who was almost to the boat ramp and Amy who was struggling to lift the heavy ropes off the wharf's bollards.

"Amy, forget those, get the Mischief moving."

One of the soldiers fired his rifle. Rex wasn't sure at whom the soldier shot. No one appeared hit. Jerome's thug blocked the top of the ramp. He had a shotgun threatening to shoot anyone who attempted to board. Rex stopped, aimed, and shot the man with Frank's revolver. Kyle batted away the wounded man's shotgun and heaved him off the boat ramp. Amy and Hokee scampered past Kyle who paused to grab the man's dropped shotgun, and headed for the pilothouse while yelling for John and Slim to open the firebox dampers and stroke the fire.

The second thug raised a shotgun and told Kyle, who was running to the Mischief's stern to help the captain, to stop or he'd shoot him. John stepped out of the engine room with his Krupp rifle and shot the thug. Jerome's man managed to fire one of his shotgun barrels at John, the pellets hitting the wall by the engine room door. Kyle then shot the thug who stumbled overboard.

19

Rex heard the soldiers shoot again. They appeared to be shooting at Kyle. Malik and Jerome were still wrestling on the stern. If the soldiers didn't get lucky, Kyle would free the captain without a problem since Durer's entourage was gone. The first thug appeared to be lying unconscious on the wharf without his revolver. Rex left the man alone and focused on the tie-down ropes. Amy had engaged the paddlewheels and was maneuvering the Mischief to remove the strain on the tie-down ropes.

One of the soldiers shot again from the alley in the market. One fortunate break, the garrison troops appeared to be terrible shots for Rex couldn't detect their bullets hitting anything near his or Kyle's vicinity. Still they needed to stop shooting before they did harm. A shot aimed at a point just above the head of the soldier peeking around the alley corner, sent the soldier scrambling for cover, allowing Rex to focus on unhooking the remaining tie-down rope.

Amy managed to remove the strain on the heavy hemp rope and the last loop popped off the rear bollard. Rex made a final check on the soldiers' location, saw no sign of them, and then glanced toward Frank, who was now lying on his back by the bar's entrance. Two grubby women had ventured out of the bar's door to either help or rob him.

Rex dragged the ramp on the Mischief. Already Amy had the boat and barges clear of the wharf by several meters. He headed to the aft end of the Mischief to confront Jerome. Kyle had the man's hands tied behind his back. Malik was sitting on one of the coils of tie-down rope along the deck's port side. The Ichneumon captain was coughing and rubbing his neck. In the distance, a dozen Ichneumon soldiers from the fort construction site were running toward the market and wharf area, shouting.

"Will we be out of rifle range by the time they arrive at the wharfs?" Kyle asked.

Rex nodded.

20

"Grab him," Malik yelled.

To everyone surprise, Jerome had jumped overboard while their attention was on the approaching soldiers. Kyle ran to the rail to shoot the escaping man.

"Let him go," Rex said.

They joined him at the boat's hand railing to watch in silence as the prisoner struggled towards the shore fifty meters away. Rex wondered if he would regret stopping Kyle, for they would have to come back past Westport on their return trip.

Jerome proved a good swimmer, even with his hands tied. The eels and icy water didn't get him and just before the Mischief rounded a bend, and Rex lost sight of him, Jerome was wading ashore.

Amy and Rex were watching the sunset from the pilothouse walkway. Malik was back at the controls. To everyone's relief, they didn't encounter the Ichneumon warship that Jerome had warned them to expect. The Mischief was now twenty kilometers below the rock quarry and rapidly leaving the Westport turmoil behind.

"News of new frontier gold finds always travels fast," Rex said in response to Amy's question. "So yes, I figure Port Delta has heard. If they haven't, our crew will spread the word. The excitement of gold nuggets lying in a creek, just waiting for some lucky soul to pick up, should help divert attention from us."

"Dreams are powerful motivators," Amy said. She appeared wishful. "If a gold rush occurs up the Great Western, steamboats are going to be in demand."

"I agree. Assuming I avoid capture and manage to get paid by the tobacco company," Rex said, "how far is Orleans?" Hokee padded over from somewhere in the back part of the Mischief and flopped down on the deck in front of them.

"You're going to help me?" Amy asked, looking hopeful.

"No, if you mean your insane idea of absconding with Purnell's machinery," Rex said. As he had feared, she had misunderstood his reason for asking about Orleans. Now she was angry. "That crabber boat is what I meant," he explained. "The one you and Saad said was a good deal."

One of the survivors from the Orleans Queen, First Mate Saad had suffered multiple injuries, but he seemed on the mend. Amy knew him from when she was a kid running around the Orleans Boat Works. She had spoken in his defense and Rex, though not trusting the man, had allowed the man to travel with them and work as a laborer in the engine room.

The man had concurred with Amy's suggestion that the crabber boat, Princess, with some boiler repairs, would make a good river tug. How to arrange the purchase of the sidewheeler hadn't been resolved. Herr Saad agreed that Orleans was a death trap for Amy.

"There's no call to insult me. It's no crazier than what you plan."

"I'm trying to reason with you, not insult you." She was right. He needed to try for a less strident tone in his opposition. "It's one thing for a couple of us to sneak into Orleans at night and deal with the Princess's owner. We might have a chance doing that. But steaming to the main dock with empty barges and demanding that Purnell's employees load the barges with the man's heavy machinery. . . Please, they'd laugh at us, and then shoot us."

The mercurial woman didn't respond. Instead, Amy kicked off her boots and with her bare feet, rubbed Hokee's back. She had that distant look she got when analyzing a problem. After a minute of silence, she spoke.

"It'll take two days at high steam to reach Orleans from Port Delta. But being fall, sudden storms are a threat. Pirates and the Ichneumon navy can be a problem, a bigger trouble than Purnell's thugs."

"Maybe I should forget the Princess."

They watched the river in silence, both absorbed in thought. Amy broke the spell.

"No, you're right. After all, if the Mischief broke down in Delta, what would we do?" She looked at him with an expressionless face. "The pressing issue is the need for a second steamboat and the Princess is the only one for sale. However, buying it is just the first step."

Rex could guess what her second step would be, the need for her presence in Orleans.

"Someone knowledgeable has to make sure it still operates and can travel safely to Smithtown. Are you going to do that?"

"My hope was Herr Saad could nurse the Princess to Westport where we could sell it," Rex said. "Double our money, and let people like Jerome worry about the maintenance."

"Who would share in profits from the Princess?" She asked after more silence.

Rex considered how best to answer. Amy had talked about them being partners, though he wasn't sure what kind of relationship the independent-minded woman envisioned between them. She wasn't aware the council had sold the Mischief, and Rex needed to tell her. He hadn't even considered her in the Mischief deal, since she had no Wapiti connections and aside from her split of Wu's gold, which she planned to buy her manumission with, no extra funds. Now he worried she might feel slighted. He wanted Amy as a friend, rather than just as a business partner.

Chief Hopkins had first raised the question of who owned the Mischief. The Wapiti Chiefs council, after much discussion, had decided it had no interest in owning or operating steamboats. Prussian legal doctrine, which the council tried to follow, stated the emperor owned all seized enemy property. Since the council was the Wapiti equivalent of an emperor, the chiefs decided they owned the Donnelly war booty.

However, the Mischief had been an Ichneumon flagged vessel seized during the Salt Furnace battle. After more argument, the council decided the vessel had been aiding Donnelly and therefore it was legitimate war booty. They resolved to put the Mischief up for sale at a minimum price of one-hundred-thousand D-marks.

Rex had learned about the council's decision and asked Andy Smith, even though he had no extra funds, to join forces with him to make an offer for the Mischief. He had approached Andy because he was Chief Smith's son. Rex wasn't adverse to a bit of preferential treatment because of nepotism. The council had accepted their offer, and they had until the first of the year to pay the hundred thousand D-marks.

The approaching deadline on paying for the Mischief didn't overly concern him. Even if the river froze and they couldn't pay until the spring thaw opened the river, no one would complain. Besides, he had the Mischief and in this frontier world, possession was everything.

"Any gain would be split in proportion to the share of money and effort each partner or person put up to buy the Princess," Rex answered while considering how best to explain the Mischief ownership.

"I suppose the gain would depend on the expenses. How much would the council expect, since we're using their riverboat?"

Rex had encountered that lady's look before. He wasn't sure if sly properly described it, and he now suspected Amy was aware the council no longer owned the Mischief. He wondered if Andy might have said something. The two were neighbors in Smithtown.

"The council has no claim if Andy and I manage to make a hundred thousand D-mark payment by the end of the year. We'll own the Mischief," Rex said. A smile formed on Amy's beautiful face. He felt relief.

"You got a great deal. The Mischief is worth several hundred thousand D-marks," Amy said. "Now help me collection my property."

Help her kill herself, was the more likely result, Rex thought. His repeated refusals to help her raid Purnell's boat works seemed to have no effect. Maybe Amy's aspirational personality allowed her see pathways where everyone else saw walls and bottomless pits.

Her machine shop idea made sense. He had initially encouraged her idea, even agreed to help, figuring Amy had arrangements to purchase the machines in Prussia. Then he had learned she planned to steal the machinery from her father. Now was as good as time as any to tackle the contentious issue of Orleans. Rex didn't want Amy taking off on her own and Purnell's thugs murdering her.

"Let me get this straight," Rex said. He was still trying to understand the dynamics of Amy's relationship with her father.

"The boiler in the Mischief is your original water tube boiler? A test unit for your design, and that Purnell paid to build, right?"

"Yes," she answered, after a pause, suspicious he had an ulterior motive. "It's the basics of the Caroom boiler patent. Since I was Benjamin Purnell's slave and used the Orleans Boat Work's shop to design and build the boiler, he filed the patent and claimed his boat works to be the inventor."

"Well, that's not unusual. It's the way it works in most companies," Rex said.

Her hackles were up. "I wasn't aware cod fishermen were so involved in inventing and patenting machinery," an indignant Amy said. "Everyone in the industry refers to the design as the Caroom boiler."

"Please, I'm not questioning you designed the boiler. I'm just saying that what your father asked for isn't unusual."

"And I suppose those Greek buyers of salted cod discussed their problems with inventors and patent provenance with their fish catchers." The lady wasn't averse to sarcasm seasoned with a few insults.

Why can't I remember that I'm not on Earth? Amy's cod fisherman remark was the result of a loquacious Wapiti warrior, Scott Belcher, who without realizing it, had made him aware that the Royal Prussian Church was a danger. The church considered anyone claiming to be from another world crazy or a devil and a threat to their dogma. The church calls such unfortunate souls false prophets and pays a handsome reward for their capture. Then after interrogation, the church burned them. Rex figured that explained why the Jesuits were often the source of new scientific discoveries and devices in the Prussian Empire.

Not wanting to attract the interest of a zealous Jesuit, and to explain his presence, he had been vague at first as to who he was, until Scott asked him if he was a cod fisherman. The question had puzzled him until the warrior explained that Rex reminded him of the heretics, the large blond haired nomads that the Royal Prussian Church often sent missionaries to save. Most of the nomads were hardworking cod fishermen, but some became vicious marauders, pirates. They lived on the edge of the northern ice fields, the most remote and uncivilized area on Erden.

What the fish looked like, or how one caught them, Rex hadn't a clue, still a fisherman he became. To explain being in the Wapiti homeland, he claimed his mother had been a Wapiti sold as a slave to Greek traders who later sold her to his father, a cod fisherman. He told Scott that he was searching for his mother's family.

Rex reckoned few people believed his tale since he was a head taller than most Wapiti and had a light complexion and blond hair compared to the Wapiti's darker coloration and dark brown hair. Most Wapiti, Amy included, probably figured he was a deserter hiding from the Prussian army.

"What are you after in Orleans, lathes and milling machines? Surely, you don't expect him to sell equipment to you or some Wapiti businessman so you can go into competition with him."

"Who said anything about buying them?" Amy said. "He owes them to me. I'm just collecting property I've already paid for."

"You don't consider that stealing them?" The lady just shrugged. "I don't want give the Prussian Navy any reason to think the Mischief is involved in piracy."

"Piracy . . .? I'm shocked you think so poorly of me," She said, smiling now. "The Wapitis are just collecting the payment owed Fraulein Caroom for assigning her interest in the boiler patent to Herr Purnell."

"Is that so? Is that agreement in writing?"

"Nope, we didn't have time. But since you're such a stickler for proper documentation, there will be bills of sales and lading for the machines. Besides, he travels to the southern islands in winter. While he's enjoying the sunny weather, we're going to steam into the Orleans boat works and load my machines on these barges with your help."

Counterfeit bills he figured. "Then why are you concerned whether your father is around when you arrive to, ah, gather your equipment?"

"To avoid turmoil, the man is forgetful and excitable."

"Excitable . . ., yes I could see that happening." Rex couldn't help smiling at that inadequate description of a murderous tyrant.

"He knows he promised those machines to me for my boiler design and not fighting his patent application. True it was a verbal agreement, but I still intend to collect the equipment."

"Well, you know my feeling on the matter," Rex said, not knowing what else to say to the bullheaded woman. "I can't stop you, but I'm not being a party to your suicide and risking the Wapitis money."

"How much money would the Wapiti have without my nut sheller? Or bagger?"

Rex knew the answer was very little. The truth was he wouldn't have two full barges of prime bagged winter sloe nuts to deliver, except for Amy's clever machines that she had concocted from scrap iron, an old water wheel, and her imagination.

"Or did you think the empty building and wooden bench . . . ah, I mean, *lab*, sufficient payment?" She appeared on the verge of tears. "Besides that, I need to see my mother and, assure her that I'm all right, despite any rumors to the contrary that they may have heard."

"Camille is your sister?" Rex asked. "Wouldn't . . . taking Purnell's equipment endanger them?" (He had been about to say *stealing*.)

"Not if they're not there. You should see Camille," Amy said. "She is the pretty one, and sweet, everyone likes that girl. She's thirteen and she wouldn't be any trouble."

"What if they don't want to leave Orleans?"

Amy waved that off, as not meriting comment, then looking crestfallen, said. "Oh god, what if he starts again?"

"What" Rex asked?

"For years, Purnell followed the Ichneumon policy of killing the troublemaker's entire family after hanging the person, or selling his family as slaves to the salt and sulfur mines. The Prussians didn't approve of that cruel behavior, and to keep their navy business he stopped. He might start again. I need to get them out of Orleans."

What a barbaric policy, it reminded him of North Korea.

"Hanson and Fritz think Purnell wouldn't harm your mother and sister in order to hold them as hostages that he can threaten in order to prevent your testimony in a Prussian court," he said.

"I had agreed with Herr Hanson, until the dead-or-alive reward poster," Amy said. She looked away, dabbed at her eyes, and then added. "Maybe he no longer fears my testimony. I'm worried he might revert back to his old homicidal habits of punishing the family."

Rex didn't know the man, but figured that if Purnell was considering punishing innocent family members, swiping his equipment might cause him to act.

"So whether my mother and sister want to leave or not, I'm taking them. I'll tie them up, if I have to."

Rescuing her kinfolk was a new consideration in favor of the raid. Worse, a number of people had told him that Benjamin Purnell was a dangerous man to cross. Amy's family could very well be in grave peril. He didn't want to encourage fatal foolhardiness, but he did owe Amy a sincere evaluation of her plan. Rex did what most men did when confronted with a situation that had no good solution. He vacillated.

David C. Brown

Chapter 3

The Mischief with its string of barges was near Port Delta, low on coal, and piloted by a very nervous captain. Captain Malik feared discovery by the Ichneumon Army and arrest as a deserter, though in actuality he had been a prisoner of war until recent. Rex understood that distinction might not matter with the authorities.

More troubling, they had yet to encounter the Clovis Belle. Had the boats passed in the fog, or had something gone haywire? Rex was amazed at the size and width of the lower Erie River. It had to be several kilometers wide, and he wondered if the boats could have passed in a wide stretch of the river during a storm or in the dark. Captain Dalporto, running against the river's flow, would favor the slack waters near the riverbanks to avoid fighting the current that tended to be highest in the center of the river. The Mischief, headed downriver, favored the center area of the river for the extra speed boost from the river flow. With the river so wide, the boats could have failed to see each other.

Since the prior day, they had passed an increasing number of plantations with private docks. One area reeked of sulfur dioxide. Rex learned the odor was from an acid manufacturing operation.

"I'd like to see the operation," Amy said. "The sulfuric acid is used to make phosphorus from bones."

31

"Is this where the matches are made?" Rex asked. Nothing that suggested a factory was visible along the riverbank, other than a large wooden dock, a guard hut, and a decent gravel road that disappeared into the west forest.

"No, the phosphorus is poisonous and very dangerous to handle," Amy said. "The Habsburg interest owns the Lucifer match patent and controls the manufacturing process. Or at least they used to. I'd heard they had sold their interest to the Staedtler Company. This is just one of many operations used to manufacture white phosphorus. They have it shipped in special glass tubes to Prussia."

"Where does the sulfur come from?" Rex asked. He had been pleasantly surprised at the quality of the matches he had encountered in this strange world. The big wooden matches seemed to always light with the first strike on any dry surface. The Wapiti matches were nothing like those puny matches common in West Virginia, the ones that required a special abrasion strip to even light.

"Sulfur and salt are mined in that area," Amy said. She pointed to several bare ridges behind the east riverbank. "They tunnel down to the salt and sulfur."

As the Mischief neared Port Delta, Rex saw more and more farm fields and fenced pastures. Cotton appeared to be the main crop. He wondered which plantation was Apophis's lair. The other manufacturing site they passed was a fertilizer operation. Amy said the stockpiles of gray material under the woodsheds were different grades of niter.

Near mid-day, in the distance on a high ridge along the west bank of the Erie, a massive stone fort came into view. As the Mischief drew closer to the fort, Rex noticed docks and warehouses starting to appear along the west bank. Wood, except the fort, appeared to be the favorite construction material, though a few red brick buildings were evident. Several ocean-going steamboats clustered about the larger bustling wharfs with many sail boats of all sizes mixed among them.

Rex spotted an Atlantic Tobacco sign painted on the side of a large warehouse. The sign reminded him of the faded Redman's Tobacco advertisements on old barns back home and he figured that building was his destination. The Wapiti crew had gathered around him at the rail to gawk at the wonders approaching. Amy was still in her room, but up, since Hokee was at the rail watching the sights with them.

The group of adventurers with Rex on the Mischief consisted of Captain Malik, Amy, John and Kyle Balers, and Slim Hoyer. They were all, including Amy, proven warriors whom he trusted.

The two teenagers, Mike Belcher and Kit Jacobs, hadn't been in a gun fight and were, like Herr Saad, of unknown quality to Rex, but Kyle and Slim spoke well of them. Slim was the Wapiti hunter who had pretended to be Cinnabar in jail in order to ambush any Purnell assassin sent to silence the man's testimony. It had been a near thing, but the assassin didn't survive the encounter.

Amy had asked that he allow Herr Saad passage to Port Delta. The former first mate had experience on the river and, though still recovering from his injuries, he had helped spell Captain Malik in the pilothouse. Saad planned to catch a ride from Port Delta to Orleans on one of the coastal traders. He wanted to get home to his family in Orleans. Rex worried the man might team up with some of his former crew loafing in the Delta waterfront bars and try to steal the Mischief. Amy thought he worried without need about Saad's loyalty, but Rex didn't intend to give him the opportunity.

Out in the river the massive Prussian battleship HMS Schlesien rode at anchor, surrounded by several smaller, ironclad paddle wheelers. All the warships were flying the Imperial Prussian red flag with the black iron cross.

"I'd love to tour that engine room," Amy said, studying the HMS Schlesien with Captain Malik's telescope.

There appeared to be one Ichneumon warship on the river, the Saukko, from the Westport quarry that Jerome had warned would seize the Mischief. Apparently, it had been steaming down the Erie ahead of the Mischief. What would have happened, had they caught up with the warship?

The huge gray stone fort wall fronting the river appeared to be twenty meters high and ran for a kilometer. The fort was located behind and above the waterfront area and most of Port Delta. Several of the Ichneumon's large blue flags with the spooky two-headed golden snake emblem flapped in the breeze at each corner. Normal-size cannon ports were visible along the walls.

Two massive cannons protruded from iron-plated turrets on top of elevated stone platforms located inside the fort walls. The two guns appeared quite capable of sinking any ship on the river. Rex hoped he had an opportunity to inspect those coastal defense cannons. The bristling armament looming above the wharf area seemed of no interest to the traders and people busy with commerce on the wharfs and markets along the river. They appeared unconcerned with being between the military might of two empires.

Rex was wondering where the notorious Delta slave market was located. He wasn't sure what a slave market would look like. Would there be cages to hold the unfortunate souls, a stage to parade the merchandise? There didn't appear to be anything like that in the waterfront market area. He spotted the Clovis Belle at a dock down river from the cotton market area. Captain Dalporto must have encountered a problem.

First, before learning what delayed the Clovis Belle, Rex wanted to check out the tobacco outfit. He told Captain Malik to dock close to the Atlantic Tobacco warehouse and to maintain steam pressure in the Mischief's boiler. He would send Kyle Baler with a message to Dalporto that Rex wanted a meeting.

"Kyle, put Herr Saad in the cell before you leave. I don't want to chance him alerting Purnell's men or seizing the ship. We'll release him after we're done."

As the Mischief docked, Rex examined the area for threats, but everything appeared peaceful. The crew had removed Panther Creek Nut Company signs from the barges and stored them away. He hadn't wanted to draw attention to the Mischief while in Delta, and no one appeared to be paying unusual attention to the boat and barges.

Windrows of dry river mud scraped off to the edge of pathways and behind stalls offered testimony that the market had recently flooded. The reeking piles of manure and clouds of flies among the windrows of mud implied the port authorities were not very concerned about sanitary conditions. He had been under the impression that the Ichneumon army enforced proper sanitation. Something seemed wrong. Hickory Ridge and even Bone Valley's limited market area had been clean, not at all a pigsty like Port Delta. Amy, in her ugly woman's disguise, joined him at the rail.

"The emperor needs to replace the garrison commander," she said. "When I was here in the summer, the Ichneumons blamed a recent flood, but the same mud is still stacked about. They don't even appear to be cleaning up the manure."

"Doesn't seem to bother business," Rex said.

The trading activity along the docks near the Mischief appeared primarily to involve timber and cotton, though in the area to his right, laborers were busy offloading numerous large burlap bags from mule drawn wagons onto a sailing ship about three times the size of the Mischief with her barges. Bags of rice and other grains he figured. Cargo headed to distant lands, since the sail-powered ships wouldn't get far up the river against the current. All the laborers were black men. *Slaves*? Rex wondered.

"Amy, Andy, I want you to talk with the local traders," Rex said. "Learn what the current military and market news and rumors are."

Andy, anxious to explore the market, nodded and hurried off. Amy didn't.

"Your concern should be a double-cross by Atlantic Tobacco to avoid paying for the cargo," Amy said. "The tobacco company has a well-deserved reputation for treachery. If they've heard about the reward, they're smart enough to figure there's a good chance the person the Wapiti trusted to deliver the annual nut crop might be the same person the prince is after. At the very least, the authorities will detain you for questioning."

"Please, I have enough to worry about. Do you know where the slave market is located?" Rex didn't need Amy reminding him of the danger he faced in Delta. He knew, just as he knew he had no other choice but to see the sale through.

"The slave market is inside the fort," she said, looking exasperated. "If you're not cautious, you'll experience it firsthand."

"I'll be careful," he promised as he studied the fort. "Do they keep the slaves in the fort?"

"I've heard there's a vast dungeon under the fort where the slaves and other prisoners are kept," Amy answered, stopping Rex with her hand, and looking at Mike and Kit who had just walked up. She included them in her warning.

"Port Delta is a nasty place full of evil people. Don't attract attention and don't get detained by the Ichneumon police."

Amy waited for their acknowledgement, which Mike and Kit did after a moment. Then she hugged Rex and said, "Please be careful." She left a startled Rex and rushed down the gangway into market. Hokee followed her.

"Only those with business are to go ashore," Rex said, after watching Amy for a moment as she disappeared among the market stalls. "Delta is not a place for sightseeing. I want everyone to be ready to leave on a moment's notice. Keep your rifle handy, but out of sight."

"Captain Malik, do nothing to call attention to the Mischief. See that everyone knows that." Satisfied he had taken basic precautions; he grabbed the case of winter sloe nuts by the gangway and disembarked.

Rex headed to the tobacco warehouse carrying one of the cases of winter sloe nuts on his shoulder. The crowd he weaved through appeared to contain men and women from all the races, with the exception of Ichneumon women. The crowd consisted of every color and shape humans came in. Prussians, a number of them women, and Ichneumon men each made up about tenth of the crowd, the rest were Clovis, Wapiti, mutts of uncertain ancestry, and black people.

Most people that Rex encountered were bare foot, except for the Prussians and Ichneumons. Many of the black men had a 7 branded on their left deltoid. Coveralls were popular with both men and women, though a few of the Prussian women wore fancy outfits, with impractical hoop skirts and burdensome hats sprouting feathers and flowers, and parasols. There were even men and women in sarongs. The older, stout Clovis women, who appeared to operate many of the market stalls, favored brightly colored baggy smocks and pants instead of coveralls.

Rex was curious to meet an Ichneumon woman. He had yet to hear a rational reason why they kept their woman hidden. But whatever their reason for not allowing their women in public, it didn't apply to non-Ichneumon women. The majority of the people present thorough out the market area were women.

Two cute teenage Clovis girls, wearing shorts and not much else, were maneuvering a two-wheeled cart loaded with several cages of noisy brown chickens through the market. He stepped out of their way. The taller girl rewarded him with a smile.

"Want some chickens?" the other girl asked, stopping. She eyed the crate Rex was carrying. "What's in the box?"

"Winter sloe nuts," Rex said. "Are you sisters?" He towered over the lanky teenagers.

"She's Sis, I'm Eddy Yoon," the chatty chicken trader said.

"Eddy, Mom's waiting on these hens," Sis said. The hens had gone quiet. The birds were all studying him. "She doesn't approve of us talking to strangers, especially Prussian soldiers."

Rex thought their mother's advice very sensible. He figured the revolver and fatigues explained his sudden membership in the Prussian military.

"Phew, you worry too much, Sis," Eddy said. The chickens appeared to agree that he wasn't a threat. The hens went back to their boisterous clucking and ignored him.

"Your winter sloe nuts, are they roasted?" Eddy asked. He nodded. "Mom likes roasted winter sloe nuts. Are they salted, Mister?"

"Yes, there are none finer than these. They're Panther Creek nuts," Rex said, amazed he had been so easily sidetracked. "Do those hens lay an egg every day?"

Rex was no farm boy, but he knew healthy looking chickens from the summers he spent on his uncle's farm in Ohio. Eddy's hens had bright red combs and shiny brown feathers. The alert birds were again examining him. Their owner appeared gleeful at an opportunity to haggle, or at least expound on the quality of her hens.

"Expecting an egg every day is not reasonable," the young trader said. "But these Ridge Browns are vigorous birds. You could expect five eggs a week from these fine hens. Do you have a sample of the nuts my sister and I could try?"

Rex had five hundred bags of nuts in the case he was carrying, but he didn't want to break the seal before the tobacco buyer could examine the packaging. He felt in his pockets while balancing the wood case on his shoulder. He normally carried a couple of bags, and found one unopened and handed it to Eddy. The waxed paper bag with the Black Panther logo had both sisters' interest, and they passed the bag back and forth inspecting the print and bag seals.

"Go ahead and tear it open," Rex said. "Try one."

"They're excellent," Eddy said after a minute, "Though there're not many nuts in a bag." Even Sis nodded while munching on the last of the nuts. Her sister wanted to know the price, and Rex explained about the Atlantic Tobacco Trust involvement.

"Ten D-marks for that small bag is pricey," Eddy said. "That's what we sell a hen for that will lay hundreds of eggs, and you can eat the hen after it quits laying. How about we trade a hen for four bags of your winter sloe?"

Rex was tempted to trade for the hens. Eggs would be good and roasted chicken even better.

"I have an appointment," Rex said. Several people had stopped to learn what the giant Prussian was talking about with the Yoon sisters. He didn't need to attract attention and said, "Tell your mother to ask for Friedrich Burgdorf at the Clovis Belle in the morning if she wants to trade hens for nuts."

"Do you have another bag Mom could sample?" the little capitalist asked. Rex was tempted to ask if she had a couple of eggs he could sample, but instead fished out his last bag of nuts from his jacket pocket and handed it to a smiling girl.

After passing between rows of cotton bales stacked three high, Rex arrived at the wood frame warehouse with the Atlantic Tobacco sign. It had the typical barn wood siding, but instead of a shake roof, had a copper roof. The two large barn-style sliding doors were open. Rex could see the building's rear wall was red brick, and several men were engaged in sorting through bundles of brown tobacco leaf. The place had a pleasant tobacco scent. The workers appeared to be repacking the tobacco in wood barrels from piles of loose leaf. They were all black men, and he asked the oldest one who the manager was.

"The man's in there," the man said. He sounded pleasant and pointed toward a windowless, unpainted wood door in the rear wall to Rex's right. "It's okay to go in."

Rex opened the warehouse's rear door and discovered a small red brick building across a narrow alleyway. Opening its door allowed him to enter a one-room office. The office walls were red brick. The left sidewall had several small windows with iron bars and a door for accessing the room behind the windows. Two Ichneumon men who reminded Rex of Manuel Prado sat behind scratched-up, painted wood desks. The gray painted desks had a file-drawer on the right side and two legs on the other side holding up the desktop. The wood swivel chairs on rollers that the two clerk-managers were sitting in looked to be of better quality than the desks. The tobacco company didn't believe in spending money on fancy office furniture.

The similarity in appearance to that wicked Ichneumon trader, Manuel Prado, made Rex cautious with the men.

"Hi, I'm Friedrich Burgdorf," Rex said. "I have the Wapiti shipment of winter sloe nuts at the wharf and need to know where to deliver it."

The younger Ichneumon with a milky eye told Rex to put the case on his desk and open it. Neither man seemed bothered by Rex's revolver in the exposed shoulder holster. Then again, the younger clerk's scars and eye implied he was no stranger to violence.

"Are they roasted and salted?" the manager, an older Ichneumon, asked. He put down the quill and ledger and walked over to examine the wooden box as Rex removed the brass screws that fastened the lid on the case.

The tobacco warehouse manager's muscular build and numerous scars conflicted with his demeanor of a laid-back accountant. Rex decided the two were soldiers masquerading as clerks as the man inspected one of the brass screws. What that might signify for a safe honest transaction between him and the tobacco company, he didn't know, but hoped he was worrying needlessly.

"Whoever made that box knew his business," the manager said. "Where did you get it?"

"This box?" Rex asked, surprised at the man's interest. The man nodded.

"They were manufactured in Rainelle," he answered, removing the last screw from the box lid. Seeing the manager's questioning look, he added. "It's up the Southern River."

"Is Rainelle in Wapiti territory?" the man asked. He had picked up one of the brass screws to study. Rex nodded while handing the Ichneumon a bag of salted winter sloe nuts.

"Neat job of bagging," the manager said, placing the screw with the other ones. He opened the bag and ate a couple of the nuts. "They're good. I thought Rahul was kidding. How much cargo do you have? Oh, by the way, I'm Alpha and that's Jar."

"I have fifteen hundred cases. The agreed price is 1,250 D-marks a case." Looking around the nondescript operation, he wondered if they could have that kind of money here.

"Sounds about right," Alpha said. "First we need the cases delivered here, and then Jar and the men need to verify the count and quality of the nuts." The Ichneumon appeared uninterested in more discussion concerning payment. As if two million D-mark transactions happened every day.

Thinking of the filthy market area, maybe doing the least possible to get by was the accepted way of conducting business in Delta, but Rex wasn't going to turn over the Wapiti cargo until he was convinced Alpha had the money to pay for it.

"You have the money--here?" Rex asked. To his surprise, Alpha pointed to Jar who lifted the picture of Emperor Ratakonda hanging on the wall to reveal a small iron door. The Ichneumons waited. It seems that they thought the sight of the safe answered his question.

"I'm a poor country guy. Show me there's money in it." He wondered what type of locking mechanism the safe used. There wasn't a dial on the door.

Alpha looked irritated, yelled for the guard. An Ichneumon soldier ran into the office holding a rifle, which caused Rex to wonder where he had come from. There had been no soldiers in the warehouse.

Jar proceeded to open the safe. Three tiny slots were visible in the door's face below the handle and Jar inserted brass pins in the holes. Each notched pin had a different length. Inserting and turning the pins in the holes released some locking mechanism hidden in the door that the allowed the handle to rotate and the door to open.

The alert guard watched Rex as Jar pull thirty-some bundles of 100 D-mark notes from the safe and stacked the currency on the desk beside the case of nuts. An impressive stack of currency, but a long way from the almost two million D-marks the cargo was worth. Jar then pulled from the safe rolls of the five-hundred D-mark gold coins.

"As you can see," Jar said. "There are a couple hundred rolls of those coins in the safe." It was a voluminous safe. Rex had to agree the tobacco company had the funds, assuming those weren't counterfeit bills.

"Thank you, gentlemen," Rex said. "I'll organize the delivery." Alpha waved his hand in a 'whatever suits you' manner and went back to entering numbers in the ledger book and Jar stuffed the money back in the safe.

Kyle and Captain Dalporto were waiting for Rex when he got back to the Mischief.

"I was hoping you'd show up," the captain said as way of greeting. "The Prussian naval board is skeptical of Captain Wolfgang's testimony that the Hendrick's boiler exploded because of the admiral's order to exceed the safe pressure. The board suspects the Wapiti sank it and the captain's injuries have affected his memory."

"No surprise there," Rex said. "What naval board is going to want to believe a fellow navy man, a famous admiral, was an idiot. So what are their plans?"

"The scuttlebutt is the admiral is waiting on two armored side wheelers equipped for salvage work and operations in shallow rivers. They're due in from Berlin. They will go and raise the sunken boat and examine the boiler. Also they want the ship's safe recovered. The Prussian navy has requested my assistance in transporting supplies and men for the salvage effort."

"Well, be sure to charge them up." Rex said trying to lighten Dalporto's worried mien. "Any idea what's in the Hendrick's safe? Purnell sent the Orleans Queen and Captain Hube to try and grab it."

"I've heard that didn't go so well for Hube," Capitan Dalporto said. "As to what's in the safe, I figure gold. What else would be worth retrieving from a sunken ship safe? The water would have ruined anything on paper like letters and orders. The other matter is General Bezdek. Before he left on Purnell's yacht for Sanibel, a detachment of soldiers escorted me to the fort for a warning. Actually, the general had two warnings. The first one was don't traffic with those pirates at River Point."

"Us, the Wapiti, the Ichneumon general called us pirates?" Rex asked. Could the Mischief be in danger of being seized? "What else did the general threaten?"

"The second warning was to avoid any entanglements with the Prussians," Dalporto said. Rex, watching the wharf area while listening, spotted Amy in her ugly woman outfit talking to three middle-aged Clovis women.

"The general and Emperor Ratakonda consider the Erie to be Ichneumon territory and intend to enforce that fact. The general warned me that the army would deal harshly with anyone who interferes. I'm a simple businessman trying to make a living. I don't need these problems."

"We don't either," Rex said. He thought of General Mehta's concerns. "Do you think the Ichneumon would start a war over control of the Erie?"

"General Bezdek is the emperor's brother-in-law, so I figure he has a fair idea of the emperor's plans," the captain said. "The general is no whiz, and Purnell provides him with lots of whiskey, drugs, and women at Sanibel palace. Vices that keep him occupied. Whatever the emperor plans, I'm sure his indolent brother-in-law won't be in charge of it. So I don't expect open hostilities until there's a new Ichneumon commander, and there're no rumors of Bezdek being replaced."

"Where is this Sanibel?" Rex asked.

"It's the largest of the Gulf islands. Too damn hot for my tastes, but it is noted for beautiful women and sandy beaches," the captain answered, before returning to Bezdek's warnings.

"I figure people like Purnell would prefer Ichneumon rule to Prussian rule," the captain said, pausing to check the wharf and market area. "A lot of the traders and plantation owners think Emperor Schnabel has become too liberal with that antislavery business. I don't think any of them would be unhappy under Ichneumon rule."

"And where do your sentiments fall captain?" Rex asked. He wondered if Amy's mother was from Sanibel.

"I want peace and to be left alone to make a living. All my wealth is in the Clovis Belle, and I've worked hard to reach this point. I don't want my boat to become another burned-out hulk in the river."

"Well, that's a worthy attitude and this world would be a better place if everyone thought like that, but as we all know, they don't. In the end, you will have to choose sides." Rex wondered how far he should trust a man who had mixed feelings over which side to support. "I need to deliver the nuts, but I need your help to . . ."

Amy returned to the Mischief a couple of hours after Captain Dalporto had left. Rex could tell she was worried.

"Most of the market stalls are owned by Clovis and Zamia women," Amy said. "They were curious where we're from and who owned Panther Creek Nut Company. As you suggested, I told them Benjamin Purnell."

"Wait, where's Zamia?" Rex asked as they leaned against the pilot house handrail and watched the activity in the sprawling market.

"Zamia is a wild land on the other side of the South Ocean where most of the tribes are black. A lot of slaves come from there," Amy said. *Africa or its equivalent in this world*, he reckoned.

"Several of the black men, slaves I gather, had a raw 7 branded on their arm. Do the bastards brand people?"

"Yes, slaves are branded. The 7 means they are, or were, property of the combine," Amy said. Shaking her head, she looked at him and added, "That people do such things is appalling, but we need to consider it a warning. The cargo needs delivered before Purnell arrives and hears about the Wapiti's large order of winter sloe, or else we'll all have 7 tattoos. The market women expect him here in the next few days to collect his slaves from Colonel Xavier."

"What is the combine? Who's the colonel?" Rex asked, wondering if Purnell was the threat everyone said.

"The Seven Combine, they're the group that controls the transoceanic slave trade. The colonel, he's over the guards and police," Amy said. "Colonel Xavier is Bezdek's adjunct and responsible for the slave market security. I figure the colonel would be agreeable to anything my father asks of him. We need gone before he arrives."

"And that means Purnell is not in Orleans," Rex said.

"So have you decided?" Amy asked. He shook his head.

Rex, knowing no one in Port Delta, had remembered the gang loading those large bags on the sailing ship. He had asked Dalporto about the gang and on his recommendation had contacted the local teamster, Isaac Haddad.

"I need to deliver the 1,500 cases of winter sloe nuts to Atlantic Tobacco Trust's warehouse," Rex said. "Can you do that?"

"Sure, that's my business," the teamster, a wiry middle-aged black man with grey hair, a few brownish teeth, and two fingers missing from his right hand answered. "How heavy is a case?"

He described the box's dimensions and weight along with the judgement that a couple of D-marks per case would be an acceptable delivery charge. Isaacs' ready smile shrouded a wily business mind that soon convinced Rex, not a gifted bargainer, hauling a case of nuts from the dock to the tobacco warehouse was worth ten D-marks per case. The delivery cost was important, but not as important as completing the transaction so the Mischief and her crew could head home.

"I might agree to this robbery if I was certain your crew could deliver the cargo in one day."

"A day would be required to transfer the cargo. The more important question is if my payment depends on your payment by the tobacco crew. I expect payment at the end of the day."

"You have mentioned that several times, and you'll be paid when I am. I did, as you suggested. I requested payment on completion of the order delivery. And the warehouse manager, Alpha agreed, with the qualification that the quality of the nuts checked out."

"Well, the nuts are excellent, so we should both be fine." Haddad said, smiling.

The sun had yet to clear the horizon when Haddad's four mule carts arrived. Amy had opened one of the cases and passed out bags of nuts to Haddad and his men before they started loading the first cart. While the cargo transfer was going on, two Wapiti warriors went around handing out free bags of the salted roasted winter sloe nuts and bags of Jacobs's hard lemon candy throughout the wharf area crowd of curious onlookers. Amy had suggested the free samples on her return the day before from scouting the waterfront markets.

All the bags, nuts or candy, had the Panther Creek Nut Company name and a logo of a black panther. Sue Sweetwater had suggested the logo. She had even talked the distiller, Herr Simpson, into having the printer he used for whiskey labels print the logo on the bags. Rex had also sent Slim Hoyer with two cases of the nuts to General Bezdek's office and the fort guards.

A concerned Slim found Rex at the barge, an hour later, where they were off-loading the winter sloe nuts on to the mule carts. "The guards liked the gift, but the colonel was asking questions about the owners of Panther Creek."

"The colonel, was he the general's aide-de-camp?" Rex asked, taking a break from carrying boxes.

"He's the fort garrison commander, Colonel Xavier," the hunter said. "Or at least I think that's his position judging from the guards' behavior. He wanted to know if the company was a Wapiti front or owned by Purnell. I told him the man giving us orders was a Prussian. Other than that, I didn't know. If I was you, I'd be ready for a visit by the Ichneumon colonel."

Captain Malik had been helping with the cargo transfer and overheard Slim. "Colonel Xavier knows me. He's an unforgiving bastard. I'm dead if he sees me."

There had been concern about the captain's safety in the heart of Ichneumon territory, and Rex acted.

"Kyle, you're the skipper of the Mischief," Rex said and then addressed the group. "If asked, we work for Herr Purnell. Malik, go to the Clovis Belle. Dalporto will hide you. Kyle, keep a fire in the boiler and be ready to bring up the steam pressure in a hurry."

Malik paused to address the small group before disembarking. "I'm not exaggerating. The colonel is a cruel man. He likes to cut off the feet and hands of prisoners that the general doesn't intend to sell as slaves."

"Cut off their feet, hands . . . the four step?" Rex asked. He remembered Chief Smith telling him about the cruel Ichneumon punishment. Malik nodded in agreement. Rex's nerves were already on edge with the nut transfer, worry over receiving payment for the crop, and Purnell's expected arrival in a few days. He didn't need that horror story.

"Yes, the bastard claims it makes the prisoners easier to control," Malik said. He wasn't done with his gruesome information. "I don't believe that is his main reason. The colonel is a monster who likes to watch humans suffer."

"Wouldn't the prisoner die, bleed to death?" Kyle asked.

"The guards stick the stump in boiling pitch," Malik said. Amy and several of the men looked stricken. Rex figured the men agreed with his thoughts. The Wapiti couldn't get out of Port Delta too quick. The captain still wasn't finished with his cautions.

"An arrest in Delta by this garrison is a death sentence, unless you know someone important, like Purnell. It's a different world here. All of you have to be careful."

Hopefully, Malik was overstating the danger.

"What a dreadful place," Rex said. "Let's finish our business and get out of this hell." Everyone went back to helping with the nut transfer. The transfer went smoothly for the next several hours. At last, Isaac Haddad left his crew loading the mule carts and walked over to Rex on the barge.

"We'll be finished within the hour," Isaac said. "I'd like my payment as soon as my crew unloads that last cart in the warehouse."

"Yes, I recall you mentioning that before."

Rex had his fingers crossed, hoping the tobacco company didn't get cute about paying the 1,875,000 D-mark invoice. Many people counted on him to deliver. To help handle the gold, he told Kit

Jacobs to meet him and Slim at the tobacco warehouse. Kit was an eighteen-year-old cousin of storeowner, Bill Jacobs. He had graduated from the Berlin Polytechnic in accounting and he was along for an adventure before settling down in Roanoke to work at his uncle's business.

"Let's walk," Rex said. He was thinking of Amy's shopping list. "I might need another crew for a different job." The teamster just nodded in agreement and fell into step beside him. "I need to locate some bulk niter."

"Do you now? Planning to fertilize those nut trees? Do you have a permit?"

"Permit, I wasn't aware a permit was required. It's for agriculture use, corn and tobacco crops."

"Ichneumons require permits for most things and Colonel Xavier handles special commodity permits. We just passed him. Want me to yell for him to stop?" Isaac asked. A column of several grim and armed Ichneumon military men had just passed them.

Rex's hope was to avoid the colonel. "No, I would hate to trouble such an important person for my trivial needs."

None of them couldn't get a read on Haddad's trustworthiness. Amy had asked about teamster the evening before, during her second swing through the market stalls. None of the Zamia women would acknowledge knowing the man. Still, Amy was convinced they knew him. However, several of the Clovis market women admitted to dealings with the teamster and spoke well of him.

Dalporto had told Rex the teamster's main business was smuggling in rum from the Gulf islands. For sure, contrary to Amy's information, Isaac Haddad was well known. People were forever greeting the man as they made their way from the Mischief to the tobacco warehouse.

After Haddad's crew had finished unloading the last cart on the warehouse dock, Rex went to Alpha's office. The warehouse manager was in a cheerful mood.

"Herr Burgdorf, first I have to tell you the quality of your winter sloe is the finest I've ever handled. We'll take all you care to send in the future," the warehouse manager said.

"I'm pleased you're satisfied. Now I'd like to complete our transaction. I have a number of operations to wrap up before heading back home. Never know when the ice will form."

If there was going to be trouble with the payment, it would happen now. To his pleasant surprise, the Atlantic Tobacco manager told Jar to bring out the payment. Rex watched the man count out the 1,875,000 D-mark payment in rolls of gold coins and some bundles of used Prussian currencies.

"Kit's one of Herr Purnell's accountants. He has a simple test to check the purity of the gold." Alpha appeared a bit taken aback by that lack of trust, Rex added, "Herr Purnell requires us to follow these strict procedures,"

He had no idea if the bastard did, but Rex didn't trust the Ichneumons. Gold-colored lead coins weren't unheard of. For whatever reason, Alpha refrained from comment as they watched Kit put drops of acid on the several coins and check the density of three other gold coins. After several minutes of silence in the room, Kit did a couple of quick calculations on a piece of scrap paper and then spoke.

"The coins are fine Prussian 500 D-marks, ninety-seven percent pure gold."

Rex told Kit and Slim to load the coins in their backpacks while he stuffed several bundles of the paper money and ten rolls of gold coins in his backpack. Everyone shook hands.

"Alpha, it's been a pleasure dealing with you. When I next speak with Herr Simpson, I'll ask him to send you a proposal on supplying barrels and boxes for the tobacco leaf."

Isaac was waiting by the warehouse entrance with two tough-looking laborers, each holding an ax.

"My office is nearby, let's settled there. My daughter should have fresh coffee on."

Rex felt a bit exposed with those backpacks full of money, but besides Slim and Kit, he had Andy Smith armed with two revolvers for added protection. Rex knew Amy was around the warehouse neighborhood in her ugly woman disguise to watch their back. She also had two revolvers.

The teamster boss sensed the hesitation. "You're safe for the moment, but we should have a private talk."

Rex needed to pay the man, but before entering Isaac's office, he told Kit and Slim to take their bags to the Mischief. The daughter had taken her looks from her father. She was a small, lean, and homely girl with her father's alert eyes. Isaac introduced her as Silva.

"Your timing's good, the coffee is ready," she said. "He's a Prussian. I thought you said they were part of the Wapiti that kicked the Ichneumon army out of River Point."

"Daughter, we have some business to complete, please see if Herr Knight's guards would like a cup of coffee." They glared at each other for a moment, until she grabbed the coffee pot and left, slamming close the office door.

"Daughters . . . Do you have children," Isaac asked. Rex said no. "She as a rule runs my hauling business, but the Ichneumons, like that Alpha character, won't deal with a female. Alas, they control most of Delta's businesses. Silva is my smartest child, has a head for business, but I'm still forced to let her brother be the manager when dealing around Delta and the port area. He's off crabbing, that's why I was involved today."

"The Ichneumons have some strange beliefs. I'm a bit surprised how prompt the tobacco company paid," Rex said while opening the backpack and counting out Isaac's 15,000 D-marks payment.

"Yeah, well the blue bloods do honor business agreements. Their cruelty is the real concern. That's why Delta is a tricky place for a stranger to do business, like their damn transaction fee."

"Fee? What fee?" Rex had a suspicion that his profits might be about to evaporate. His nagging apprehensions proved real.

"The port authority charges a ten percent fee on all transactions in Delta. The tobacco company should have withheld the fee from your payment."

"Alpha paid the full amount. The man never mentioned any fee."

"Then the tobacco boys did think they were dealing with Purnell," Isaac said. "Purnell has a deal with the colonel and doesn't pay the fee."

"Who says we're not working for Purnell?" Rex asked. Now he was worried, and he weighed Isaac's Purnell remark and trustworthiness. He tasted the coffee. He didn't want to appear overly concerned. The coffee was excellent, but that didn't mean it wasn't poisoned.

"Where is the coffee from?"

"Haven't a clue. Ask my daughter," Isaac said. "You of course know that the Ichneumon army is the real law in these garrison towns. If the garrison commander is a reasonable and sane person, things tend to be peaceful and prosperous. Hickory Ridge has such a commander, but not here. Colonel Xavier, who is the acting commander, is a cruel fool. Delta is not peaceful, nor prosperous. On the off-chance you're not with Purnell, but a stranger, you might want to consider leaving now."

Amy was waiting in the goat corral located across from the road below the tobacco warehouse. She was no fan of goats. The animals were difficult to control, though they did eat weeds. The vegetation around the goat enclosure and the ditch providing water to the animals was trimmed. Amy liked fresh goat milk. But having seen the locals' idea of sanitation, she wouldn't touch milk in Delta. She then wondered how her print order was coming.

Earlier, while the men were transferring the nuts, Amy had visited her mother's friend, Sitar Jain, who lived in Port Delta. She had told Amy where to find a printer. She had then gone to the establishment recommended by her mother's friend, Krause Printing. The shop was located in one of the few brick structures in the lower market area of Delta.

On arriving, Amy wasn't sure the printer was still in business. The front door had looked unused and someone had painted the inside of the front windows on the street level black. The stout iron bars protecting the windows spoke volumes about the character of the neighborhood.

Looking for the entrance, Amy walked behind Krause's print shop and found a large loading dock. Across from the dock, and a stone paved lot, was a wood barn and corral. The large pen had several draft horses that appeared healthy and, on spotting her, trotted over to investigate. Two freight wagons, parked off to the side of the corral, appeared in good repair. Krause's operation had an organized, flourishing appearance. *At least the rear did*, Amy thought, thinking of the boarded-up appearance of the building's front.

On entering Krause's shop through the dock door, Amy encountered several men working a noisy iron frame press. They were busy printing posters advertising a large slave auction. The room smelled of linseed oil. She asked the red-faced, fat Prussian who was handing poster board sheets to the press operator if Herr Krause was available.

"That's me, young lady," the red-faced man answered. "Hank, feed the press while I deal with this customer."

"Madam Jain said you could help me," Amy said.

"She did, Sitar Jain?" Krause asked, wiping his face with an ink-stained cloth.

Amy nodded and the printer motioned for her to follow him into the front room. She had expected difficulty with her request. To her pleasant surprise, Herr Krause was very accommodating after reading the note Sitar had told Amy to give the printer.

Chapter 4

Amy had been waiting at the goat pen about an hour when Rex's arrival to collect his payment snapped her attention back to the present. Half hour later, Rex, Kit, and Slim exited from the tobacco warehouse and met with the teamster, Isaac, who had been waiting on the sidewalk. She was preparing to cross the ditch and climb the corral rails to follow the Wapiti group when the arrival of four Ichneumon soldiers at the warehouse stopped her.

An Ichneumon lieutenant led them. He entered Alpha's office and a moment later rushed back out. Amy realized something was wrong when the patrol jogged off around the same corner that Rex had disappeared. She quit worrying about where that water snake had gone, splashed through the ditch, and climbed over the corral rails. Maybe the goats would do something useful like trample that snake, as she cleared the rails and pursued the soldiers.

Isaac wasn't finished with his alarming news.

"The real money maker for the army is the rule that failure to pay the port fee can trigger a forfeiture of the entire amount," Isaac said. "I suspect the colonel who we passed earlier was headed to seize some unfortunate's vessel for nonpayment of the port fee, or to checkout your boat."

"Forfeit the entire amount? That's robbery. No one ever mentioned a ten percent fee. Do you pay the fee?"

"Sure, when Ichneumon parties are involved, like the tobacco company. Rest assured your friend Alpha reported the pending Panther Creek transaction to the colonel's office."

"There's always something. Where do you pay the fee?" Rex asked. He thought of those long-range rifled cannons at the fort, might be better for him to give up ten percent, than risk the Mischief and her crew.

"As a rule, it's withheld at the time of the transaction. However, since Alpha didn't collect the fee, now if you pay they will know you're not with Purnell and that it was Wapiti cargo. You should also be aware the colonel hates all Wapiti."

"I gather you now know we're not part of Purnell's organization," Rex said. Nightfall was about two hours off. The best option, he decided would be for the Mischief to slip away after dark.

"After that cheerful news, think you can locate the niter without the need for a permit and the colonel's fees?"

"I might know a dealer," Isaac said. "You have any problems dealing with a woman?"

Silva opened the office door and told her father an Ichneumon lieutenant wished to speak with him.

The day before, after Rex's initial trip to the tobacco warehouse, he walked by the fort on his way back to the Mischief. Fort Delta was a larger stone fort than the one at River Point. Both Ichneumon forts had one thing in common: the lack of bastions. The Ichneumons seemed not to realize the importance of being able to fire along the front of the walls. The only way the defenders could engage attackers at the base of the fort's massive walls would be to lean over the edge, a very exposed position.

Caroom's Raid

The nature of the stonework that made up the Delta fort's walls had caught Rex's attention. The rock used by the builders appeared to be a hard, weather-resistance, yellow sandstone. River Point had used a local grey sandstone that already showed signs of spallation from the freeze-thaw cycle. The workmanship displayed in the stonework at Port Delta had impressed Rex. Skilled masons had built the fort's walls. They had cut and trimmed each block to fit tight against its neighbors. The workmanship was far superior to the mortared rock walls at Hickory Ridge and River Point.

Three Ichneumon army troopers, armed with rolling-block single-shot rifles, stopped Rex by the fort's main gate and asked his business. The guards had been laughing over some comment made by the younger guard. The soldiers looked clean and in good physical shape. Their black Ichneumon army uniforms pressed and their boots shined. They were polite and wished Rex a good day when he told them his name and said he was just sightseeing.

The lieutenant in Isaac's office was also polite, but insistent.

"Colonel Xavier has questions about where you acquired that boat and asked that you accompany us to his office."

"My boat? You mean Herr Purnell's boat, the Mischief," Rex said. He had assumed the soldiers were there to collect the fee.

If the Ichneumon colonel had recognized Prince Cherukuru's steamboat, he was in trouble, serious trouble. Rex had assumed Colonel Paget and the freed Ichneumon royalty, Prince Cherukuru, would have stopped here on their way south to their capital, Cusco. He also had figured they might have asked the Delta garrison to watch for a Rex Knight and to arrest him. He'd changed his name to Burgdorf, but he hadn't given the repainted boat much thought.

"It's Herr Purnell's boat," he repeated. "I'm his foreman, here to handle the man's winter sloe and timber sales. If your colonel has questions he should speak with my boss when he arrives in a couple of days."

A silent Isaac offered no help. Silva, who had opened the door for the lieutenant, looked frightened.

"Be that as it may, Colonel Xavier has ordered your appearance. Come with us, the colonel doesn't like to be kept waiting." The Ichneumon officer snapped his finger and two soldiers seized Rex's arms. The other two pointed their rifles at him.

"No need for a scene, lieutenant. I'll be happy to speak with the commander and clear up this misunderstanding."

At a nod from the lieutenant, the soldiers let go of his arms, after relieving him of his revolvers. They then all walked out of the teamster's office and the Ichneumon patrol escorted him to the fort's main gate. Rex's backpack had been on the floor by Isaac's desk and the lieutenant had thought it was Isaac's bag.

The guards at the fort's main gate were the same ones Rex had talked to yesterday.

"Looks like you're going get a tour of the fort, Herr Burgdorf," the older gate guard said. Rex just nodded, not in the mood for banter.

Amy was in the alley across from the weathered shed the soldiers had entered. Probably the building that Rex and the teamster had been heading for. She had just caught her breath after the jog from the goat corral, when the soldiers exited the building with Rex. He was walking unrestrained with the soldiers, but ominously, his revolver holsters were empty. Was he a prisoner? Amy followed them.

A calamity, the Ichneumon soldiers had marched their prisoner into the fort. Had they discovered Rex's identity? She was wasting time fretting by the fort's main gate, and hurried back to Haddad's place, a two-room shed attached to a barn. She shoved open the door and was in a kitchen, but could see through another open door the teamster and his daughter talking. The daughter was looking in Rex's backpack.

"Why did they take Rex?" Amy asked. They both looked up with surprised expressions, and she realized they thought his name was Friedrich Burgdorf. "Burgdorf, where is he? I'm his engineer."

"Who are you," the teamster asked, pointing a muzzle-loading flintlock pistol pointed at her. His daughter just stood there. She had a bundle of D-marks in her left hand and the backpack strap in her right.

"Please, just tell me. Why did the Ichneumons take him? Is he in danger?"

"Yeah, Burgdorf is in grave danger if those bastards learn he's not working for Purnell. What's your connection to him? You don't look like any engineer I've ever encountered."

Amy had her new revolver in her hand, cocked, but still hidden in her shoulder bag. She weighed whether to grab the daughter and threaten mayhem or trust the teamster and rumored bootlegger. Then again, the old man was holding his ancient junk pistol quite steady on her.

The man's caution was understandable, but Amy didn't have time to waste.

"I have to warn the crew. I don't have time for games. Why did they take Burgdorf?"

"Colonel Xavier sent the soldiers to bring Herr Burgdorf to him," the daughter said. Unlike her father, she sounded welcoming, but Amy had no way to know if the Haddads were involved in the treachery. "I figure the colonel is suspicious it's a Wapiti operation using the prince's stolen steamboat. Your friend is in serious trouble, especially after Purnell arrives in two days."

"That's his backpack."

The daughter nodded. Then the senior Haddad lowered the hammer on his muzzle-loading pistol. Amy pulled her revolver out of the bag and carefully lowered its hammer, before returned it to her shoulder bag. The senior Haddad shook his head, and then laughed.

"Come on Silva. This is getting interesting."

The lieutenant led his party through the gate and across a large open area to a two-story stone building. Crossing the cobble-stone-paved area to the office, Rex wondered if he was about to learn firsthand where the slave pens were located. Even though the place had a neglected air along with no sentries manning the walls, he was in a dangerous bind with little time to resolve an escape.

The cannons behind the parapet had windblown debris and leaves piled around their carriage wheels. The iron plates of the turrets hid the massive cannons from Rex's view and he couldn't see their condition. However, numerous sea gulls were perched on the turrets and extensive white streaks from bird droppings coated the turrets sides. It suggested the garrison wasn't maintaining the turrets any better than the parapet guns. Fort Delta, like the market area, had an unkempt appearance.

The quiet inside the fort allowed him to hear their boots hitting the cobblestones and the flags flapping on the walls. The lack of activity caused Rex to wonder how large of a garrison manned the fort. The room they entered had a small waiting area with two wooden benches along the left wall. It had a strong vinegar smell. The back wall had two solid wood doors. Along the right wall, a partition with two bank-teller-style openings divided off part of the room. The lone occupant in the room, a bored-looking older Ichneumon soldier sitting behind one of the windows, started to ask Rex his business and then saw the lieutenant and stopped.

The lieutenant ignored the clerk, crossed the room, and opened the far door in the rear wall. The room they entered was a working office with file cabinets and tables with maps and, more ominous, a wet stone floor reeking of vinegar. At the center desk was the fit-looking man in the black Ichneumon uniform of a ranking staff officer. The same man who Isaac and Rex had passed in the market earlier and Isaac had said was the garrison commander. The Ichneumon had the demeanor of a man in charge. He sat sipping coffee from a white porcelain cup while studying Rex, who the guards had stopped in front of the desk. The officer reminded Rex of a spider sizing up his prey. He placed his delicate cup on its matching saucer on the desk before speaking.

"I'm Colonel Xavier, Herr Knight. I'm very happy you chose to visit Delta and stop by."

"I'm afraid you have mistaken me for someone else. My name is Friedrich Burgdorf, and I work for Herr Purnell." He strived to appear unconcerned despite the chill from hearing his name. The smirk on the colonel's face didn't help Rex's composure.

"I very much doubt that. The prince's description of the Prussian leading the Wapiti matches you. Besides, Herr Purnell deals in raw winter sloe nuts. The tobacco company manager, knowing of my interest in a certain large Prussian, had informed me earlier in the month that a sizable shipment of roasted bagged nuts from the Wapiti was expected. Alpha was kind enough to notify my office that the nut shipment arrived today and here you are."

The heavy iron door behind the colonel's desk opened and two unarmed Ichneumon guards entered carrying chains and a slave collar. Rex weighed the chance of overpowering the three guards, but with three rifles pointed at him, he didn't have a realistic chance of success. The only feasible option was to hope one of the three slave-collar keys in his boot fit that collar the guards were placing around his neck. Otherwise, he was doomed.

"However, on the off chance you are who you say you are," the colonel said, "I'm placing you in a cell until Herr Purnell arrives at the end of the week."

"My boss is going to be upset with your foolishness. General Bezdek will hear about this."

"You're in no position to issue threats. Cause trouble and I'll removed a foot tonight."

The colonel motioned for two solders to help the prison guards, which they did with brutal efficiency. Had the Ichneumons seized the Mischief and Amy? Rex prayed not. As they dragged him and the chains out of the office, the colonel added,

"The prince said to start on the four-step punishment as soon as you were captured, but I'll wait until Herr Purnell arrives. In case you haven't heard of it, you get to decide which hand or foot you want chopped off, and then each year we chop off another hand or foot. Of course we're not cruel, wouldn't want you to die, so we provide boiling oil to seal your injured limb. Use the next few days to decide which hand or foot you want me to start with. Get him out of here."

General Paget had warned him the man was big, but the massive size of the suspected Wapiti leader had still caught Colonel Xavier by surprise. He had dealt with enough Wapiti to know the man he had just sent down to a cell was no more Wapiti than he was. The man was a Prussian and that was his quandary. Could the tobacco buyer, Alpha, and the lawyer, Rahul Malhotra, have mistaken one of Herr Purnell's men for the Wapiti leader, Rex Knight? The colonel remembered the man's boat needed secured.

"Lieutenant, take your patrol and seize the Wapiti boat and any money until Purnell arrives and we can resolve the ownership."

"I just released my squad for dinner. Okay to let them finish?" the lieutenant asked. "With Burgdorf in custody, his crew won't leave without him."

The colonel knew the lieutenant was lazy, General Paget's pet, and Purnell's spy. If the delayed impoundment of the Wapiti boat caused problems, and he rather hoped it did, he'd have an excuse to replace the lieutenant. The Saukko was in port. It could chase down the Wapiti boat and capture the crew while the lieutenant explained his delay in carrying out his orders to the navy board.

"If you think an hour won't matter, go join your men. Let me know if there's a problem."

After the lieutenant left, the colonel thought about the prisoner as he waited for the cocoa water to boil. The man didn't act fearful. He seemed more concerned about Purnell's reaction. Colonel Xavier knew Purnell and the Wapiti have been waging a war on each other over the last year. Those northern savages had even managed to sink three of Purnell's large steam-powered boats, so it was difficult for him to imagine a supposed Wapiti leader-chief claiming their most bitter enemy, Herr Purnell, was his employer. His information about Herr Purnell visiting Delta hadn't alarmed the man, though the description of the four-step punishment had. So the man wasn't nerveless and therefore maybe he was Friedrich Burgdorf.

The smell of the cocoa brewing reminded Colonel Xavier of Prince Cherukuru. The prince's safe return had resulted in an immense celebration that the Ratakonda succession was intact. In passing through Port Delta on his return to Cusco, the prince had promised a general star to the Ichneumon officer that captured the Wapiti leader who had humiliated him.

Colonel Xavier had always heard the prince was a simpleton and disregarded the offer. Then Emperor Ratakonda had promoted Colonel Paget and several other officers involved in the release of the prince, along with issuing a promise of a promotion to the rank of general for the officer who captured Rex Knight. The emperor's action had ambitious officers across the empire excited. A few weeks later, Colonel Xavier's friend and mentor, General Paget, had ordered him to return to Cusco and attend a meeting at the palace.

Colonel Xavier tasted the cocoa, added more sugar and, satisfied the brew was sweet enough, carried the mug to his desk. He should check on the Wapiti boat. Instead, he lit another cigarette, settled in his desk chair, and let his thoughts return to that day of his audience with the emperor, the most exhilarating day of his life.

The massive throne room entrance had solid gold doors seven meters high and rumored to weigh two thousand kilograms apiece. Despite the weight, the doors balance on its smooth hinges allowed one guard, admittedly a powerful one, to swing the door open and closed. To walk through those famous doors had always been his goal, but Colonel Xavier had never dreamed, in his wildest fantasy, that a request from Emperor Ratakonda for his presence would provide the opportunity.

"We're meeting in the emperor's private office," General Paget told him when they entered the gleaming marble throne room and gold throne.

Xavier knew he had been gawking. The spectacular room had been empty, except for two Royal Guards and an old man. The click of their boots was lost in the massive room. Flags and banners from defeated foes hung along the west wall, including several scorched Prussian Imperial flags.

"Notice, there's no Wapiti flag in that collection," the general whispered. "The emperor expects us to correct that."

Colonel Xavier realized with a start that the old shriveled bald Ichneumon male with alert, clear golden eyes who greeted them by the throne was the emperor. The public pictures of Emperor Ratakonda always depicted a vigorous large man with a stern mien.

"I see I'm not quite what you expected," the emperor had said. Horrified he had insulted the emperor, Colonel Xavier had prostrated himself on the floor in front of the emperor's bare feet. The emperor had been in a forgiving mood that day.

"Ah, get up, Colonel, we all get old," Emperor Ratakonda said. "General Paget speaks well of you and I don't have time to waste on court protocols."

They followed the emperor into a luxurious office, the walls paneled in dark wood, thick carpets, and stunning floor-to-ceiling glass windows that provided views of the royal gardens and distance snowcapped mountains. Colonel Xavier had never imagined glass panels of that size were available. He wondered who had manufactured them. Their cost would have been astronomical.

"I want you to return to Port Delta and lay a trap for the Wapiti military commander, a man named Rex Knight," Emperor Ratakonda said. "The general will fill you in the details, but it's important that you capture the man and send him here, alive. Some of my advisors believe he may be a magus, so as you can appreciate we want him delivered able to answer questions. Accomplish that task, and I'll make you a general."

Colonel Xavier didn't need told his fate if he failed. "Thank you, Your Majesty, for the honor to serve. I will not fail."

"General, see that the colonel has all the resources needed to ensure success."

The meeting was over.

Over those two weeks he had remained in Cusco, he had assembled twenty volunteers from the imperial guard garrison that he knew to be good men. He needed them for the Delta garrison had gone soft. Xavier knew that was true, but the garrison hadn't been his responsibility. Besides, everyone knew the emperor's brother-in-law was useless as a commander. Emperor Ratakonda had realized that and had given General Paget permission to replace General Bezdek as the Fort Delta commander.

The Delta garrison was understaffed and the troopers there were lackadaisical in their approach to duty. Prior to his promotion, Xavier's responsibility had been the slave market and prison, which were both profitable enterprises. For that reason, he had escaped the emperor's censure.

The main problem with the garrison personnel was that they shared General Bezdek's opinion that there was no one who would attack them. The Prussians could, but they were in no condition to start another war. Even he had to agree that General Bezdek had a valid point. The Prussians still had their hands full on the eastern front with the Mongols.

However, from the recent news reports, Colonel Xavier had begun to sense the Prussians were winning in the east. The arrival of Prussian warships at Port Delta, while he had been in Cusco, gave credit to the belief that Prussia's eastern war was winding down. If that occurred, then Emperor Ratakonda's planned attack to take advantage of the Prussian preoccupation with the eastern war might start too late. Mobilization of the necessary Ichneumon forces to throw out the few Prussian soldiers in the Erie Valley had been underway when he left Cusco. General Paget was to use part of the force to reinforce the fort at Port Delta and guarantee Prussian access to the Erie River was blocked.

Those Prussian warships riding at anchor below the fort's cannons offered a tempting target. Unfortunately, Colonel Xavier knew the garrison troopers hadn't fired the cannons in years. He didn't know if the emperor and General Paget altogether appreciated how unprepared the garrison was for war, and he had lacked the nerve to tell them.

The discovery of excessive gunpowder being stored in the tobacco warehouse had clued him into the problem. He had been shocked to learn the garrison's various commanders, starting at least ten years before under General Meringa, had stopped the annual gunner practice. The general hadn't wanted to explain the lack of gunnery practice to the emperor and the Cusco headquarters. It was easier to store the annual allotment of gunpowder and iron cannon balls intended for target practice.

General Bezdek, along with the waterfront merchants and captains of the docked boats, didn't like the noise, smoke, and grime from cannons firing overhead. The merchants and captains got angry and sarcastic when a misfire sent an iron ball caroming through the stalls. At least the garrison had never used exploding cannon balls for practice. As a result, the fort's two powder magazines were full, and large conical stacks of cannon balls were scattered throughout the fort.

With more investigation, Xavier learned that for the last three years, the yearly 750 barrels of black powder allotted for practice had gone into the rum aging-and-storage vault under the bonded tobacco warehouse. The north rum storage vault was now full of gunpowder. Colonel Xavier had even discovered that thirty-five barrels of gunpowder and twenty barrels of rum were stacked among the tobacco barrels in the old wooden warehouse over the south rum storage vault. An inspection showed that rum vault was full of unused practice gunpowder. He should have advised General Paget about the problem and have restarted gunnery practice, except now the Prussian warships were in the way.

Instead of lighting another cigarette, the colonel checked the time and discovered it was time for his supper. He locked the office and crossed the courtyard to his quarters to wash up.

While washing his hands, Xavier decided to play it safe. He was certain the prisoner was Knight and in the morning, he would have the guards cut off one of the prisoner's feet. The pain and healing period to recover would ensure the monster didn't overpower his guards and escape before General Paget's arrival next week. The colonel knew from experience there was little danger of a prisoner dying from the first amputation. The general had met Rex Knight, and he would be able to verify they had the correct man. The news of the capture would help mollify the general's response to Xavier's failure to warn him earlier of Delta's excessive gunpowder.

The guards slammed back the heavy iron bolt on the solid door behind the colonel's desk and prodded Rex through the opening into a dark circular stone shaft with a set of wooden stairs that spiraled down to another door about ten meters below. The neck collar was tight and choked him if he didn't hold his head up. The attached iron chains pulled on the collar, adding to the weight against his neck. The air in the shaft had a foul odor, which didn't help his breathing difficulties. The faint hydrogen sulfide odor and warm humid air reminded him of a sewer.

Two scruffy middle-age thugs in gray uniforms opened the lower iron door after the soldiers hammered on it. The jailers, Rex reckoned as he inspected the large arch-stone hallway revealed behind the iron door. It disappeared into a dark void. Curtains of cobwebs graced the dirty uneven stonewalls that formed the passageway. Small oil lamps, irregularly spaced along the walls provided a meager illumination and added a smoky tang to the unpleasant, damp atmosphere.

As Rex's vision adjusted to the twilight, he could see the passageway ahead appeared to run for hundreds of meters with cell doors every twenty meters or so on both sides. He realized that a huge dungeon existed under the fort. The first of the cells they passed were empty. Now about a hundred meters into the dungeon, he passed two cells that contained handsome young black men who Rex figured were slaves awaiting the auction block.

The male prisoners watched in silence as the soldiers, guards, and Rex, in chains, shuffled on down the dark hall. After several empty cells, they came to two cells that contained women huddled in the dark cell interior. The prisoners appeared mostly dark skinned, though several of the women appeared to be Wapiti. None of them had clothes.

All the men and women prisoners that Rex could see in the poor light from the smoky lamps appeared to be sleek and healthy individuals. Each male prisoner had a raw number 7 branded on his shoulder. The women had their brands on the left buttock. They hadn't been here long. No human would remain healthy in the dungeon's noxious environment.

Prime stock to sell as slaves, Rex figured, while wondering what had become of the rest of the black people from which the slavers had culled these prisoners. The guards had stopped at one of the female cells to allow the two soldiers from the colonel's office to ogle the silent women who turned their backs to the guards. The women didn't respond to the guards' lewd remarks.

The sight of those nude women prisoners had riled the soldiers' libido. They were asking the guards if they could sample the merchandise. As the party continued walking down the hallway away from the women's cells, the guards boasted to the soldiers that every day they dragged one of the women out of the cell and took her to a room where everyone sampled her. The soldiers wanted to know if they could join in the fun. The guard leader and soldiers then haggled over what the soldiers had to trade for the favor of 'sampling' a prisoner.

"You mean rape her," Rex muttered. That remark resulted in him getting a painful jab in his back by a rifle barrel and a warning to shut up. The bastards knew their behavior was despicable and referring to their depraved conduct as 'sampling' changed nothing.

Rex wasn't certain hell adequately described this reeking place as they arrived at a side hallway. The intersection appeared to serve as the guards' office area. A wood table with several wrought iron chairs beside it sat off to the side of the passageway. Behind the table, bolted to the wall, were two large wood cabinets and a rifle rack. Two coiled bullwhips draped over the rack added to the awful aura.

The filth of the place appalled Rex. There appeared to be no regular effort to empty the buckets of waste. A cast iron wood stove in the hallway intersection had pieces of split hardwood scattered beside it. The various rusty iron pokers and pincers hanging on the wall behind the stove made clear the purpose of the stove wasn't to heat the hallway.

Ash piles against the wall and flung about on the floor told Rex the guards had little supervision. The Ichneumon army garrisons Rex had seen, prior to Delta, were clean, and he wondered if the slave market ran this operation. The group stopped at the intersection to complete the haggling over the woman.

A screech from the cell across from the side hallway caused everyone to look. A slink watched them. Its large pitiless eyes focused on Rex. The Wapiti had claimed slinks could see in total darkness and bled a blue blood when cut. The Ichneumons used the ostrich-sized carnivorous flightless birds as guard creatures. After seeing the one in Panther Creek that Amy killed, Rex had hoped never to encounter one. Now in this hell, he had.

Slinks reminded him of the prehistoric terror birds. The guards ignored the beast. He couldn't. The creature and Rex studied each other. Then he noticed a part of a thin forearm with the hand attached and another amputated hand lay on the floor in front of the slink's cell door. Some horrifying event had occurred.

"I need one of those revolvers," the head guard said. The guards and soldiers were still haggling over his revolvers.

The guard who wanted a revolver then walked over the slink's cell and kicked the forearm to where the beast could reach it. The crunch from the creature eating the arm bones, and men haggling over a revolver for a chance to rape helpless women, left Rex dismayed.

"I want a hundred D-marks along with a woman," the soldier said. "They're better than the new revolvers the colonel brought back to Port Delta."

"That's your problem, no samples without the gun," the head guard said as he then kicked the amputated hand into the slink's reach, and said. "Buster, you need to be neater." The other guard laughed at his remark. The head guard noticed Rex's disgusted look.

70

"You think this is bad, if I know the colonel, Buster will be eating your foot in the morning," the thug said. Both guards laughed at Rex's look.

"That looked like a woman's hand. Do Colonel Xavier and General Paget know what you're doing with the women?" the soldier who wanted to do a deal asked. The head guard was shrewd enough to recognize a threat of exposure.

"Just messing with you," the head guard said. "Let's get this bastard caged and then we'll have some fun."

If his hands were free, Rex could have overpowered the distracted guards and two soldiers as they negotiated. But his hands, chained to a leather belt that the colonel had insisted the guard use, were useless. So he passed the time examining the surroundings, trying in vain to ignore the crunch of bone from the slink's cell.

A look in the open wooden barrel he stood by explained why on the first opportunity that offered any hope of a successful escape, however unfavorable the odds, he must make his move. The water had clumps of what appeared, at first glance, to be greasy scum floating on the surface, though the lack of light prevented him from being certain. The clumps could be decomposed drowned rodents. The metal dipper hanging on the wall beside the barrel suggested it was drinking water. Rex hoped he wasn't in here long enough to be forced to have to drink that lethal-looking liquid.

The side hallway went a short distant before ending at a large cell. The cell containing several cowed men missing various hands and feet. The air reeked from human waste.

"Take a good look, Wapiti man. Soon you'll have to tell me which foot you want chopped off," the older guard said.

The guard jerked the chain attached to the iron slave collar around Rex's neck. His hands chained together to a leather belt around his waist prevented using them to help break his fall. The guard kept pulling on the chain causing the collar to choke him as he struggled to regain his feet. The other guard and soldiers laughed at his awkward efforts.

One of the men in the large cell, the one missing a foot and hand, started begging for water. Then another one started yelling they hadn't gotten their food or water for two days. The older guard nodded to his younger companions. They unlocked the cell door with a simple skeleton key and using short clubs, beat the two complainers into silence while Rex waited in the hallway. The rest of the prisoners cowered in the back of the cell.

"Let that be a lesson, speak if told to, otherwise no talking," the guard holding Rex's chain said. "If I hear one more sound, I'll leave your cell open for Buster tonight. He's hungry."

The guards then put Rex in the small cell across the hallway from the larger cell with the mutilated prisoners. The senior guard locked the collar chain to an eyebolt anchored in the cell's stonewall, and asked,

"Are you going to behave?"

Rex meekly said yes and the guard unlocked his hands. Then the cell door slammed shut and in a moment, the faint yellow glow from the guards' rest area at the hall intersection was the only light. The cell was an empty stone cove, no bed, no chair, not even a night soil bucket. Having seen the drinking water, he couldn't imagine the food this hell served to the prisoners. He'd wait until midnight, after the guards had settled down, before making his move.

Chapter 5

The woman's crying had ended about an hour before and Rex could no longer hear the guards in the hallway. He couldn't be sure how much time had passed since he entered the fort, but he figured several hours had passed, which meant night had fallen. His right boot had a tiny slit in the lining where he carried the three common slaver collar keys in use along the Erie valley, a steel pin, and a tiny razor sharp folding knife that had been in his backpack from Earth.

Indira Hopkins had suggested the idea of always carrying the collar keys. At the time, they had been thinking of freeing rescued Wapiti, not himself. He prayed this collar wasn't some off brand and tried opening it. No luck with that key, but the second key he tried did open the collar. He sent a blessing to Indira.

As Rex rubbed his neck, he considered the rusty cell door lock. The Ichneumon builders had fabricated the door and wall of the cell from thin flat iron bars riveted together in a grid. From experience, he knew this world depended more on neck collars chained to walls than on the cells to contain prisoners. As a result, most of the prison-cell-doors he had encountered on this world were simple affairs. He hoped Fort Delta's dungeon didn't prove the exception.

Iron plates encased the cell lock mechanism with a key hole in the exterior plate. The lock's bolt used a rectangular hole cut in the flat iron bar of the cell's front wall. The bolt had barely entered the hole due to misalignment, and Rex tested his strength against the door. He was able to flex the door a little. Next, he tried the wall frame and discovered the corroded anchor bolt in the floor allowed the doorframe to swing in about a centimeter. A moment later, he had popped the bolt out of the hole, allowing the door to swing open with a rusty squeal.

A couple of the maimed prisoners had heard the sound of the cell door opening and they were standing at their cell door watching. He didn't need them making any noise and walked over to their cell. In a whisper, he told them he'd be back after dealing with the guards. The prisoners in frantic whispers begged him not leave them.

"I won't, get ready to move," Rex said. "I'll be back."

"They release the slink as they leave for the night," the terribly maimed prisoner said. "You don't have much time."

The intersection of the hallway was empty of guards. The slink quietly watched from its cell. Rex could hear them back down the main hallway about fifty meters in the direction of the women's cell. He looked around for a weapon and saw none. The locked rifle rack offered no help. The one item suitable for a weapon was the ax by the stove, and it wouldn't be of much use against two rifle-armed guards down an open hallway. The locked large wood cabinet, beside the rifle rack and across from the side hallway, cast a dark shallow along the wall from the light of the torches by the stove.

When the guards returned, if their attention was toward the cell with the maimed prisoners, he might successfully ambush them. Rex hurried quietly back to the prisoners and told them in a few minutes to start screaming for the guards.

"If we do, and you don't kill them, we're all dead," the youngest prisoner said. He appeared to have all his limbs.

"Cheer up. I will be too, so get the bastards to come."

The guards were still down the hallway when Rex returned to the shadow area by the cabinet. He could hear a woman plaintively begging someone to stop, but didn't see her. A few minutes later one of the prisoners yelled for the guards, which got the terror bird hissing. He pointed the ax at the slink, causing the creature to jerk its head back from the cage door and go quiet. He could now hear the guards' curse and quarrel over whose job it was to check.

One guard returned to check on the racket from the cell. The other guard disappeared back in the cell from which Rex had heard the woman whimpering. He figured that was the 'sampling' room, the guards and soldiers had referred to earlier. He still didn't know if there were armed soldiers in there.

The guard sent to investigate had a rifle and stopped to get one of the torches by the stove. He slung his rifle over his shoulder to free up a hand to hold the torch. The slink was restless and had its head back through the cell door bars, chirping loudly. The guard ran to the cage and jabbed the burning torch at the slink, causing the creature to jerk its head back in the cell with a squawk.

The man stepped away from the cage toward the entrance to the side hallway and held the torch up to illuminate the area. If he had looked, he would have seen Rex off to his left by the gun rack. The guard proceeded to yell questions at the prisoners trying to determine what their problem was, without walking down the side hallway to their cell. Rats were attacking them was the answer. He laughed and told them to eat them. By then Rex had crossed the distance and buried the ax in the guard's skull.

The torch went flying into the short hallway in a shower of sparks and the rifle clatter loudly on the stone floor. The guard's rifle was one of those Ichneumon army copies of the Krupp rolling block design. Rex made a quick check. The rifle had rusty spots, but was otherwise clean and loaded. The guard's belt had a metal cartridge box with six of the 11.6x65 rounds. The guard's belt also had a sharp steel sword about half-meter long within an attached scabbard and another scabbard with a hunting knife. He put on the bloody leather belt, the hallway too dark for him to determine the blood's color.

A quick glance around showed no one in the main hallway. The slink had its foot through the cell door bars, straining to hook a claw in the guard's body. The rivulet of blood from the guard seeped across the floor toward the floor drain by the slink's cell was exciting the beast, but the body was still out of its reach.

Rex turned and ran to the end of the short hallway where he handed over the guard's key ring. "Get ready, I'll be back."

Walking fast as possible and still avoiding making noise, Rex hurried to the room he had seen the other guard enter. It was a small cell similar to the one the guards had locked him in, except two torches on the wall provided considerable light in the room. A nude black woman was stretched face down across a wood table with the guard who had locked him in the cell busy raping her. The guard's pants were down around his feet. Two soldiers, each had one of the woman's arms, were holding her down.

The bigger soldier holding the victim's left arm, looked up and recognized Rex. Before he could yell a warning, Rex shot him. Dropping the gun, Rex yanked out the short sword and slashed the rapist across his neck. The other soldier let go of the woman and ran to get his rifle in the corner. Rex was around the table and on him in a flash. With a mighty swing, he decapitated the soldier.

Blood sprayed him and the woman. Total silence reigned, except for ringing in Rex's ears from the rifle shot in the confined quarters. He hoped the rifle shot didn't bring more guards and proceeded to retrieved both rifles and his own revolver from the soldier. After reloading the firearms, he checked the hallway, and seeing no threats, went to free the rest of the prisoners. The rape victim who crept past him to the hallway, the rapist's blue blood still dripping off her, wandered in a daze.

One lucky break, the rapist had a large ring of keys and a five shot 9 x 19mm revolver that Rex added to his collection of weapons. He figured the heavy bolted door between the dungeon and the colonel office would block escape that direction. With a bit of luck, one of the prisoners knew another way. He opened the women's two cells. The dozen or more females were cowering along the rear wall of the cells. The key that opened the women cells wouldn't open the cells with about twenty men. The thin small middle-aged black man asked what had just occurred and who he was.

"I'm Rex. What's your name?" He figured he might as well use his real name. Only a fool would allow the Ichneumon to capture him alive after learning of their four-step punishment.

"Zolfo," the black man answered while Rex sorted through the various keys on the guard's ring to find one that fit the cell door. Seeing the guard's key ring, he asked. "Is the bastard dead?" The blood-splattered woman stumbled past. "Lulu, is that your blood?"

The woman started crying in earnest and told him between sobs the blood was from the guard while Rex opened the men's cell. Zolfo went to the woman and hugged her. Still hugging her, he asked, "Are we free?"

"Free? I'd say it's more we're loose. I just killed the guards and need directions on how to get out of here."

"I know how the guards enter. But we'd never get out that way, since it goes through the guards' barracks."

"There's always a way. If you want to leave, come on," Rex said to the group. He headed on towards the men's cells and opened those doors. The maimed prisoners he could see milling in the hallway intersection. Three of the women had ventured out of the cell. He told them to help the rape victim.

At the hallway intersection, the two prisoners, each missing a hand, were helping the man who had lost a foot as well as a hand. The fourth prisoner, Pete, the Ichneumons had held the longest and had one hand remaining. He had stayed in the cell. The big Wapiti man missing a hand and foot spoke.

"I can't imagine how you managed to escape, or how we'll get out of the fort, but thanks for coming back. I'm Bill Hopkins. I used to be Chief Hopkins. My helpers are Tammo and Ravi."

Tammo was a large Wapiti who was missing his left hand, which meant he had been prisoner for less than a year. Ravi, who appeared to be Clovis and missing his right hand, was a recent prisoner. A left-handed man, Rex figured.

"Pete is near death, helpless with one hand. He can't move," Bill said. "He asked that someone go and end his suffering." The slink hissed and thumped against the cage door. "And shoot that damn slink before it gets loose."

"You want me to handle Pete?" Zolfo asked. The Zamia had misunderstood the cause of Rex's dismay. It was the vision of a man with only one hand that had appalled him.

What a nightmare the day had become. Fear of not escaping the evilness in the dungeon threatened to unnerve him. Rex vowed to kill himself before allowing that to happen. Pete, the crippled prisoner, had the right of it.

None of them had a future unless they managed to find an unguarded exit and a severely maimed Pete would endanger all of the thirty-two men and women waiting in the hallway. Plus, what possible future could a man with no feet and one hand have in this world? The prisoners in the hallway were quiet, but fearful as they waited for directions.

"Make it painless," Rex said, realizing there was no other option. He handed Zolfo the knife he had taken from the first guard he had killed.

The women told Rex about two other men in a cell on down the hallway. He freed them. One was a Wapiti; the other was a Prussian.

Rex waved them forward and asked their names and background. It would help take his mind off Pete's fate as Zolfo ran

78

down the short hallway to deal with the man. The Prussian prisoner told him that his name was Helmick, a sailor by trade.

"I got drunk, resisted arrest and ended up here to be sold as a slave to pay my fine. I'd rather die than be recaptured." *Amen to that* Rex thought. "Can I have a rifle?"

Rex handed him one and Helmick checked the condition of the rifle, working the action to verify the rifle was loaded. Obviously, the sailor was familiar with firearms.

The Wapiti was a thin short and young nervous man, a dwarf.

"Martin Johnson is a good man," Bill Hopkins said.

"God, what did they do . . .," Martin said.

"Just Ichneumons being their usual evil selves, how did you get in here?" Bill asked

"They tried to sell me as a slave, but no one would buy me. Too small and ugly, they said. Now I'm scheduled to lose a hand next week, so I have nothing to lose. Can I have the other rifle? Do you have a plan?" Martin asked Rex.

"Martin was with me when the Ichneumon captured us two years ago," Bill said. "Don't let his size fool you, he's a good hunter with a recurved bow and knows the Krupp rifle."

The slink, unable to reach the guard's body, was now screeching at the prisoners, and Bill again asked Rex to kill it. With its head thrust through the cage door, the slink made an inviting target. Figuring the creature was too fast for him to reach, Rex still wrenched the ax from the dead guard's skull and walked across the hallway intersection to the cage. The slink eyed him approaching with the ax for a moment, before bolting to the back of its cage out of reach. The creature went silent.

"Another gunshot might draw unwanted attention. So the creature is safe for now," Rex said, handing the ax to one of the women. "Let's find a way out of this hell."

The group set off to explore the dark hallway ahead for an escape route. Helmick followed a few steps behind with a torch to illuminate their way. The women had two more torches behind them. After about hundred meters, though in the darkness it could have been more, they arrived at a dark circular stone shaft with a set of wooden stairs that spiraled up to a door about four meters above where he stood. Zolfo had by then returned to Rex's side and whispered that the door opened into the garrison's quarters.

They were in no position to take on a hundred armed soldiers and guards, even sleepy ones, and Rex considered their options. Another hallway, unlit, went off to the left of the stairs in the shaft. He figured they had a couple of hours before the relief guards would arrive and discover the escape. No one in the party knew where that dark hallway went.

Figuring they had no other choice, Rex turned into the dark opening and soon discovered its floor had a slight downward grade, along with no side cells. The stone passageway went on for about a hundred meters, and then the stone floor turned damp with a thin coating of slippery mud. Their tracks in the mud would ensure the Ichneumon guards had no problem discovering where their prisoners had fled.

A bit more disconcerting were the numerous large, three-toe tracks in the mud. The tracks had to be from the slink. Then Rex realized the hallway floor ahead of them had standing water covering it, which explained the slink tracks. It was Buster's waterhole.

After taking the torch from Helmick, Rex waded into the water. The clear water was ankle deep, but watermarks visible on the walls indicated the water had been waste deep in the past. The passageway ended at a vertical circular shaft that had a wood stairway winding around it. Visible up the shaft was two doors, with the top door a good ten meters above them. It didn't take Rex long to discover the doors blocking the shaft exits were locked. Prying open one of the doors constructed of thick wooden planks and reinforced with iron bands, didn't appear to be an option, given their lack of tools.

Of more interest, the roof of the shaft was of wood construction and appeared in poor shape with missing boards. A heavy block and tackle hung from a massive wood center beam at the top of the shaft.

"I'll bet the Ichneumon troops used it to move heavy items between levels," Helmick said. "I wonder why they closed that passage." Different textured stone had sealed what appeared to be another hallway off the shaft.

"Maybe we could break the seal," Helmick said, "if we can't open the doors."

They tried the shaft's lower door again. It was still unyielding.

"Be a noisy undertaking. Besides we lack hammers and pry bars," Rex said as he examined the seal's stonework and mortar joints. The masonry workmanship was first class. "First, I want to check the feasibility of escaping through the roof."

Rex handed his rifle to Helmick, and the torch to Zolfo, then tested the moldy thick hemp rope with his weight. It held his weight and he climbed up the dirty rope to the beam. After a bit of awkward twisting about, he gained the top of the stout timber beam.

"Zolfo come on up and bring my rifle."

The roof was within reach. Even better, it was rotten, allowing Rex to soundlessly pried away several of the shingles to make an opening to look out. It was night. The surprise was the shaft roof was less than five meters above the courtyard level and located about thirty meters from the outer wall, but still inside the fort. He then, with Zolfo's help, dragged up the heavy rope and feed it through the opening in the roof. The sound of slashing water caught his attention. The prisoners were washing off in the bottom of the shaft.

The roof structure was rotten, and Rex had to exercise care crawling out the hole and to the edge. He didn't need falling debris attracting the guards, but everything held and he was on the courtyard pavement in a moment. The shaft was part of a large stone warehouse. The fort walls appeared unguarded, but he could hear guards talking nearby. Zolfo stuck his head out of the roof to check, and he motioned for him to pull the rope back in, out of sight.

Easing along the warehouse wall in the shadows, Rex looked for a door. At the corner of the wall, he could see several guards by a fire pit across the courtyard. They were quietly talking. It appeared to be a shift change, as after a moment two of the guards walked off toward the main gate. The other two guards climbed the wall steps that bracketed a man size door in the main wall.

Rex reflected on their luck. If the Ichneumon soldiers had been on the wall when he broke through the roof, they might would have noticed. When the guards reached the walkway behind the wall's parapet, they stopped to look over it. The guards' attention elsewhere, Rex hurried around the corner to a doorway and the loading dock. Several empty wood barrels, missing lids, were stacked on the dock. The barrels provided some shelter from the guards as he studied the loading dock doors. They were barn-style sliding doors.

Rex paused behind the barrels to consider his next move. If he was to survive this nightmare, time to ponder was a luxury he didn't have. The maiming that the Ichneumons had inflicted on their prisoners had horrified him. Fear of capture and suffering amputations was threatening to emasculate his sense of honor and courage, tempting him to slip away. One person had a real chance, but thirty strangers, some crippled, it seemed a hopeless endeavor.

His indecision was wasting precious time. He wasn't going to abandon his fellow escapees. All or none it would be. He crawled over to examine the dock door lock while vowing, if by some miracle he did escape, he was not going on to Orleans. A moot point anyway, since the Ichneumons would have seized the Mischief and his crew.

Rex was about to try prying the door away from the frame when he spotted movement at the building corner he had just come around. A guard stepped into view, not ten meters away. The shadow from the barrel hid him from the guard, who was looking towards the fire pit by the main wall. He would have been helpless if the guard had come by a few moments sooner while he was sliding down the rope. Still, the guard would discover him if he walked on to the dock. Waiting for the guard to make his move, Rex wondered if his luck had run out.

The absence of Ichneumon soldiers and a whiff of smoke visible from the Mischief's stack gave Amy hope she wasn't too late. Kyle had seen her coming down the wharf and greeted her at the gangplank.

"Where's Rex?" Kyle asked. "Slim and Kit have been here about an hour." He nodded greetings to the teamster and his daughter Saliva.

"He was arrested and taken into the fort. I expect soldiers here at any moment. Fire up the boiler, you need to embark at once."

"But what about Rex?" Kyle asked. "I can't leave him."

Slim and several Wapiti had heard them and crowded at the gangplank.

"The Mischief must be saved. Without the boat, we're all trapped," Amy said. "Take two men and tell everyone else to come with me." Kyle seemed torn as to what to do.

"Kyle, don't freeze up," she said. "Get the boat out of here!"

"What about the cannons, won't they just sink us?" Kit asked. Everyone looked towards the fort but her. She searched the waterfront for Ichneumon troopers.

"Those cannons are the least of our worries, now get the Mischief out of here," Amy repeated, getting angry.

"They haven't fired those cannons in years," Haddad said.

"Forget the history lesson, Kyle, you have to get moving."

"You should listen to your engineer. Soldiers will be here at any moment, and then you'll be in the slave pens."

"Go man, we'll figure out a way to rescue Rex," Amy said, resisting an urge to slapped him. "Hide the boat and gold, and then send word to Haddad's office."

"Dad, I just saw the policeman who checks manifest. He probably waiting for soldiers," Saliva yelled. "He'll be here in a minute."

Kyle, still dubious, at least turned and yelled for the engine room crew to stroke the boiler.

Amy, getting livid, asked, "Am I going to have to do it?"

He shook his head and raced to the pilothouse. She realized he had forgotten to order the deck crew to release of the ties fastening the barges to the Delta dock.

"Kyle, stop. Give them slack to untie the barges and boat from the dock," Amy yelled on feeling the paddlewheel engage. "Slim, Kit, and anyone not needed onboard grab your weapons and come with me. Hurry," she yelled while running down the gangway to the wharf.

In short order, the Mischief crew had the barges untied and the gangway back on the deck. Even better, the boat was several feet from the dock and safe from soldiers jumping aboard from the dock. She scanned the market area for Isaac and hostile soldiers.

Then Amy heard yelling. The policemen who had earlier checked cargo and shipping manifests had spotted Isaac. The port official was yelling for Isaac to stop. Looking where he was pointing, she spotted the teamster. The official then realized the Mischief, no longer tied to the dock, was leaving and he started to bellow for the boat to return.

"I can't run, he knows me," Isaac said, as Amy ran up to him.

"You can't be standing here when the soldiers arrive," she said to the Wapiti warriors that were with her. "Slim, you guys disappear into the market."

Without a comment, the four Wapiti followed Slim into the market area. She hoped their rifles didn't draw unwelcome attention. Glancing towards the bay, she saw Kyle had cleared the wharf area and the Mischief was picking up speed. The sight gave her hope. The policeman was fat and slow covering the fifty meters to where Isaac and she waited. Amy had cautioned the Wapiti not to run, but Slim and his men were gone when she made another check. She relaxed a bit, but Isaac didn't.

"He knows I did business with Burgdorf and the Mischief," the teamster said in a low voice. "He'll want to know why the boat left without his clearance."

"Tell him the Mischief captain went to intercept Herr Purnell," Amy said, thinking fast. "The Mischief is a much faster boat and will bring Herr Purnell back here to talk with Colonel Xavier."

"Rajal, what brings you out at dinner time?" Isaac asked, dredging up a smile.

The policeman was red in the face and sweating profusely. He took a moment to catch his breath and cast a brief glance at Amy who had her hand on one of the revolvers hidden in her shoulder bag. She was not surrendering to these animals.

"That boat wasn't cleared to sail. Soldiers are coming to impound it," Rajal said. They all turned to look. There were no soldiers in sight.

"That's the boat you're talking about?" Isaac asked, pointing toward the Mischief. The policeman nodded, mopping his face. "Don't you know that's Purnell's fast boat? It's going to intercept Herr Purnell's boat and hurry him back here to clear up some issue at the fort. They'll be back tomorrow, with the man."

The policeman had no response to that news and they watched in silence, for a moment, the Mischief steaming toward the Prussian battleship, Schlesien. Amy reckoned the Mischief was safe. Kyle must have realized the fort wouldn't chance a cannon shot that might hit a

Prussian warship. Isaac and Amy then walked off and left the policeman staring out at the disappearing Mischief while waiting for the late soldiers to arrive. The labyrinth of market stalls and alleyways soon had them hidden from the wharf area. Amy stopped Isaac.

"How can we free Burgdorf?" She knew he would try to escape.

Rex was willing his heart not to beat so loud. The Ichneumon guard had stopped beside the loading dock stairs. The soldier was a few meters from the barrels by the door where Rex hid. He had been about to open the loading dock doors that sealed the warehouse entrance when he heard the guard. The doors were heavy wood, barn-style sliding doors hung from a top roller system. The door's bottom appeared unfastened, but until the guard turned away, Rex feared to investigate and attract attention. Then one of the men by the fire yelled to the guard, who then walked over and spoke with the wall guards.

Safe for the moment from discovery on the warehouse dock, Rex tried opening the loading dock door. It wouldn't slide, but it had enough slack that he could swing the bottom edge of the door slightly away from the wall. By lying on his back, he was able to squeeze through into the warehouse.

The floppiness in the door was due to the fact someone had forgotten to latch the hook on the inside of the door to the wall frame. No shouts from the wall guards meant they hadn't noticed his entrance into the warehouse, but just in case anyone came to investigate, he hooked the door latch back in place.

The interior was dark, but Rex's night vision was good and he could make out stacks of large iron cannon balls and wood barrels stacked three high. The strong tobacco smell had him wondering if the barrels were some of those he saw earlier in the day at the Atlantic Tobacco warehouse. Smaller barrels, the size used for gunpowder, were stacked among the large tobacco barrels. Rex figured they were empties awaiting return to the arsenal, until he lifted one and discovered it was full of something. Surely, it wasn't gunpowder. Gunpowder should be in a secure magazine.

The cut stone block construction of the loading dock's rear wall was the same as the shaft, not the grouted stone construction of the outer warehouse walls. Rex saw a heavy wood door in the rear wall. The door's location was about where he expected the door from the dungeon shaft. Two corroded iron bolts locked the door. The bolts required all his strength to slide open. It was obvious that no one had opened those bolts in a long time. With a low moan from the hinges, the door opened onto the second bench in the stone shaft stairs. The escaped prisoners let out a sigh of relief on recognizing him.

"It's critical, not a sound. There are guards nearby," Rex whispered to caution the group. He noticed Zolfo and Sammy were still perched on the upper beam and motioned for them to come down. Martin was in the bottom of the shaft watching back down the hallway.

"Bring the rope, Sammy. Put out the torches and follow me."

Bill Hopkins had a terrible time getting up the shaft's steps, but at last managed to enter the warehouse. The group filtered in among the stacks of barrels. Zolfo and Sammy dragged the rope into the warehouse before Rex closed and slid the bolt home, locking the door.

"I've been here before. The rum storage vault is below," the Zamian man said. "The door is over there, but it'll be locked. The man pointed off into the darkness on their right.

"Zolfo, do you have any idea on how to escape the fort?" Rex asked in a whisper. They had managed to escape the dungeon, but not the fort. After discovering the dead dungeon guards, it wouldn't take the guards long to find them.

Rex crossed back to the loading dock door and looked through the crack between the sliding doors. He could see two guards were still across the courtyard by the fire pit. Two of guards were missing, and then Rex spotted them standing on the upper walkway at the top of the outer wall. They appeared to be looking over the parapet wall.

"Zolfo, is that gate across the way locked or just bolted?"

The wiry black man looked through the crack. "I'm not sure. As a rule the doors are just bolted." He turned away from the warehouse door and pointed. "That door over there goes to the stairs for the rum vault, but there's no exit from the vault."

"Is there powder down there?" Bill asked. The maimed Wapiti looked in terrible pain with his leg stump now bleeding.

"There's not supposed to be, but I've heard they were using it for a powder magazine," Zolfo said. "There're powder barrels here." He pointed to several smaller kegs among the large tobacco hogsheads.

A fort this size would have several powder magazines. A powder magazine detonation might offer a great distraction to cover their escape, if it didn't kill them. He told Zolfo to give him the unlit torch.

Bill, Zolfo, and Rex then carefully dodged around the prisoners to the vault door. He passed several of the women prisoners clustered around a bundle of burlap that they were unfolding and cutting with a knife stripped from one of the dead guards. Rex hoped they were making wraps to cover their nakedness. It was very distracting.

Unlike the shaft door, the well-oiled bolts and hinges on the vault door slid open smoothly, revealing stairs descending into total darkness. The only way to see was to light a torch. He told Zolfo to strike a spark. Holding the torch up, Rex entered the stairs that had a ramp running alongside to use for rolling barrels up and down from the cellar. There were many barrels stacked in the cellar, but what they contained wasn't clear.

"Zolfo, hold the torch."

A tense Zolfo remained on the top stair with the torch as Rex pulled the short sword and pried the bung out of the first barrel. It contained a liquid that he had no trouble identifying, rum. He told him to come down a few steps with the torch to illuminate the room better. The man's hand was shaking so violently, Rex feared the burning rag might come apart and fall into the magazine and land on spilled gunpowder.

"Zolfo, let me have the torch," Bill said.

The first row of barrels consisted of oak whiskey barrels and he figured contained rum. Behind those barrels were rows upon rows of 15-kg wood kegs of gunpowder, stacked four high. The room was full of those kegs, at least a thousand, maybe many more. Rex opened one to taste the powder. It was corned black powder with the course texture used in cannons and large blasting charges. He checked two more barrels, same powder.

Rex went back for better light and found Bill with the torch. They watched as he tossed a few grains of the powder on the torch. It flared with the satisfying flash of good quality gunpowder.

Rex hustled up the steps and organized a work party from the five male prisoners who had been watching. He put them to work carrying the powder kegs among the tobacco hogsheads to the dock door. He planned to form a train of gunpowder from the vault to the man-gate in the main fort wall across from the loading dock.

"Seventy-five kilos of gunpowder should be plenty. Stack the kegs by the main warehouse door," Rex told them as he returned to the vault. Bill was struggling on the vault stairs. "Bill, careful you don't fall down those steps."

"Make sure you open several kegs down there, those wood kegs tend to protect the powder and we can't chance a misfire."

Rex agreed. He then realized many more gunpowder kegs were stacked behind the tobacco barrels, and he could use those kegs to blow the place. Save them from having to depend on a powder train down the stairs, always an iffy proposition for a fuse. It was a careless way to store gunpowder, especially in a fort subject to attack and receiving enemy fire. One rifle bullet could detonate a barrel of gunpowder.

Still, Rex set to work opening a keg in the vault and pouring its contents around and on several rows of the gunpowder kegs. He then used another barrel to pour a generous trail of powder up the barrel ramp to avoid the vertical risers of the stairs. Rex crowded past Bill to complete the powder tail to the top of the ramp and then went back down the steps for a final check.

"Be careful with that torch, Bill."

Rex next poured more gunpowder from the stairs to the kegs by the tobacco hogsheads.

"Might as well tie everything together," he said, making a final check in the vault.

Next, with the fuse set, Rex knew they needed to determine if the man-door in the outer fort wall across the courtyard from the warehouse offered an avenue of escape. He didn't know how much time had lapsed, but the guard shift change and the discovery of their escape had to be near. Then the unexpected happened. Bill slapped away Zolfo with his left arm stump and kept the torch.

"Get everyone out! I'm staying," the triple amputee said, knocking Zolfo off the top step and taking his place.

Rex grabbed the stunned Zolfo and stopped his fall. He realized what Bill had in mind.

"Don't, we can make a powder trail from outside to set off the magazine."

"You don't have the time and I'm done living as a cripple. Tip another barrel over for me before you go so the torch can't miss."

Rex could understand Bill's feelings, but suicide still didn't sit well with him. To buy time he tipped a barrel over and rolled it back and forth to create a pile of black powder at the bottom of the stairs. Thankfully, the powder in the barrel was properly corned, screened, and dust free. One spark and they'd all be history.

"Don't do anything stupid, Rex." Bill said. "Just leave. Save the other thirty people so I can pay these animals back for their barbarous conduct." He held the torch away from Rex and Zolfo as they crowded by him on the stairs.

"Tell my brother, John, that I gave the bastards a good lick, and to hang Bret Paget. He's the one that double-crossed us and sold us into slavery."

"Bill, know that Bret Paget was killed in the fight for Donnelly's fort," Rex said. "The bastard got his due. We may have to shoot our way out of here. I'm going to go for that gate across the courtyard. I'm not sure how long it'll take to get everyone clear. You want the door closed or open?"

"Leave it open so I can hear, I'll wait for the Ichneumons to arrive, but give me another torch."

Rex told the young Wapiti warrior to find another fresh torch. Zolfo brought the torch and laid it on the step beside crippled man, along with an extra flint and steel.

"Those are of no used," Bill said. "Bring me a couple of unlit torches for backup. In case the bastards didn't discover the prison break until morning."

Zolfo, embarrassed, realized that a one handed man couldn't use a flint and steel.

"We need to move. Bill thanks, and if by chance Colonel Xavier escapes, I'll see he receives justice," Rex promised.

He then went to the main door and learned that the guards were still on the wall. They hadn't moved. What a quandary, with the four rifles in their possession they could kill the wall guards, but the shots would bring the garrison out in force. If that man-door in the wall was locked, than the guards would have them trapped in the open courtyard.

"Any suggestion on how to find out if that door is locked?" a frustrated Rex asked.

If Amy were the prisoner, she was confident Rex would figure some way to rescue her, not stand around frustrated and wringing his hands. But, she couldn't think of a solution. Finally, in desperation, she had asked Salvia if there was any way into the fort, besides the guarded gates.

"Along the fort's wall are several access doors used by the fort's maintenance crews to clear brush and repair cracks," Salvia said. "They're locked from the inside, but occasionally the crew forgets to lock the door. Other times the men will leave one of the doors unlocked so their girlfriends can sneak in. But it's no help. The prisoners are in the dungeon, out of reach."

Unless these Ichneumons were idiots, they wouldn't trust a wooden door to keep enemy soldiers and saboteurs at bay. Amy had visited several Prussian forts and figured the Ichneumons designed their forts in a similar fashion. At the very least, there would be a portcullis, a heavy iron grate in the ceiling poised to drop and block the passageway. Standard design was for a murder hole above the grate, to allow the fort defenders to protect the grate. Whether a small passage would rate a murder hole, Amy couldn't know. She hoped not. Still, to go in the passageway without a way to deal with a dropped iron grate would be foolish.

After the sun set, Amy, Slim, Kit, and Saliva had hiked up the tree-and-brush covered ridge behind the market area and below the fort's massive rock walls. The group had stopped at the edge of the fifty-meter wide clearing along the fort's wall. They could see the door Saliva had told them about at the base of the wall. It wasn't wood. The door was an iron plate.

Two bored looking guards rested on the wall's parapet, smoking.

"They'd be easy targets," Slim whispered, "But so would we in the clearing."

Amy agreed their presence had stymied her plan to gain entry into the fort through a maintenance door. Then the guards stood up and turned. She could hear them asking someone in the fort whom they were. Then the guards disappeared from the parapet.

"What's going on?" Amy asked. Salvia just shrugged her shoulders. She wished Hokee were with her to warn them of approaching strangers. Instead, the wolf was with Kyle on the Mischief. Hokee tended to attract attention that she didn't need in Port Delta. Then several quick rifle shots and in the stillness after the shots, Amy heard several voices, someone shouting, "Move, move."

David C. Brown

Chapter 6

The tall striking black woman who had organized the burlap fashion show stepped up to Rex. He was happy to see they had wrapped burlap around their torso, though only about half the black men had chosen to use the rough burlap for a loincloth. He would have passed also, having felt the dirty, coarse, and prickly fabric.

"I have an idea," the woman said. "Those guards are wearing gray uniforms. They're local men, not those Ichneumon bastards. I can pretend to be a whore that lost track of time and walk over to the gate. Those guards will be down from the wall in a flash to check me out. If I imply I'll grant some favors against the outer wall, I think they'll open the gate. When they do, have them shot and we'll all run."

The woman's forthright discussion of using her sexual charms to distract the guards surprised Rex.

"There has to be an outer gate," stalling while he wrapped his mind around using a naked female to help clear a way for escaping. "What if it's locked? And what's your name?"

"I'm Salma. Wouldn't you figure they'd just use an inner bolt on the outer gate?" The lady was focused and all business.

"In normal circumstances, but in a fort you wouldn't want an outer door that anyone could open," Rex said. She nodded while again taking a moment to look through the door crack to check on the guards.

If they had sufficient ropes and a bit of time, they could go over the wall. Well, not the mutilated prisoners, and he wasn't about to abandon them. *Besides how tough could the lock be? The one holding the bolt closed,* Rex thought.

"Why wouldn't they think you're an escaped prisoner or spy and arrest you?" He knew he was still hesitating with the question, but they were about to commit to a life-or-death decision.

"Two reasons, first no one has ever escaped from here."

"That's encouraging news," Rex said. Salma smiled and continued.

"The second reason is that they would expect a spy to sneak through the shadows," she said. "Not me, I'm going to noisily sashay across that open courtyard with you, my last client, waving to me. You game, big boy?"

The woman appeared less concerned than Rex about the irreversible choice. Actually, she was ahead of him and had realized they had no other choice. Either chance the deception or sure death in the dungeon.

"If the guards sound the alarm, it won't work," Zolfo said.

"No shit," Rex said. His outburst was a sure sign his anxieties had his nerves stressed. He could feel the entire group's attention on him. If the tunnel through the outer wall had a lock he couldn't open, they would all be doomed. But if they dithered in the warehouse until the guards discovered the prison break, they'd be doomed.

"Salma, you're okay. I like your idea."

"I found a hammer that I'll bring," Zolfo said. "It might help if there is a lock."

Rex nodded and then organized the sharp shooters. "Zolfo, Martin, Helmick, agree on which guard you're targeting so you don't all shoot the same one." Rex said, unhooking the sliding warehouse door. Salma had stripped off the burlap and asked for his shirt. He slipped his revolver under his belt behind his back after handing over the shirt.

"You stay on the dock bare chested and wave," the stunning female said, "While I flounce across the courtyard in your shirt. If you have a God, now would be a good time to ask him to keep their commander from showing up."

"Alright, girl, start the show," Rex said, sliding warehouse door open with a bang. They were committed. He walked out on the dock with Salma wearing his shirt. They kissed in front of the speechless guards. She then walked down the steps to the courtyard. The two guards, who had whirled around on hearing the door open, had recovered and demanded an explanation.

"Relax, boys. It's just the captain's girl. Goodnight, Salma," Rex said loud enough for the guards to hear and then walked back into the warehouse, adding in a whisper to the snipers, "Not yet, wait until I say to fire."

Watching from the warehouse's dark interior Rex listened to Salma tease the guards about having to work while everyone else was sleeping. One guard wanted to cross to the warehouse and find the big stranger, but Salma had let the unbuttoned shirt flop open and neither guard beside her could take their eyes off that magnificent body. The guard on the wall was hurrying down the stairs to join the party.

She said something and after conferring among themselves, two of the guards went and sat on the stairs near the wall exit. The other guard pulled out a key and proceeded to unlock the exit door. Rex felt a vast relief when the guard swung open the gate and shoved Salma ahead into the passage.

"Now," Rex said. Three rifle shots shattered the night's silence. The three guards were down, and Salma was rifling the one guard's pockets and picking up the key ring.

"Two minutes, Bill," Rex yelled as the prisoners leaped off the loading dock and ran to the exit door.

Arriving with Martin, Rex found the passageway full of prisoners. The word was a locked gate blocked the tunnel exit. Already two guards had materialized and were firing at the entrance. One of their bullets hit a prisoner, and his screaming added to the group's rising panic. Helmick and Martin returned fire and the guards scattered. Rex forced his way to the blocked exit telling everyone to stay calm.

Salma and Zolfo were in front of a heavy iron door with stout brass hinges and two large bars that slid into holes in the rock blocks forming the doorframe. The problem was a small iron pin that locked the top bar in place. It was held in position with a key lock that none of the keys fitted. The lock looked fragile to Rex, but all they had was Zolfo's hammer and knives for tools.

"The commander must have added the lock to prevent the guards from using the passageway for illicit entry of their, ah, girlfriends," Zolfo said. "Look, there's an iron grate above us."

Rex knew what that was and yelled for Helmick, the Prussian sailor.

"The magazine's going to explode any moment. Helmick, there has to be a room above the passageway. Find its entrance and don't let anyone in it to drop the iron grate." The Prussian sailor was gone in a moment.

Rex crowded past Zolfo and Salma to reach the door. He was trying to find a favorable angle to use the short sword to pry the bolt out of the bar when the ground moved, followed an instant later by a stunning blast. The pressure wave entered the tunnel and shoved people into a tangled mess throughout the tunnel. The grate fell about halfway and jammed as the tunnel wall cracked.

Rex was deaf. All he could hear was ringing. The tunnel looked unstable. Two more cracks had appeared and several bricks had fallen from the ceiling. Had the tunnel collapse? Between the darkness and dust, he couldn't be sure. He put that worry aside and concentrated on the pin. He got the right fulcrum and the pin snapped. He then pried the two bolts back and the heavy iron door swung open.

A dazed and dust coated Zolfo stumbled out the opening. The fresh air was a relief after the rank tunnel air and unwashed bodies. Salma was crawling toward the opening, so Rex went back the tunnel toward the fort's interior. Chaos had a firm grip on the prisoners in the tunnel. He shouted orders and directions to reorient the confused escapees and, in a few moments, had the survivors scrambling toward the correct exit. The guards' blind gunfire into the tunnel had killed several prisoners. As he crawled across the rubble partially blocking the tunnel opening into the fort, he hoped the garrison had suffered worse from Bill's explosion, and that Helmick had survived.

The gunshots and shouting from inside the fort had puzzled Amy. Could it be a prison break? Then the fort exploded. She watched mesmerized as several flaming objects arced up through the rising pillar of debris and dust. Even as pieces of rock and wood debris rained down on them while they hugged the tree trunks, Amy knew that somehow Rex had caused it. Behind her, down the slope from her location, a ball of fire landed. It had looked like a comet, arching far up into the sky, before turning and crashing down into the trees in a burst of fire. Flames momentary licked at her. The smell told Amy the flaming object had been a burning barrel of rum.

Were her hopes like that barrel? Amy wondered. If Rex had perished, and the massiveness of the explosion inside the fort sure made it likely, then her dream of a life with a man she respected had died. The surviving Wapiti and she would be fortunate to escape and reach River Point.

The door that sealed the service entrance in the fort's wall opened and several Zamia men and women staggered out of the smoke filled passageway. Some people had survived the explosion. Amy ran to the opening to help, praying Rex had been one of them.

From the light of fires, Rex could see a crater existed where the warehouse had been. Things were burning all around, but the darkness, smoke, and dust limited his view. Fires appeared to be burning thorough-out the entire fort and there didn't appear to be a single live Ichneumon soldier or guard in the area.

A shout made Rex look up. A dust coated Helmick was crawling out a partially caved-in room that was missing its outer wall above the tunnel.

"Help me, my leg's not working right," the Prussian sailor said.

The fires were becoming intense in the rubble piled around the warehouse crater and that created another danger. Unexploded barrels of gunpowder and rum buried in the burning rubble might explode. That realization sent him scrambling up the unstable rubble to reach the sailor and help carry him to the tunnel. They had almost made it back to the outer door when Amy, holding a revolver, met them.

"Thank the Lord, you made it," Amy said. She hugged him and Rex could smell singed hair. "What happened?" she asked.

"We have to keep moving, the guards will be after us. I'll tell you later." He'd preferred to hold her, but they didn't have the luxury. "We have to go," Rex broke the embrace to help Helmick who had slumped to the tunnel floor.

"How bad is it? I want to take a quick look." Curious, she started toward the tunnel's fort side inlet.

"Is the Mischief okay?" He asked, picking up the wounded sailor.

"I told Kyle to hide it," Amy said, stopping. "Ouch, damn, where'd that rock come from?" Part of a brick from the tunnel ceiling had fallen and grazed Amy's arm, causing her to look up. "I fear the tunnel is on the verge of collapse."

"The entire outer wall may collapse, help me with Helmick, before we're trapped" Rex said. She grabbed the man's other arm to help.

In a moment, they were out of the tunnel. Clouds of dust and tobacco smoke were swirling in the air outside the fort's wall, as they carried the battered sailor across the clearing to the woods. Slim and Kit spotted them and rushed over to relieve them of the unconscious Helmick. Then a section of the wall above the tunnel exit collapsed with several pieces of the wall rock tumbling as far as the trees. The tunnel entrance was covered. They had escaped just in time.

Colonel Xavier's room, located near the fort's south gate and next to the main barracks, was the upper floor of a plain two story wood structure that reminded him of a clerk's office. His humble quarters were nothing like General Bezdek's plush quarters by the north gate. Dare he hope to get those quarters, if his prisoner was Rex Knight and the emperor made him a general? The colonel was sipping the local dark rum that had a hint of molasses and weighing rather to have another glass of rum or go to bed.

The next day would be a busy morning. He wanted to be present when the guards questioned the Prussian. Lieutenant Kakani's information on the missing boat and the captain going to find Herr Purnell had him wondering if he needed to wait, not cut off his prisoner's foot. His experience was that all those animals begged and pleaded for him to spare them. By holding out that hope, he might actually learn the man's identity. The colonel decided against another drink and went to bed.

The sound of gunfire woke Xavier. Not sure what he had heard, he stayed in the comfortable bed debating whether to investigate, and then he heard more gunfire. The colonel rolled out of bed and started dressing when he felt the ground move. A flash caused him to look out the room's window in time to see the entire barrack and warehouse area of the fort's interior erupt in a massive fireball. The sight riveted Xavier. What had happened?

Then his room's window exploded in his face as the shockwave hit. The blast left him flat on his back and racked with pain, his eyes felt like the glass had sliced them open. But worse was the dawning realization that the explosion had shredded his hopes of a general's rank.

Then Xavier heard a loud whistling sound. It reminded him of the sound a cannon ball makes as it passes overhead. Were the Prussians attacking? His last awareness of the horrible night was the sound of the roof ripping open and things crushing him. Colonel Xavier never saw the large iron cannon ball that smashed through the room, taking off his right foot.

The escapees had collected in the woods on the slopes below the fort. Most had no clear idea where to flee. Rex, watching the dense smoke and occasional tongues of flames visible above the fort's walls, decided they were safe for the moment. The raging fires would have the surviving soldiers occupied.

"Some of the escapees are by the edge of the swamp washing off the worst of the grime," Slim said.

"We need the Mischief," Amy said. "Kit, go and see if Kyle left word. Try Captain Dalporto, he may know. We'll meet you at the dock."

Amy told Rex about the Ichneumons soldiers' attempt to seize the Mischief after his arrest. He learned he had Amy to thank for saving the Mischief, as they jogged to the swamp's edge. They found Zolfo, Sammy, and Salma in the swamp cleaning off the grime. Martin, the dwarf, was with Salma. Rex had lost track of Martin in the confusion of the escape and blast.

"What's your plan, Zolfo?" Rex asked. He noticed that Amy was eyeing the nude Salma and the shirt.

"Most of the prisoners are slaves and their owners will organize a pursuit to recover their property," Zolfo said. He had been rinsing his shirt and paused to check the hillside before adding. "Erdogam's minions are most likely already headed to the fort to check the slave cells."

Zolfo wrung his shirt to help dry it while explaining Erdogam was the man, a former river trader, who, along with Colonel Xavier, supervised the slave market. Since the colonel's promotion, Erdogam was now responsible for the safekeeping of the market's property, meaning the slaves.

"He'll hire Apophis who is remorseless in pursuit of runaways," Salma said. "Our best hope is Erdogam thinks we're buried in the rubble."

"Do you know Apophis?" Amy asked. Salma nodded.

"What about the ring?" Zolfo asked. "If the explosion freed them, Erdogam will be too busy to hunt us."

Rex asked what they were talking about, what ring.

"Two large shipments of Zamia slaves landed last week, nearly seven hundred men and women," Salma said. "The ones that escaped with us were part of the fancies that the colonel had selected from the new group. The auction was to be Saturday. The rest of the slaves are still in a ring stockade behind the fort, and I figure the explosion smashed it and the ones that weren't killed are now free."

"I was told the Prussians had ended the slave trade."

"That's nonsense, they're involved, though the emperor has had for the last year the Prussian navy patrolling the easterly trade winds and arrested any slavers caught," Salma said. "These were the first new slaves in Delta in over a year. The navy must have ended the blockade."

"I'm headed up the river as soon as I reach the docks and find the Mischief," Rex said. "I'm escaping this hell. I can take a few extra people like Martin, Helmick, and any other Wapiti that want to return home, but I plan to embark immediately before the Ichneumons shut down the docks."

The sound of another explosion within the fort caught their attention for a moment. Rex had hoped another magazine would explode and finish the destruction of the evil place, but the explosion they heard must have been just a single barrel of gunpowder.

Bill Hopkins had dealt a massive blow to the blue bloods and their prized fort. The Wapiti chief had gotten his revenge. Rex was still having difficulty believing their luck with that outer gate and escaping the outer wall collapse. Depending on lucky breaks was a loser's strategy. He wanted gone.

Amy couldn't allow his plan to proceed. He was thinking short term. Something had unnerved the man. Rex was just fleeing. She needed the Mischief for her trip to Orleans, then to hunt Apophis. She owed that monster a bullet in the head. And . . ., and that willowy black woman, how did she come to be wearing his shirt and nothing else? Was she a slave?

A good night's sleep is what Rex needed, and she had just the thing back at the Mischief. This morning, she had visited her mother's friend, Sitar Jain, an herbalist from the island, a real witch who had a small store near the Delta wharf area. Amy had used part of her share of the money found in the Orleans Queen safe to buy medical supplies, medicines, and tonics to take back to her lab. One of the tonics she had stocked up on was the red poppy infusion. It was for the Wapiti doctors. It aided sleep and alleviated pain.

Amy also needed to pick up her order from Krause at the printing press. She figured the explosion would have bought the man back to his shop to check the building.

The gunfire and a heavy boom brought Colonel Markel running to the port side of HMS Rhine Mar, a new Prussian armored sidewheeler troop ship. A large explosion had occurred within the Ichneumon fort, and he sensed it might herald an opportunity for a general's star. The whispered rumor among the fleet's officers was that Emperor Schnabel had asked Admiral Scheer to seize the fort at Port Delta. However, the admiral had managed to blow the boiler on the HMS Hendrick and kill himself before finalizing the attack plans.

Acting fleet commander Admiral Wilhelm was still holding hearings on what caused the Hendrick to explode. All the witnesses had testified that Admiral Scheer had ordered the safe maximum boiler pressure exceeded. Wilhelm's refusal to accept that a fellow admiral had made a foolish mistake was proof, in Colonel Markel's opinion, that Wilhelm was an even bigger fool than Scheer. However, the navy brass wasn't concerned about an infantry colonel's opinion and plans for seizing Fort Delta remained incomplete.

The Rhine Mar captain was a congenial man for a navy officer and he agreed with Markel's suggestion that they dock and help the injured at Port Delta.

The Prussian infantry unit on board the Rhine Mar was the 88th Highland battalion, trained to fight in snow-capped mountains. The colonel had expected orders sending the battalion into the Pyrenees to fight bandits. Instead, the new orders had assigned the 88th battalion to Admiral Scheer's fleet. They would provide ground troops for the planned Erie River campaign. Sending trained mountain troops to patrol swamps and do garrison duty along the Erie River basin seemed a huge waste of talent to the colonel.

On arriving at Port Delta, Admiral Scheer had requested an attached infantry group from the 88th. The admiral wanted troops to garrison River Point should the Wapiti prove uncooperative. Colonel Markel had sent Captain Beck. He was the battalion's best infantry captain and he would know how to handle Wapiti.

Well, for sure, something hadn't cooperated with the admiral. He was dead, his boat sunk. Of more concern to the colonel was why

Captain Beck and his men hadn't managed to secure the fort at River Point. No one in the group of survivors attending the Admiralty hearing seemed to know.

He hadn't much cared where Berlin sent him, but after a month on a ship, he just wanted off the ship, even an assignment patrolling swamps looked attractive. He had eight hundred well-armed and trained troopers, enough to garrison every Ichneumon fort on the Erie. Even more important, in the battalion he had five other capable infantry captains, besides Captain Beck. The command structure of the battalion's five line companies that formed the heart of his battalion was solid. Fort Delta was as good as place as any to start a 'garrisoning'. He called the captains to the bow.

"The fort is a large facility with many underground passageways," Colonel Markel said. "I suspect one of the magazines exploded. For sure, the explosion appears to have been massive, and I figure it has the garrison disoriented. I know General Bezdek is in Orleans, so that flunkey, Colonel Xavier, is the commander. The speculation I heard in the market is the garrison is understaffed, but reinforcements are expected. I want companies A and B to storm the main gate and setup strong defense points inside the fort. You're to seize the colonel, if he shows up. If asked, we're there to provide protection from looters. Company C, since your training is to scale cliffs, I'll give you the job of crawling through tunnels."

"Do I detect a bit of sarcasm," Captain Bromberg asked. He was the battalion's wiseass, nephew of the emperor, and the youngest captain.

"Pay attention, captain," Colonel Markel said. "Company C's job is to flush out hostile forces hiding in the dungeons, which I've been told are vast. Free every one that looks like a slave, which I've heard there're hundreds of."

"Isn't that hell hole famous for selling young Zamia females?" the captain of Company D asked. "Naked, beautiful Zamia slaves that might embarrass, even distract a young and inexperienced officer. Company D would be proud to handle the odorous duty."

"Watch it, pal, I don't want to call you out," Captain Bromberg bristled, then catching himself, laughed and added, "Besides, I'll be fine as long as there no nude Wapiti females among them."

That remark resulted in a round of teasing from the other captains. They knew Bromberg's much-decorated cousin, Major Caprivi, had fallen hard for a Wapiti maiden.

"Enough nonsense, Company D, you're to secure the wharf and market area. Company E, you're in reserve. Keep in mind that speed is critical. I don't want the Ichneumons to recover and try to stop us. If no shots are fired, that would be best." Seeing several questioning looks, the colonel added, "Use a club or your fist."

The ship docked and the Prussian force disembarked at double time as the horizon lightened. They encountered dozens of dazed Zamians wandering about the waterfront.

Unaware of the Prussian assault occurring at the fort's main gate, Rex and Amy, after locating Martin, had jogged to the wharf where the Mischief had last been. Zolfo and Salma, both familiar with Port Delta area, told Rex that they would take charge of the surviving Zamia prisoners.

The Delta waterfront was teeming with worried citizens wondering what had occurred in the fort. To Rex's relief, the Mischief was back at the south wharf where he had left it less than twelve hours earlier. Even better, he learned on boarding that the Mischief's boiler was up to pressure.

"Hi Amy, I see you found him," Kyle said. "When I heard the explosion, I figured you caused it and the Ichneumons would be too occupied to be concerned about us. So I returned." The young captain had acquired a black headscarf that gave him a piratical air.

"Bill Hopkins did that, bless his soul," Rex said. "Thanks to him, those evil bastards are occupied."

"Bill? I thought he died two years ago in a boat accident. That's what those Ichneumon traders told us."

"Bill was a prisoner, about to start the third part of the four-step sentence," Rex said. Kyle and Amy, both familiar with the cruel Ichneumon's punishment, gasped.

The whistle blasts alerted them to the approach of another Prussian warship. "You think the Prussians are coming to help or to seize the Ichneumon fort?" Kyle asked. The entire fort appeared to be burning. The flames had given the cloud layer a reddish glow.

"Maybe if we're lucky, another magazine will explode and finish the destruction," Amy said. "I have to pick up some paper supplies, be back in fifteen minutes." She was gone before Rex could object.

In the process of trying to spot Amy, Rex noticed the large number of Prussian soldiers headed toward the fort.

"The Prussians, do you suppose they're coming to help?"

"The Prussian naval officer is not by nature given to impulsive behavior or helping the Ichneumons," Saad said.

Rex, thinking of Admiral Scheer, wasn't sure he agreed. He also wasn't sure Kyle had made a smart choice freeing the first mate. He just didn't trust the man, but agreed with Kyle that since their enemies now knew they were in Port Delta, there was no point in worrying about Saad warning Purnell's men. The first mate was still useful as a pilot.

"If I was the Prussian commander, I'd seize that fort and bury those cruel bastards in their own dungeon," Rex said.

Kyle pointed at two Wapiti women and other strangers on the wharf. The two women had the typical Wapiti comeliness, looked to be in their late twenties. Kyle told him they wanted to talk with the man in charge.

"You're the captain. They wouldn't talk with you?" Rex asked.

He studied the two women, as Kyle relayed their unreceptiveness to his and the crew's offer of the restroom and a set of clean dark gray cotton fatigues to replace their burlap wraps. Rex remembered them being in the cell with the Zamia women.

"The taller one's response to the crew's offer had a guarded, almost bitter tone."

"Well, they have been in hell, so their caution is understandable," Rex said. He asked their names.

"I'm Ly and she's Wendy," the taller one said. "Who are you, why were you in the dungeon, and who's he," The antagonistic woman asked, pointing at Kyle.

The Mischief's crew seemed as curious to hear Rex's answers, as was Ly. The Prussian marines were still pouring off the second warship that had docked near the Mischief, reminding him that they needed to leave the port. The Mischief didn't need entangled in a battle between empires for control of the fort.

"I'm Rex. He's Kyle, the boat's captain. It's none of your business, but we had just delivered our cargo of nuts to the tobacco company. I was in the fort paying the fees when the colonel had me arrested on some trumped-up charge. And, like you, I joined the prison break to escape. We're headed back home to Smithtown. You can come or stay."

"What a crock of . . ." Ly said. "We're not to be your slaves. We're free just like that?" She snapped her fingers for emphasis, looking at the silent audience, before focusing on Rex. His patience with the hostile woman was exhausted.

"Look, we're freemen. You're a Wapiti and welcome to join our crew as a free woman. No slaves allowed. Just for the record, which tribe are you from?"

Ly just glared at him. The younger woman, Wendy, started trembling. She was clearly on her last energy, but seemed to find some reserve of energy and in a weak voice told him.

"I'm, well, both of us are from Johnsontown. We were visiting West Port with Chief Chin to inspect the construction of the new fort. A couple of Ichneumon traders, a man name Prado, drugged us and sold us to Tyler Reed. Reed's brother needed money and sent us to Port Delta to be sold."

"Come on, look at them," Ly said. "They're no better the Reed brothers or that bastard, Chief Chin. You can't trust these river rats."

"But Erdogam's out there. How are we going to escape his men? He did come back for us. He could have left us. He even helped Bill."

Kyle was one of the handsome Wapiti males with an outgoing nature, when not mad. "What's wrong with you guys? Get them some fatigues to wear. That burlap has to be itchy." He then noticed the sailor still holding the fatigues. "Let me have those." Kyle snapped his finger. Rex thought that was an even better snap than Ly's.

"It is itchy," Wendy said, "but we didn't want to accept them and be ah obligated to ah . . ."

"Good lord, girl," Kyle exclaimed. "We're not like that."

Ly and Rex exchanged surprised looks while the two of them had their own private exchange. Several rifle shots in the distance added to the tension.

"Well, if you're fool enough to fall for assurances from a pretty face, I'm not. Good luck, girl." Ly turned and jumped back on the wharf and disappeared into the market area. The crew looked disappointed and one of the men put the other set fatigues back in the trunk.

The sun would be up soon and Rex wanted gone from Port Delta. Memories of Bill's suppurating partially scabbed over stumps and Pete, with one hand and laying helpless in the filthy cell, haunted Rex. Zolfo or Isaac could worry about Ly. Now, where had Amy gone?

"Rex, Rex, wait." The shouts caused him to turn. He looked and saw Salma and Silva Haddad running toward the Mischief. Then there was another round of rifle shots from the area of the fort's main gate.

"Erdogam saw us," she said. "He shot Zolfo and is now after soldiers to arrest us."

"Kyle, Saad! Get over here." Rex yelled. He didn't need this complication. The two-armed men ran over to him while Wendy rushed to Salma. He heard her tell Salma that Ly had ran off. While Wendy had Salma distracted, Silva was helping Zolfo and a couple of dozen escaped slaves silently gather by the walkway.

"Please don't leave them," Salma said. "They have no place to go."

It wasn't fair to ask him to risk everything, Rex thought. They were strangers, didn't even speak the language, and were sure to be trouble, even dangerous. Then there was the winter sloe gold to protect. They're desperate and meek now, but later when they hear rumors of the wealth hidden on the Mischief and realized that they outnumber the Wapiti five to one, then what. Then he thought of Bill and Pete's fate.

"Load them on the barges, but first take anything they could use as a weapon. I want to embark in two minutes," Rex said. "Salma, Silva, tell them to board, now. We're leaving."

The confusion was vast as the Wapiti paddle wheeler crew prepared to pull away from the dock with everyone. Amy, to Rex's relief, ran out of the market and scurried up the gangway with several brown bags.

"I'll fix you a cup of coffee," Amy said. Pausing a moment to watch the confused scramble by the Zamians to reach the front barges, she added, "Oh, good, you're taking them."

Then she disappeared into the engine room. *Had she risked another trip into the market for coffee?* Rex wondered as he went to find Salma. He found Zolfo, who appeared in a bad way. Silva was tending to him in the horse stable where Slim had put Helmick.

"Your father will wonder what happened to you," Rex said. "They're pulling the walkway in a minute."

"Silva, you need to disembark," Salma said rushing into the horse stable. "I'll look after Zolfo and Helmick. Your father will need you, and you can help those that didn't reach the waterfront."

A hesitant Silva left the wounded men and was the last person off the Mischief. During the slight delay, no Ichneumon or Prussian official or soldier arrived to stop them, which was fortunate. Rex would have shot them before allowing them to stop the Mischief's departure.

Rex divided the unexpected passengers, ex-prisoners and escaped slaves between the two front barges. Not knowing anything about them, he felt prudence required keeping the Zamians isolated from the boat and cargo. In good conscience, he couldn't refuse them passage, but he spoke bluntly with Salma.

"The Wapiti will help them escape Port Delta, but only on the condition the prisoners stay in their assigned barge. Make that clear to your friends, Salma. I can't risk losing the Wapiti boat or cargo. The guards will shoot any ex-prisoner that attempted to board the boat without permission."

"Fine with me," Salma said. "I'll make your warning clear. After all, I know only a few of the new slaves. Most of them just arrived in the past week on two Combine ships that slipped through the Prussian blockade of the Zamia coast. Chances are there's a felon or two in the group. What about food?"

"We'll share our rations, but I hope you like fish."

Rex, watching the water, then wondered how the Prussians were making out with seizing the fort. He hoped they killed Colonel Xavier and sent those murderous Ichneumons packing. For sure, the fighting had sent the boats and ships docked at the Delta waterfront fleeing. Malik and Kyle had threaded their way through the chaotic harbor traffic with no collisions.

Rex caught a glimpse of the Clovis Belle churning up the Erie before losing sight of it in the smoke and darkness. Captain Dalporto, no fool, was clearing out of Delta. Since the Mischief was also embarking up the Erie, and was a faster boat, Rex figured he'd catch Dalporto in the morning. The experienced river pilot would knew how to avoid the Saukko and rock-hauling duty at Westport.

The fires inside the fort appeared to be fading as the Mischief with her barges full of prisoners headed towards the open river. The delicious mug of sweet coffee hadn't helped. Rex figured the abatement of his adrenaline spike, relief of having escaped amputation, and worse, accounted for his drowsiness. He knew Amy wanted to go to Orleans, not River Point, and he needed to explain his reason for not going after the machines, but first he needed to rest a moment.

The bright sunlight woke Rex. The few hours of sleep seemed to have cleared his head, and then looking again at the sun, he realized it was more like midday, not morning. He walked to the pilothouse to check with Kyle on the Mischief's progress. Judging from the bow wake, the Mischief appeared to be traveling at its full speed. Kyle was determined to beat the ice.

Looking down on the barges from the pilothouse stairs, he could see most of the passengers were asleep. A glance around the river revealed that he couldn't see the west riverbank, nothing but blue water. He hadn't realized the size of the Erie River. Looking east, clouds hid the riverbank, looking north, he could see land, but it was distance.

Rex looked again at the clear water. Blue water, where was the familiar muddy water? He rushed to the pilothouse where he found Amy.

"Kyle's checking the boiler," Amy said, "Malik is resting." She looked guilty.

"Where are we?" Rex asked, knowing the answer.

"We're in the gulf, headed to Orleans."

Benjamin Purnell had felt a sense of relief on learning that the Prussian naval blockade of the Zamia slave trade had ended. That blockade had been the result of the Prussian emperor's antislavery effort. At first, he had thought the Prussian emperor had realized how unpopular his antislavery policy was and had ended it. Then rumors started. The fame security of Prussian General Staff's command and control of the empire's armed forces and spies apparently was vulnerable to manipulation.

With some effort and a few bribes, the Orleans businessman had learned the details behind the ending of the Zamia blockade. Harlem Penton and several of his fellow cotton-growing plantation owners had paid Archduke Habsburg to arrange bogus navy orders. Purnell figured Harlem's oldest daughter was the brains behind the idea. Regardless of whose idea it was, the scheme had been successful. Several hundred Zamia slaves had arrived at Port Delta, thirty of which Purnell had paid for and needed yesterday in the sulfur mine.

Over the last two years, his loyalties had switched to the Ichneumon Empire, though the Prussian navy remained his Orleans boatyard's most important client. That business would end if the Prussians learned he was now an active agent for the Ichneumons. Or they'd kill him and seize the Orleans boatyard for their navy. So learning others had fooled the Prussians gave the businessman a certain comfort.

Then news arrived that the Ichneumon fort at Delta had exploded. Even more surprising, a Prussian army colonel had seized the opportunity offered by the garrison's disarray to grab control of the fort, along with the recent cargo of slaves.

Events called for drastic action. Remembering the bogus navy orders, Purnell realized a Prussian mail boat might offer him a chance to help the Ichneumons. He checked the arrival schedule. There was a Baltic mail boat scheduled to stop in Orleans for firewood that afternoon. It would do.

"Razo, take your crew out to the abandon Orleans fort," Purnell said. "Use the cannons to disable the mail boat."

Razo was Orleans official executioner who also ran firewood crews for the boat works. He was an experienced Prussian artilleryman who the army had sacked for stealing supplies.

"I'll send the Aruba out to rescue the crew. All your crew needs to do is damaged the boat enough it's dead in the water." The Aruba captain would make sure none of the mail boat crew, with the exception of the royal messenger, survived the mishap.

The ambush was successful and Purnell's well-equipped Orleans office had the talent and material to counterfeit new navy orders. Within two days, the comatose royal messenger with the bogus fleet orders was on his way to Admiral Wilhelm on the Prussian warship Schlesien anchored at Port Delta. The Prussian acceptance had been a near thing. The warship's captain had grilled Purnell on the events that had resulted in a civilian delivering a dying diplomatic messenger with a lock satchel. In the end, the admiral had accepted his story, thanked the businessman for his help, and told him to leave. A convoy of Ichneumon warships had entered the Erie.

The Aruba passed the Mischief during its first night out of Orleans.

General Paget was proud of the Ichneumon convoy. His flagship, the Kura, and an older armored sidewheeler, the Helot, both carried the new breech-loading rifled cannons in revolving turrets that fired the fifty-kilogram exploding shells. The rifled cannons made obsolete the armament of the Prussian navy, except for those smooth large bore breechloaders on the Schlesien main turrets. Accompanying the warships in the convoy were three clipper ships carrying six hundred Ichneumon marines. Even better, his convoy was the vanguard of the main force that would arrive next month to seize the Erie River. Emperor Ratakonda wanted the Prussians out of the Erie valley and those Wapiti savages taught a lesson.

The cargo on one of the clipper ships included six of the new rifled cannons for the fort. Paget would need a month to whip the garrison into shape and install the new cannons. His hope was to use the enemy warships foolish enough to remain in the harbor for target practice. He intended to send them to the bottom of the harbor before the main force arrived.

The sun had just cleared the horizon when General Paget on the lead Ichneumon warship, Kura, entered the Delta harbor. Tentacles of black smoke were visible rising from several areas behind the massive fort walls. Even more unusual, the waterfront was empty of boats and ships, except for three of the Prussian warships docked at the large wharf below the fort's main gate and Purnell's Aruba docked at the cotton wharf.

The large Prussian battleship, Schlesien, still rode at anchor, dominating the center of the harbor. The powerful ship wasn't asleep. Its two rear gun turrets were tracking the Kura and Ichneumon side-wheelers as they approached.

"The Prussian flag is flying from the main fort tower," the naval captain beside General Paget said. The man was studying the fort with a telescope. The general grabbed the captain's telescope to verify the information.

"Should I sound the general alarm?" the perplexed Kura captain asked.

How could the fort be in Prussian hands? Paget looked again at the battleship they were passing on port at about three hundred meters. All four of its massive turrets were tracking the various Ichneumon side-wheelers. One broadside from those cannons would destroy the Paget's convoy.

"No, don't sound the general alarm. Proceed to dock," General Paget ordered. "Then secure the vessel against a hostile boarding party. We're too out gunned to challenge the Schlesien." He wore the dress uniform of a general, which would help with the only option open to him to salvage his career and regain the fort.

A dozen no nonsense Prussian troops from the 88th Highland battalion, with a lieutenant in command, blocked the Kura's gangway.

"General, with all due respect my orders are to prevent Ichneumon troops from disembarking," the lieutenant said.

"I won't trouble you with a protest of this illegal action. After all, you have your orders. As you can see, I'm unarmed." Paget said, making a show of turning around with his hands held away from his body.

"Sergeant, wait here while Lieutenant Weidman escorts me to his commander."

The Prussian lieutenant looked surprised to learn he was to escort an Ichneumon General.

"Sir, those are not my orders."

"Show a bit of initiative lieutenant. You think your commander wouldn't want to meet and try to avoid a war?" He wasn't going to debate the matter with a lieutenant. His next stop would be the Schlesien and Admiral Wilhelm.

"If you understand I can't guarantee your safe return, fine," the young lieutenant said. Paget nodded. "Then follow me general."

Before leaving the wharf, the lieutenant told his sergeant to maintain the walkway blockade. Lieutenant Weidman then escorted the Ichneumon general to the fort's main gate. A dozen alert Prussian troopers guarded the gate. They told the lieutenant where he could find Colonel Markel.

"Colonel Paget, you're a general now, congratulations. What can I do for you?" the Prussian commander said. He had been inspecting a large crater that had once been the bonded tobacco-and-rum warehouse. A crew of Zamia laborers was busy gathering up and stacking iron cannon balls. The size of the crater and debris field, damage to the fort's southwest wall, and collapse of guard barracks had required a substantial explosion.

"What exploded?" General Paget asked, looking in the crater. No wonder the Prussians were able to take the fort, the explosion would have killed everyone in the barracks. "Where is Colonel Xavier?"

"The colonel is barely alive. The blast from the magazine injured the man terribly. Only about a dozen of his soldiers survived," Colonel Markel said. He saw no need to tell the enemy general they had killed about forty of the surviving Ichneumon soldiers when they tried to stop the Prussians from entering the fort.

"That wasn't a powder magazine. It was full of tobacco and rum," Paget said.

The Ichneumon general studied the crater. He could see smoldering bundles of tobacco and pieces of whiskey barrels scattered across the courtyard. Did the Prussians have a new secret weapon? There were rumors bandied about in the officer's clubs of a Prussian mortar that could cast a thousand kilogram shell a couple of kilometers. He hadn't believed them. Now looking at the crater, he wondered. General Paget needed to interview the survivors, learn what had happened here. But first, the Ichneumons needed to gain back the fort.

"It was decent of you to help the garrison, but I have men waiting on the ships to disembark and assume control of the fort. You need to tell the lieutenant to stand down and allow us to enter."

"That's not going to happen," the Prussian colonel said. "This den of horrors is not going to reopen. The emperor has outlawed slavery. This place was a holding pen for Purnell and Erdogam's slave market. Plus the Erie Neutrality Treaty outlawed building forts along the Erie. You need to sail back to Cusco."

The feldwebel in charge of the main gate walked over, saluted, and informed the Prussian commander that a Herr Purnell wished to speak with General Paget. The man was waiting at the main gate.

"Is he with your entourage, General?"

"No. I figure he's here to check on his property. You're forgetting Prussian law doesn't rule in the Erie valley and that the fort is Ichneumon property."

Colonel Markel had never met Purnell, but he had heard the Orleans businessman was obese. The man was round, but not flabby. He was dressed neatly with dark trousers, a white-collar shirt, and a tailored navy wool jacket that would be suitable attire for a meeting with Emperor Schnabel. More concerning to the colonel was the demeanor of the Rhine Mar captain, who was with the businessman and looked worried and aggravated.

General Paget and Purnell obviously knew each other and after greetings walked off a short distance to confer away from the gate. The Rhine Mar captain watched the two walk off.

"Colonel Markel, Admiral Wilhelm asked I escort you out to the Schlesien," the Rhine Mar captain said.

"It was the coffee?"

Amy nodded. She had been dreading Rex's awakening and discovering her treachery. They were alone in the Mischief's pilothouse.

"You realize that your action risks the loss of the Wapiti's only steamboat, all the gold from the winter sloe sale, and a number of their warriors' lives?" Rex asked in a quiet voice. Amy wasn't sure if he expected an answer and waited.

"All to steal machine shop equipment from Purnell. How could you be so selfish?" he shouted.

The acerbic words stunned Amy. The tears that threatened to erupt didn't help. "Rex, we can do it . . ."

"And the money, do you have any idea how many families are counting on us to return and pay them?"

"We can always turn away if it looks to dangerous." Amy was disgusted with her passivity. Where was her temper?

"If it looks dangerous, do you have any idea what those animals do to captives at Delta?" Rex paused, studying her as if she was a stranger. "Not sure? Perhaps you think they're just rumors. Well, I'll tell you. The fiends chop the prisoners' hands and feet off. Women they rape first. Afterward you get to lay rotting in a cell without a hand, or a foot, or without both, until you die in the filthy dark cells."

That, Amy realized, explained her friend's loss of nerve. The horrors he had witnessed in the dungeon. Sadly, she was all too familiar with the Ichneumon barbarism and could imagine the horror of seeing the results would have on the strongest mind. Could he not realized that if the Wapiti were to prosper, to have their own territory, then risks would be unavoidable? Sure, she had deceived and doped him, but his caustic attitude was unwarranted, well for the most part.

"If by some fortuitous stroke of luck, you manage to steal the tools," Rex said. "The opponents in New Hamburg fighting the Wapiti's territory request will claim it shows we're thieves and pirates."

Amy had had enough.

"No, you are wrong. I wanted you to go because I know that the crew won't go without you. I believe the raid's odds of success are favorable, if you help."

"You admit it's a raid, robbery."

"Who in this lawless world will care?"

"Purnell will," Rex said.

"He is the only one," Amy said, "I'm collecting a debt. That fat spider owes me the equipment for my cooperation on a patent deal. You know he tried to renege on his promises by having me murdered, or worse in Panther Creek."

Rex seemed less agitated, even nodded. Temper and angry words would not win him over. She tried a smile, but in her exhaustion state, it felt more like a grimace.

"You're familiar with Andy's futile efforts to repair those salvage boilers. You can't repair a damaged boiler with a forge and hammer. Blacksmithing can't make those repairs. You need milling machines, lathes, drill presses, plate rollers, rivets, and iron tubing. The Wapiti need this equipment just as much as I do."

"It's still reckless behavior," Rex said, sounding weary. "What if the boat breaks down in Orleans? The Wapiti will hold me responsible if their gold is lost."

"Those mishaps could happen anywhere on this trip," Amy said. Rex just shook his head. "At least listen to my plan, you'll like it."

"Do you realize why I'm here and not lying in a filthy dark cell without a foot and a leg stump that's been cooked in boiling tar to stop the bleeding?"

Amy wasn't sure if it was a rhetorical question, but asked anyway, "Why?"

"Because I had a key that fit the slave collar, otherwise, I would have been helpless. It was blind luck that the key I had fit that collar. Only a fool keeps depending on luck."

"There's another word for it, planning. I'll bet that you had more than one key. Knowing you, several to increase the odds of having the right key," she said. "That's not depending on blind luck, that's strategizing, weighing the odds, planning. Please help me, together we can pull this off and help the Wapiti."

Rex shook his head. "I'll wake Kyle, you need some rest," he said and walked off.

The Prussian guards refused to allow them into the fort. Purnell wasn't pleased, but the Orleans trader was sensible and didn't argue. He suggested they wait on his new sternwheeler, Aruba, but General Paget preferred they wait aboard the docked Ichneumon warship, Kura.

"Whoever allowed this disaster to happen needs to be shot," Purnell said.

"I was as surprised as you. Colonel Xavier is no fool," General Paget said, worried far more about the emperor's reaction than the Orleans businessman's opinion.

"If I'm successful, Colonel Markel is not going to like his new orders," Purnell said and in a few words explained to the skeptical general.

"Admiral Wilhelm is not the brightest commander, but I can't believe he would abandon this fort because of new orders from Berlin that you had a hand in delivering. He's not stupid. Everyone knows you have dealings with the Ichneumon Empire. It would be like me giving the admiral his secret orders," General Paget said.

"I also have dealings with Berlin and the Prussian navy. Your Ichneumon understanding of the human psyche needs work."

General Paget wasn't in the mood for lectures from a Prussian traitor, but did say, "Please explain."

"First, I set the scene by delivering to the admiral's battleship the burned and incoherent, but alive, Prussian courier with his locked satchel still attached to his charred wrist. While the crew members were trying to save their man, I explained that a boiler explosion had sunk the royal mail boat near Orleans. The few other survivors are at Orleans, but the courier had begged us to take him to Admiral Wilhelm."

"Did the mail boat boiler explode?" the general asked. It seemed like boilers were exploding with alarming frequency.

"Let's skip those details. They're unimportant to the story. Besides, what loyal citizen wouldn't help an Imperial courier? That was all I said to the Prussian officer in charge of the crew that had boarded to take the courier to the battleship's infirmary. I never referred to orders or the locked satchel."

The Orleans businessman paused while one of the Kura's better looking black women slaves served them hot fresh coffee. The Ichneumon navy had started using Zamia female slaves on board the ships for housekeeping tasks. Paget suspected the Orleans trader was wondering if the use of slaves on a warship meant the Ichneumon manpower issue was worsening.

"Your coffee is hard to beat. This is excellent, better than Zamia coffee," Purnell said while adding two more heaping spoons of sugar to his cup. "The hard part was the satchel lock. It gave my man a fit. He couldn't risk awakening the courier, but in the end, he managed to open it without leaving a mark or the Prussian any wiser. My office has every paper type in use, so making a new order wasn't hard. The new orders are for the Prussian fleet to rush back to the Baltic. We should know in a bit if the admiral fell for my deception."

Could this man be serious, General Paget wondered. If he is, it would be an incredible stroke of fortune. "Let's hope. What did the actual orders say?"

"Here, read them," Herr Purnell said. "You'll see fate is a fickle creature. Just think, if the mail boat's boiler hadn't, ah, exploded, Admiral Wilhelm would be reading those orders."

The Berlin orders included Colonel Markel's promotion to general rank, along with orders for him to seize the Ichneumon forts on the Erie. Admiral Wilhelm was to place the two armored sidewheelers, Rhineland and Rhine Mar, under Markel's command to use in seizing all the Ichneumon forts on the Erie. Admiral Wilhelm was to use the rest of the fleet to block the Ichneumon navy from entering the Erie River and reinforcing Delta.

"This is amazing," General Paget said, better understanding why the emperor held the Orleans businessman in such high regard. "I need to get word to the Hickory Ridge garrison. Also, if the old fool follows these orders, he'll dispatch the Rhinelander to River Point. General Mehta has to stop the Prussian vessel before it can reinforce River Point."

"I'm on a quick trip to Fenwick's plantation," Purnell said, "There are problems at the sulfur mine. I don't think the river ice has set yet below River Point. I'll have Aruba's crew run your man to Hickory Ridge while I'm at the plantation. You might consider sending the Saukko to follow the Rhinelander, cut off any retreat."

"If the rest of the Prussian warships lift anchor, I'll send the Saukko. Now, I need another favor," General Paget said. "I have my family on Kura with me. I wasn't expecting this disaster, and it's not safe for them to remain in Delta. Would you take them to Fenwick?"

Colonel Markel had told the feldwebel to close the gates and allow no one entrance until he returned. The trip in the admiral's harbor boat with its ten rowers required fifteen silent minutes to reach the battleship and another few minutes to reach the admiral's office.

Admiral Wilhelm was another old school naval man with a bushy grey beard. The man had a scholarly air, though the colonel had heard the man suffered from a weak memory and tended to live in the past. The admiral's orderly offered tea, and Markel figured why not. If the purpose of the meeting was to cashier him, he might as well be alert.

"Colonel, it was good of you to help the Ichneumon, but now that their resupply convoy had arrived, we can wash our hands of this place. I have new orders. Berlin has recalled the fleet to the Baltic. One of the sidewheelers will proceed to River Point to investigate the sinking of the Hendricks. Pick a hundred or so troopers and a captain to travel with the sidewheeler and provide protection. As to the fort, it belongs to the Ichneumon army, and I want you to turn it over to General Paget."

Could this fool think that was a humanitarian effort?

"With all due respect, sir, Admiral Scheer's orders were for me to take control of the forts along the river. Fort Delta controls the entrance to the Erie. We can't just abandon it to our enemies. It would be the equivalent of abandoning the whole river valley."

Colonel Markel's fear was the navy would give away the strategic position that fortune had handed them, and now the admiral was preparing to do just that. Worse, judging by the red face, his blunt remarks had offended the stupid man.

"The emperor's orders are clear. I am not debating them with a colonel," the admiral said. "The emperor and I expect you to do your duty without delay. The Rhineland is going to River Point, and it is bringing up the boiler pressure and will depart in an hour. Have those men on board. The fleet is departing as soon as the battalion is back aboard the Rhine Mar."

Colonel Markel sent Company C of the 88th Mountain Battalion to River Point to reinforce Captain Beck's survivors.

Rex had listened to Amy's plan without comment. No surprise, her plan was solid and had a slight chance of working, except for her being non grata in Orleans. With a ten thousand D-mark reward on her head, no sane person would believe Purnell had sold or given her the equipment. What a quandary, and every hour carried them closer to the point of no return. The number of things that could go wrong was many, a broken valve, a snapped rod, a hurricane, pirates, any one of the calamities could cost them their lives. If he were a sensible leader, he'd lock her up and reverse course for River Point.

Then again, how many young men were wise when a beautiful woman was involved? After an hour of pacing the deck, Rex had rationalized it made sense to help her abscond with Purnell's equipment. He was honest enough to acknowledge he was guilty of thinking with his c**k.

The Mischief was by now closer to Orleans than Delta. Amy was a managing woman, and for whatever reason, he couldn't seem to resist her. Besides, any bastard involved in the Delta slave market deserved some kind of retribution. Helping Amy make a fool of her father would be a start. Towards sunset, from his perch on top of the Mischief's pilothouse roof, Rex spotted serval black smoke columns on the southern horizon. Captain Malik told him the smoke was from warships.

"Do you suppose it's more Prussian support for Delta?" Rex asked, as he studied the smoke.

"Going the wrong direction for that," Malik said. He realized the captain was correct and felt a bit stupid. "From the volume of the smoke, whoever they are, they're at full steam, probably Ichneumon ships fleeing the Prussians at Delta."

"Let's hope. Think the Ichneumons will mount an effort to recover the Erie River?" Rex asked.

Malik shrugged his shoulders.

"You don't care?"

"Oh, I care," the captain said. "But Hickory Ridge is our real obstacle to reaching safety. At Delta, the river is so wide the fort gunners can often not see the far shore in poor weather. Regardless of which empire is in charge, we should be able to slip by Delta, especially at night."

"Well, one hurdle at a time, this Orleans business of Amy's will be risky enough." He still wondered if he had lost his mind to acquiesce, but added. "I'd prefer not to have to fight our way by Port Delta or risk a grounding along the east shore. I want to be back past the fort while the Prussians have control."

Malik nodded in agreement.

Chapter 7

The following afternoon, the Mischief arrived off Lafayette's dock, which was across the Orleans bay entrance and down the muddy east gulf shore about a kilometer. A weathered elderly man, a Prussian, had greeted them as the Mischief's johnboat bumped against the dilapidated wooden dock. Rex had to pause disembarking to allow a two-meter long brown snake time to slither off the dock's bumper block of old hemp rope. The creature vanished in the murky water.

The grim gray-bearded man had a double-barreled shotgun pointed at him. In fairness, Rex knew he didn't appear that peaceful with his two revolvers, one in a shoulder holster and another shoved in his belt.

"I'm looking for Herr Lafayette. I'm Herr Burgdorf, and I'm interested in purchasing the Princess," Rex said, reckoning it was best he got to the purpose of his visit without delay. Sunset was a few hours away. He wanted to see the steamboat Amy had told him was for sale while there was still light to inspect the boat.

"That's me," the man said. "Where'd you get the Ichneumon boat?" The shotgun remained pointed at Rex.

The Mischief with the barges was anchored a couple of hundred meters off the mangrove-covered muddy east coast of the Orleans bay inlet. The steamboat with Amy and several armed crew members was visible to anyone on the dock who looked. Captain

127

Malik joined Rex on the shaky wood plank dock after tying off the small rowboat. Verifying there were no more snakes lurking about Lafayette's dock had delayed the captain.

"I'm Captain Malik," the captain said. He offered his hand, but Lafayette ignored it, preferring to keep his hands on the shotgun. *Definitely not the trusting sort* was Rex's thought.

"I'll be damned. An Ichneumon, what are you, pirates, slavers?"

Rex couldn't determine if the man was worried about them being pirates, upset with Malik being an Ichneumon, or relieved. However, the old man still kept the shotgun pointed at them.

Three younger hard-looking men jogged onto the wood dock, causing it to vibrate violently. They stopped beside the older man. Rex was starting to worry the weak dock would collapse and dump them in the water with the snake.

"Who are they, Granddad?" the tall man with a full dark beard asked. He also had a double-barreled shotgun. His two pals were clean-shaved. All three men were shirtless, dressed in gray coveralls, barefoot, and wore leather belts with canvas holsters holding ball-and-cap revolvers.

"Pirates, that's the missing Ichneumon boat with the witch's engine," the grandfather said. The other men all studied the Mischief for a moment before nodding among themselves.

"You're too late. I sold the Princess," the man added while lowering the shotgun hammers. "Where's your home berth?"

"Delta," Rex answered, blithely dissembling. "Delta Hauling, I move heavy freight and I'm in the market for a tough river boat. I'd heard you might know of any available."

The young man with the black beard and the elder Lafayette exchanged looks. "I might," he said. "Give us a moment." They walked away a short distance for privacy.

"I'm Stefan, this is Pauli," the youngest grandson said as his grandfather and older brother walked away. "How'd you get that boat? The Ichneumon navy never sells a boat."

"Why would you think it's an Ichneumon steamboat?" Rex asked. He hadn't thought the Mischief would be that noteworthy. They were even flying a Prussian flag.

"It was built across the bay," Stefan said. He studied Malik for a moment. "You're the Ichneumon captain. I remember you from the test run last year. You made a fuss about allowing women on the boat."

"A memory like that could get you killed," Malik said. He wasn't smiling and Stefan appeared alarmed. The grandfather returned in time to catch Malik's remarks for he glared at the captain.

"I have a small sternwheeler that was used in the island trade," Lafayette said. "The Heron's title is in dispute." The grandfather paused to learn if that bit of news was a deal killer. Rex shrugged.

"Well, if that is not a problem for you, I might be able to help you. I was planning on selling it to avoid the hassle and lawyer fees."

"Is it nearby?" Rex asked. Lafayette nodded. "Then I'd like to see it. Tell me about the boat."

"Is Benjamin involved?" Rex shook his head. Satisfied, Lafayette explained, "The Heron was built by Focke Wulf for an Ichneumon gulf trader. It's eight years old. The Prussian Navy seized it for smuggling rum and sold it to a timber cutter for back taxes, import duties, and court costs. The fool gambled it away and I ended up with the boat. I'll sell it for two hundred thousand D-marks."

Rex didn't know if that was a deal or not, and said, "Show me."

Before he left to follow the Lafayette gang into the woods, he sent Malik to bring the Mischief into the Orleans bay entrance.

"While you're moving the Mischief, tell Amy that I'd like her and several armed guards to follow me."

129

Amy was the one who could tell him if the Heron was seaworthy and worth the price. Since she was in her ugly woman disguise, Rex figured no one should be the wiser as to her identity.

Lafayette's small dock was on the gulf side of a narrow ridge that marked the east side of the entrance to the Orleans bay. Rex learned the ridge was a sandy peninsula that hid a small cove off the main Orleans bay. Lafayette's crab-and-oyster operation was located around that cove. Standing on the high point of the ridge, he could see across the bay a small island with a stone fort. It was a couple of kilometers away, but the flags flying from the walls appeared to be Prussian.

"I had Kyle help me row the other boat over when I saw you leave. Malik will bring the Mischief around," Amy said, catching him at the ridge top. Lafayette had gone on as Rex stopped to wait and take in the view. She looked hot and uncomfortable in her ugly woman disguise padding and wig hat.

"Is that a Prussian fort?"

"No, my father runs it," Amy said. "What flag is flying depends on whose navy he expects. He must expect the Prussians. The fort is not as a rule garrisoned."

"Good, those cannons could block the narrow harbor."

Looking in the direction Lafayette had gone, Amy said, "Those half dozen farms and two long irregular wood wharfs with several small warehouses is his family's place."

The crab and oyster man had constructed the warehouses from rough-cut timber planks and shake shingle roofs. The buildings looked solid. Three small sailboats shared the moorings at the wharf with a steamboat. Unlike the warehouses, the wharf looked flimsy.

"That's not the Princess," Amy said. In addition to her ugly woman disguise, she had worn heavy leather knee boots. *Fear of snakes*, Rex wondered.

"He told me he'd sold the Princess, but might sell that boat. He called it the Heron," Rex said.

Caroom's Raid

The steamboat was a sternwheeler freighter about twice the size of the Mischief. Dark streaks marred the gray paint. Rex couldn't tell from the ridge if the streaks were burn marks or dirt. For sure, the boat appeared in poor condition. The Heron's two dented smokestacks were in series, instead of the more typical side by side seen in riverboats. The pilothouse was in the center of the boat with a truncated cabin area behind it. All the cabin and pilot house windows appeared to have the glass panes missing or broken. Most of the boat was open deck area for bulk commodities such as cotton bales and logs. A sturdy gin pole-style crane was in the center of each deck area.

Walking through the small community Rex noticed that a number of the families were Zamians. *Slaves*? Rex wondered. A shout from the wharf caused them to look toward the water. Lafayette met them at the top of the steps to the wharf.

"This is Fraulein Haggard. Her father is my partner," Rex said. Amy gave him a pained look on hearing the name. "Kyle, meet Herr Lafayette. He's interested in selling that old sternwheeler. Kyle is my first mate."

"You can't be serious," Amy said. "That piece of junk is one of those Kiel river freighters that have a nasty habit of rolling over in rough seas when loaded."

"That's ridiculous, there's nothing wrong with that steamboat," the man snapped. Grandfather had a temper, and Amy had stoked it. Rex wondered if he was another misogynist.

"If you take your orders from hags, then just leave," the elderly crabber said, having no appreciation for how close to the mark his cantankerous statement was.

The hag had that gleam in her eyes Rex was learning to recognize. It meant she had identified the problem and solved it before most people were even aware there was a problem. Amy winked at him and proceeded to vilify the Heron.

"That's why those stacks look odd," she said, shaking her head.

"Odd? What do you mean? Those smoke stacks work fine," Lafayette snapped.

"They're not the original Focke Wulf elliptical stacks," she said, sounding disappointed. "That boat has rolled and lost it stacks. Where'd you get those pipes? From the boat works junk pile across the bay?"

"They came with the boat. Maybe the Prussians shot the other ones off," an exasperated crabber said. After glaring at Amy for a moment, he addressed Rex. "What difference do the smokestacks make? And who is she, some witch?"

"I'm not interested in a boat that will dump my cargo in bad weather," Rex said, ignoring the question. "Did it capsize?"

"Not that I know of," the crabber hedged. "I won it at poker."

Maybe he had, but if the boat's design was as unstable as his partner thought, the crew may had abandoned boat during a storm, and Lafayette had come across the hulk and salvaged it.

"Did the Heron arrive on its own power, or was it towed?" Amy asked.

Lafayette, much irritated by a woman questioning him, answered, "I towed it to save fuel."

Rex figured the boat was a floating wreck and of no use to them, but since they were there, Amy might as well inspect it.

"I'd like to see the engine and boiler," Rex said, causing Amy to smile. He had obviously said the right thing.

The party resumed their walk to the wharf. Several black and mixed-breed children tagged along behind them. Amy opened two bags of the cherry drops and handed each kid a couple pieces of the hard candy. They loved the sweets. Lafayette grumbled about spoiling them.

While Lafayette's grandsons were opening the hatches, Rex walked through the mildew and stripped cabins with Amy. Kyle went to the pilothouse to check the control linkage. *If the boat had capsized,*

132

then why didn't it just sink? Rex wondered. He had a number of questions, but they would wait until they had some privacy.

Amy asked the crabber for permission to examine the boiler and engine. Lafayette just shook his head, and Rex thought he might refuse her request.

"Stefan, Pauli, go with the hag. Open the inspection plates for her and watch out for those snakes," Lafayette added. "On second thought, don't look too hard."

"Let's try not to hurt any creatures, boys," Amy said, smiling at Lafayette lame attempt to discourage her inspection.

"I've never heard of your partner, Herr Haggard, or Delta Hauling," the crabber said, watching Amy disappear down the open deck hatch with his younger grandsons. The older grandson, with the heavy beard, waited with Rex and his grandfather.

"It's a big world," Rex said. "I had never heard of you until Captain Malik told me about your operation." The grandson asked what bought him so far from Port Delta.

"I have a contract to deliver a heavy lathe and some other machines from the boat works to Delta. Your neighbor is expanding operations. What's your name?"

"Albert. Granddad's social skills are a bit rusty, but that Haggard woman would rub most people wrong. Women should know their place."

"Let's stick to business," Rex said. "You worry about your crew, and I'll worry about mine."

Stefan had returned to get an oil lamp for Amy to use for inspecting the boiler. Rex followed him down the stairs from the deck. They landed between the rear of the boiler and two massive vertical iron cylinders with manifolds and linkage. Stefan crawled in the boiler while Rex examined the steam engines. Amy, from the sounds, was inside the front boiler banging on pipes, and he walked around the boiler's horizon tanks to find her.

Light flooded the area when Albert removed a second hatch. Rex could see the area had been the coalbunker, though only few small pieces of coal remained. He picked up a piece of the coal to examine, curious to see how its quality compared to the Wapiti coal he sold. The Heron coal was hard and had smooth glossy surfaces. It was anthracite, an expensive coal and excellent fuel. Rex wondered how the dilapidated vessel managed to have prime military coal in its bunker.

"It's a twin-tube Cornish boiler, and it has seen better days," Amy said from inside the firebox. She then emerged on her hands and knees from the left firebox, brushing spider webs from her wig. The stuffing part of her disguise made the square iron firebox door opening a tight fit. Stefan emerged next from the small door. She then went towards the stern to check the engines and drive linkage.

Rex checked the bow. The timbers appeared solid, and he looked in checked the bilge. It contained water, but he couldn't tell how much and wondered where the pump was located to drain the sump. Then he heard Albert yelling at Amy and hurried to the stern.

"Look at this pin. Whoever was in charge of maintenance never greased it," she said, shaking a short worn brass pin about the diameter of a broom handle in Albert's face.

"These engines are junk," she said. "A scrap yard might be your best bet, but it would require a tow to get it there."

"You broke it," Albert yelled. "You had no call for messing with that engine. Now I'll have to fix it. Damn women." He snatched the offending pin from Amy's hand and handed it to a startled Stefan.

"You figure how to get it back together since you let her tear it apart. Tour is over."

Rex started to tell Albert *not so fast* when he caught Amy's wink. She had something else in mind to bedevil the Lafayette men. They followed him to the deck where the elder Lafayette waited with Kyle.

"Your son was very rude to Fraulein Haggard," Rex said. Not knowing what Amy had in mind, he complained. As expected, Albert griped about Amy's disassembly of the crosshead linkage on the port steam engine.

"I was just trying to help," Amy grumbled to Rex, ignoring the Lafayettes, but speaking loud enough for them to hear. "The boiler firebox looks okay, but after seeing the neglect in the engine linkage, I fear the boiler pressure vessel will prove to be full of mud and much corroded."

"Too dangerous to fire up, you think?" Rex asked. Amy nodded. He had grasped her strategy. The grandfather, no fool, was listening and realizing the Heron sale was in danger.

"I'd be willing to reduce the price to cover repairs," he said. "We could ask the experts at the Orleans boat yard what they thought the repairs would cost."

"I'm not trying to be difficult, Herr Burgdorf," Amy said. "But I've seen the aftermath of boiler explosions. One of my father's business is scrapping boats that boiler explosions destroyed. I fear the Heron is too far gone."

"Would your father be interested?" Albert asked.

"For scrap? Sure, if you towed it to Delta, he'd make an offer," she brazenly suggested. "But I figured Purnell across the bay would buy it. There's no need to pay someone like him twenty-five thousand D-marks to tow it to Delta." She pointed her thumb at Rex.

"We're headed to Orleans," she added. "If you'd like I could tell Herr Dunlap that you have a boat for sale."

Amy felt a bit guilty taking advantage of the old grouch. He wasn't a hateful person, nothing like Razo who ran Purnell's firewood crews. She knew Lafayette was a not-so-secret abolitionist who didn't approve of slavery, or use slave labor. But on the other hand, the fool disapproved of educating girls. None of the Lafayette women could read. That, in her opinion, was a crime, since women were, more often than not, smarter than men were.

From working in the boatyard, she knew about the family's dealings with Purnell. The last she had heard, the clan had owed the Orleans Boatyard over one hundred thousand D-marks for past repairs, late payments, and two sail-powered sloops. Looking around the hardscrabble operation, Amy figured they still did and if her father learned about the Heron, he'd have the sheriff seize it for past debts.

The Lafayette business wasn't just crabs and oysters. Bootleg rum made on the gulf sugar islands paid most of their bills. Amy figured if she looked, at least one of those barns would contain several rum barrels and have a bottling operation. Lafayette was fortunate in that her father hadn't bothered, so far, with bootleg rum. Otherwise, he would be dead or in prison.

"I'm not interested in repairing it," Herr Lafayette said after exchanging some unspoken message with Albert. "I'll offer you an, as-is-where-is-deal. One hundred thousand D-marks, today."

"What do you figure your father's scrap price would be?" Rex asked. He wished he knew the boat's real condition. He hadn't had an opportunity to talk in private with her. Since she had bought up scrapping boats, he'd play along. See where she went.

"Fifty, maybe sixty thousand D-marks," Amy said, looking regretful to have to suggest such an inadequate amount.

"Listen to you two, you're nothing but pirates," Albert said.

"Are you willing to stand by the boiler while it's bought up to full rated pressure?" Amy asked. Albert appeared vexed, knew she was maneuvering him, but shook his head.

"Sixty thousand would be a fair offer, Herr Burgdorf. I'm sure my father would pay that," Amy said and then added, "if the boiler appears repairable."

After Rex had two private meetings at the end of the wharf with his partner, and another hour of haggling with the crabber and Albert, the parties arrived at the final offer. Rex would pay the crabber seventy-five thousand D-marks for the Heron, if that included the use of the wharf and Lafayette's forge and tools for three days.

"With the understanding there is no title for the Heron, I'll accept your miserly offer," Lafayette said. He looked at Amy and shook his head. "Women . . ."

Rex worried the hulk might prove a death trap for the Wapiti crew. He had agreed to part with his gold D-marks from the winter sloe nut sale because Amy was confident they could repair the Heron boiler, engine, and drive linkage enough to ensure the boat could make the trip to River Point. Then after the Heron had delivered her cargo of machines, Rex could decide whether to replace the boiler, or sell the Heron to the gold miners in Westport.

A needed item that Salma and the Zamian women had accomplish during the trip across the gulf was finding outfits and clothing for everyone. The sartorial effort had exhausted the Mischief's inventory of Prussian fatigues and required some skillful alterations, but at least there were no naked men or women walking around the wharf. Rex figured the Lafayette wives would have rebelled at such heathen behavior as he gathered his polyglot crew on the wharf to review job assignments for making the Heron seaworthy and the pending raid across the bay.

"Salma, make sure your people understand they need to act like slaves. Kyle and I will carry whips and shout orders. Herr Malik will issue the orders, but I don't want them to think we have turned on them. They're freemen."

"Lord, that outhouse stinks," a cheerful Amy said, joining them on the wharf. The challenge of making the hulk seaworthy had her in a good spirits. Salma and her, both fluent in the Zamia language, would serve as the main translators. She then cautioned the crew.

"Everyone needs to remember, if anyone asks, we're here to load the machines for the new Purnell machine shop being built at Port Delta."

"The women want to help. They're strong." Salma said.

"Good, their help would be welcomed. First, we need to get the Heron running. I need those inspection plates removed from the two boiler pressure vessels," Amy said, nodding to Salma. "Rex, the corroded bolts that hold those plates will require a large wrench and a strong man to loosen them. Kyle, I want . . ."

The amount of black muck that they removed from the pressure vessels amazed everyone. Parts of the boiler flue tubes and the shell of the pressure plates had deep corrosion pits, but Amy assured them the boilers would hold, if they didn't exceed her calculated safe upper pressure limit.

"How do you know that gage is correct?" Rex asked. The glass face on the brass gage was cracked and salt crystals coated the bottom section of the dial face.

"I don't. I'll scrounge one from the Mischief and look for a replacement at the boat works." She said, and left to supervise the crew reassembling the steam engine on the port side.

"At least it cleaned up well," she later told Rex, after gripping most of the afternoon about the engine's obsolete design, lack of a condenser, and the amount of clean water it would consume.

The empty coalbunker forced Rex to deal with Lafayette. Any kind of coal was an expensive commodity along the gulf coast and not available in Orleans. Pinewood was the only fuel on the peninsula and the old pirate knew that. He charged an outrageous price for his firewood, and having no other option, Rex paid. The Zamians, willing workers, loaded the fuel on the Heron.

Salma, who was supervising the firewood detail, asked. "Do you need a distraction?"

Rex already appreciated the Zamia woman was a quick study. She wasn't privy to the fact this was a raid, but she must have sensed something wasn't quite legitimate. He nodded and she outlined her idea for a distraction. It made him laugh, but he nodded in approval.

On the afternoon of the second day, they fired both boilers. Three of the Zamia men volunteered to run the Heron's boilers and Amy and Kyle trained them on the finer points of using dampers to help control the fire. The boilers didn't leak at the planned operating pressure, and later, the Heron made a circle around the backwater bay. Rex wasn't optimistic the Heron patched together boilers and engine would last until River Point, but that was a concern for another day. Today, deceiving the Orleans Boat-Works management was the task.

Rex agreed the papers that Amy had drawn up based on her knowledge of how the boatyard operated looked authentic. He then handed the counterfeit manifest to Malik. The shop workers knew the Ichneumon captain from past dealings and their hope was that Purnell's men would never suspect an Ichneumon navy captain of working for a Wapiti or Purnell's daughter.

"The boatyard manager, Herr Dunlap, knew about my father's offer to set me up in Port Delta with a machine shop," Amy said, explaining to the dubious Ichneumon captain why the ruse was believable. "The manager will just reckon Purnell had found another dupe to buy the old iron and the man had hired Delta Hauling."

Amy, Malik, and Rex were in the Mischief pilothouse holding a final council as they approached the main wharf. Slim would guard the Mischief while docked at the Orleans Boat Works. Kyle, Andy Smith, Stefan Lafayette, and Herr Saad were on the Heron, which trailed behind and off the Mischief's starboard side.

"Here's the map. It shows the location of the machines in the boat yard. At least, where they were the last time I saw them," Amy said. She would stay in the Mischief, out of sight, and be available to resolve any questions that arose. "Use it to keep the boatyard manager from picking the wrong machines," she cautioned and then added. "While you're liberating the lathe and milling machine, Saad is going to try to convince his wife and four children to leave with us."

"I hope you're right about the man's loyalty," Rex said. "If he warns the guards, we'll be in a world of hurt."

"He won't," Amy said. "First, he'll introduce Malik and you to Dunlap, then leave. He won't be there to help while we're at the boatyard."

Amy was counting on her mother being at the boatyard and Rex finding and telling her that her daughter was hiding on the Mischief.

With the exception of Malik and Saad, only the Wapiti in both crews knew the truth. They all were a bit nervous and anxious to get the raid behind them as the Mischief and Heron steamed into the inner Orleans harbor, flying Ichneumon flags, with a beautiful rising sun behind them.

The brown water made Rex realize the Orleans harbor was another river delta with shifting channels and sandbars. The inner harbor was smaller than he had expected. The boatyard dominated the western shore and was the first industrial area he had seen in this world. Gray smoke poured from two large truncated stone pyramids that he recognized were cold air blast furnaces. Amy hadn't mention the iron works.

Surrounding the boatyard area were numerous one-story houses, and further out in the treeless hills along both sides of the river he could see many fields of corn ready for harvest.

On the crest of the west ridge jutting towards the gulf was a large white colonial mansion that overlooked the harbor. Based on

Amy's description, that had to be Purnell's home. He hoped their information was correct that the tyrant was on his yearly vacation to some southern island.

"May God smile on our endeavor," Rex prayed as the front port barge bumped up against the wharf. "Malik, take Saad and find the yard manager. He'll know where we can find Herr Dunlap."

"Dunlap isn't an early bird," Amy said, easing closed the steam valve to stop the port side engine. She would pilot the Mischief while Malik was ashore. "The yard manager may have to send a laborer to his house."

They all watched Kyle maneuver the Heron into the position along the main wharf. The spot Amy had told him to use. The strongest crane for lifting machinery was there. Curious boatyard workers were collecting on the dock as the two steamers docked. The Zamia laborers emerging from their tents in the Mischief's starboard front barge swiftly had the complete attention of the dock and machine shop workers.

"What's Salma doing?" Amy asked. "Those women are naked! They'll start a riot."

Rex looked. With the women facing away from the pilothouse, watching the approaching dock, it did appear they wore nothing. Rex wasn't about to admit that Salma and he had agreed to use them as a distraction.

"They're not naked. They have on thongs," Rex said. "I'm going to grab that firewood." A considerable amount of prime split oak and chestnut firewood was stacked along the dock.

"Did you know about this?"

"Our boats needed firewood for the boilers," Rex added, rushing from the pilothouse.

The Zamia women were enjoying their audience of workers, instead of loading firewood.

"Bitch, tell your lazy-ass crew to start carrying firewood, or they'll get a taste of my whip."

The crack of his long bullwhip had both the boatyard workers and the black ex-slaves nervous. The boatyard personnel appeared to have accepted he was a brutal henchman willing to use mayhem to accomplish his assignment. He gave another vicious snap to the whip while Salma screamed some order. Whatever she said got the women moving and their audience of boatyard workers scattered. In moments, the firewood was flying into the Mischief and Malik had disappeared into the warehouse across from the wharf they had docked with his entourage of a dozen male slaves.

"That's a prime bunch of female slaves. Who are you with?" a rawboned Prussian asked. He had been with the several workers across the yard by another firewood pile. They had been yelling malicious taunts at Salma's gang of women.

"Delta Hauling," Rex said. "Are you with the boatyard?"

"I'm Razo. I run the firewood crews up the river. Would you consider selling some of those women?"

"Not my call, I do what the captain tells me, and right now that's to fill the wood bins on both boats. If you want him, he's in there looking for the manager," Rex said pointing towards the warehouse and then snapping the whip again at the firewood crew.

As if on cue, Malik emerged with the male slaves trailing behind him and another Prussian, a grey-haired thin man who was holding the sham shipping order papers. The man saw the firewood loading and rushed over to where Rex and the firewood crew foreman stood.

"Who gave them permission for taking the firewood?" Dunlap asked, and then realized the crew was different. "Those are women . . . naked women. What's the meaning of this?"

"Ask him," Razo said, pointed at Rex.

"They're loading firewood," stating the obvious.

142

The middle-aged man seemed as concerned about the attire of Salma's crew, as with the firewood disappearing aboard a stranger's boat. A justified concern on Dunlap's part, since the boatyard workforce appeared more interested in watching the women than working iron.

"Herr Burgdorf, this is Herr Dunlap, the yard's manager," Malik said. He appeared amused. Not Dunlap, the flustered manager seemed at a loss.

"Pleased to meet you," Rex said, sticking out his right hand, which after a moment, the man shook.

"Take it off my invoice for moving your boss's junk to Delta," Rex said. "Now where should I place the barge so you can load the iron?"

"Who are you?" Dunlap asked. "What iron?"

"Didn't you and Saad give Herr Dunlap the manifest?" Rex asked.

"It's all there on the manifest," Captain Malik told Dunlap. The arrogant Ichneumon officer was back as he jabbed his finger at the documents the flustered manager was holding.

"Remember I want to clear the harbor before it gets dark," Rex said. He then turned to Malik. "As soon as those worthless bitches finish with the firewood, they need to load that pipe and plate over there."

He pointed at a stack of iron pipe visible through the open warehouse door. He then realized Dunlap had a stricken look.

"Did you say First-mate Saad was here?" the boatyard manager asked. Rex nodded. "Oh God, he was accused of sabotaging the Orleans Queen. Herr Purnell had his family hung as a warning to other turncoats. I have to tell Razo."

The news stunned Rex and Captain Malik. Amy's fears for her mother and sister weren't groundless, but first he had to stop Herr

143

Dunlap. Any clamor to locate the first mate would threatened to expose their scheme.

"Not that Saad, you fool," Rex madly fabricated. "Our man is from Westport. Apophis captured Purnell's first mate at Hickory Ridge." He hoped the manager thought he was mad, not horrified. "The Ichneumons are holding the traitor at Port Delta for Herr Purnell."

The manager seemed to buy the story and Rex added, "They know how to deal with that kind. We need to attend to business."

Dunlap looked sad and after a pause, said, "You're right. However, I need that pipe to finish a boiler repair."

"If it's on Purnell's list, it needs loaded, or he won't pay. If I have to wait around while you clowns decide whether your boss knows what he's doing, I'll add on demurrage of ten thousand D-marks a day for each boat. Now let's get with the loading."

Malik, nodded, and then yelled at Kyle to come with him and the boatyard manager to learn where the lathe was located. Rex walked over to inspect the pipe, while wondering if there was any way to warn Saad. There wasn't, and Dunlap's news had him worried about Amy's family. As soon as he had the pipe loading underway, he'd go find her mother.

The pipe was heavy wall 5-cm inside diameter wrought iron pipe in 5-meter lengths. It appeared to be seamless pipe, and Rex wondered how this primitive industrial society had managed to make seamless iron pipe. Amy had told him quality boiler pipe was the hardest material to find in the western territories, though rolled iron plate was also rather scarce. Take all they could safely carry was her advice.

Salma and Razo were laughing when Rex emerged from the warehouse. He didn't like that a bit and walked over to them.

"Quit loafing and help your crew," he said. "I want them to start on the pipe."

Salma didn't like the reprimand and both she and Razo started to respond when Rex cut them off.

"Does Purnell know you're lollygagging on the dock and interfering with work?"

"You might push those women around, but watch your mouth around me, or I'll put manners on you."

The firewood crew foreman gave Rex a hard shove. Several boatyard workers and Zamians, including Salma, paused to see how the stranger with the whip handled the challenge to his authority.

Rex's fist in Razo's face sent the man reeling back. A flurry of blow and kicks left the man bleeding and whimpering on the dock in a fetal position and the boatyard manager screaming. He stopped and waited for the manager to arrive. Salma and several of the women who happened to be on the dock to get more firewood were staring at him in shock.

"Salma, we don't have much time," he said, rubbing his knuckle. Razo's teeth had cut it. "Finish the firewood and start loading the pipe."

"Any more fighting and I'll have you arrested and held for Herr Purnell's return tomorrow," the manager said. The man looked terrified Rex would turn on him, but still tried to do his job of maintaining order.

"Sir, I'll behave, but that scum bag was bothering my slaves, and I need to get the cargo loaded." He said, gesturing for the still procrastinating Salma to move.

The manager checked the moaning man, decided his injuries weren't life threating, and lost interest in Razo. Rex figured the man just wanted the work done. After a moment, to be sure the fight was over, the manager walked back into the warehouse. By then, Salma had the women hustling, though several were sneaking fearful glances toward him.

The Mischief's firewood bin was full and the Zamia crew had started filling the Heron's larger coal bin with split oak. That would require more time since it required carrying the wood to the other dock, a distance of about fifty meters. Rex decided to check on Kyle and Malik's progress on loading the milling machine before looking for Amy's mother. He also wanted to learn if they knew where Saad went. With Purnell due back at any moment, the Wapiti needed gone.

It wasn't difficult to understand why the boatyard manager seemed unconcerned with losing the machines. Both machines were in jumbled dust-covered piles of heavy cast iron parts carelessly covered with ripped green oilcloths for protection from rain. Each of the machine's parts required several strong men to carry it over to the barge. Kyle was on the Heron showing the men where to place the pieces.

In a way, if they didn't miss a critical part, having the machines disassembled was a blessing. Neither Wapiti boat could have managed the milling machine in one piece. Based on the displacement of the Heron after loading, the milling machine weighed in the neighborhood of six thousand kilograms. The lathe's parts weren't quite as heavy, five thousand kilograms. The weight of the machines wouldn't sink the Heron. The question was if the old boat's structural keel, the boat's spine, was strong enough to resist buckling in rough seas. His other worry was if its boiler could push the load up the Erie River.

Rex found Malik helping the men gather the lathe parts.

"What are you going to do about Saad?" Malik asked. He looked nervous.

Rex shrugged and added, "I just hope he doesn't do something to attract the guards." He was more concerned about Amy's family.

"We best are gone," Malik said.

"Amen, but first you needed to find Dunlap," Rex said. "We need the tool holders, cutting bit stock, drill bits, chisels, grinder wheels, belts and anything else you can wheedle out of the man. Oh, and a steam gage or two. Take a couple of the ex-slaves to carry the items. Remember Ichneumon captains don't do manual labor. Did you locate that small steam engine?"

"Yes, Kyle has already loaded it in the Mischief's port barge. Why'd you hit that guy? You know we don't need the guards stirred up."

"The guards were watching. I figured if I did nothing it'd be out of character. Plus he irritated me," Rex said. "Go find Dunlap. Let's plan on embarking in an hour." He then went looking for 15 mm diameter rivet blanks and Amy's mother.

Amy had wanted one thousand rivets. The machine shop was the largest building in Orleans, a rambling wood structure with a high ceiling. Looking up at the long spans of unorthodox wood king post construction of the roof trusses, Rex wondered how the structure could withstand a snow load, until he realized snow was improbable this far south. The shop was noisy with much pounding on metal plates, and the workforce seemed recovered from Salma's show.

An assortment of disassembled gearboxes, steam engines, and a contraption of pipes that had to be part of a boiler were scattered about the cavernous space. Groups of two and three men in oil-stained dark grey coveralls were working among the pieces. No wonder Amy Caroom was so different from other women: he was standing in her childhood playground.

"Are you the foreman over the slaves?" a wiry older man working on the pipe contraption asked.

Rex nodded. He had paused to watch him using a heavy tool to flange the end of a pipe that projected through a plate. He couldn't recall if one of those tools was on Amy's list, but it looked useful.

The thick iron plate was about a meter in diameter with a series of holes drilled in it that the men were feeding pipes through for the man to flange. They all seemed uneasy, almost hostile toward him, probably the result of his earlier conduct with the bullwhip.

"Who bought the old machines?" the pipe man asked.

"The stuff is going to Delta," Rex said. "Purnell is setting up a machine shop. At least that's the rumor. Is that a boiler you're working on?"

"It is a Caroom boiler. Ever heard of her?"

"What's your name? I'm Burgdorf." Rex learned the man's name was Sam. "Captain Malik tells us his boat has a Caroom boiler. He says it's the best kind, even if a female designed it."

"Amy Caroom, she used to design our boilers, but had a falling out with Herr Purnell," Sam said. The machinist stopped working on the pipe flange and elaborated. Rex wasn't surprised to learn that the worker had revered her, but time was short and he couldn't afford to visit.

"Dunlap told me about Saad's family," Rex said. Several of the ironworkers commented on Purnell's despicable policy of murdering of entire families before he could ask about Amy's family. He never got a chance. Sam told him Amy's mother and sister had gone missing last week.

"This place is getting crazy. Even the Ichneumons aren't that bad," Sam said. Rex didn't agree, but kept quiet as Sam added. "If whoever is buying this junk needs experienced ironworkers, tell him several of us would go to Delta."

"I'll pass that on, but I'm on a tight schedule," Rex said. He didn't comment on Amy's missing family and dreaded telling her about Purnell's behavior. Instead, he asked, "Where are the rivets located?"

Sam volunteered to show him. They headed back toward the warehouse where the pipe was stored. He was happy to see that Kyle was about finished loading the two heavy machines, and some of his crew had gone to assist the women with the iron plate. With any luck, they'd be gone within the hour.

His guide was very spry and set a fast pace across the dock area to the warehouse where Salma's gang was standing behind the wrought iron pipe rack. The women were talking, not carrying the pipe and pieces of iron plate to the Mischief.

"Those are some fine-looking women to be carting pipes," Sam said, shaking his head. "Next time tell them to wear some clothes. As it is, our wives are going to be in an uproar. I'm surprised none of them have arrived to protest."

The man looked around, verifying he still had the right of it, no wives at hand. Rex learned that wasn't what had the machinist's interest.

"That milling machine they just loaded on the Heron is the one that was promised to Amy," Sam said. "Do you know Captain Dalporto? He's the captain on the Clovis Belle."

Rex, ever cautious, considered for a moment on whether to admit knowing the man. "Yes, I've met the captain."

Sam stopped again outside the warehouse entrance and asked if he was familiar with Panther Creek.

"Sam, I've been around, but until you explain why you're asking these questions, I think you need to focus on rivets."

"Herr Burgdorf, you match the description of the Prussian the captain said was in Panther Creek when Amy Caroom was murdered by Cinnabar's savages. I was hoping you could tell if that's true."

"Why would you think it wasn't true?" Rex asked. Sam's inquiry reminded him that finding Amy's mother was next on his list.

"The men and I were wondering why our boss would bother putting out a reward on a dead person."

"Sam, not to be unfriendly, but I don't have the time. Besides, I never saw the body. The only person who was there was an Ichneumon sergeant that survived the battle and told about a young woman being killed. He didn't know her name." The machinist stopped and studied Rex.

"On the chance Amy's alive, and you happen to talk with her, tell her that her mother and sister, Camille, were hung the day the reward was posted," Sam said while watching Rex. "If Amy is alive, tell her that Purnell wants her dead."

God all mighty, is there no limit to the evilness. Rex thought. He wasn't good at hiding his emotions when it involved Amy, he could feel tears forming. To protect the deception that this was a Purnell sanctioned project and not a raid, he should have pretended indifference to the Caroom family, instead he asked. "Why would Purnell kill them?"

"He has always been a murderous bastard," Sam said, pausing to look around. Satisfied no one was near, he added, "Lately, he has started killing the victim's families, probably to terrorize and silence anyone who might consider opposing or testifying against him."

Sam resumed his hurried pace into the warehouse. The man had realized he had been discussing a taboo subject with a stranger.

Salma was still at the pipe rack, along with a couple of the black women, laughing. The Zamia workers apparently had difficulty remembering they were to act like slaves who feared the whip. Christ, this act of cruel overseer was wearing on him. He needed to find and comfort Amy, but completing his assignment was critical to accomplishing her goals. Resigned that the deception needed maintained a bit longer, Rex uncoiled the whip and snapped it in Salma's direction. The loud crack of the bullwhip stopped the women's laugher. The two ex-slaves beside Salma hurried off with two sections of pipe.

"Salma, I need four laborers to carry rivets," Rex yelled. A pair of Zamia women walking back from the dock rushed to him. Sam gave him a hostile glance, and looked a bit unsure.

"I'm not kidding about the lack of time." On a whim, he decided to increase the number of rivets. "I need 1,500 of the 15 mm ones, a mix of lengths."

Rex endeavored to stay focused on completing the gathering of parts, but worry over Amy's reaction on hearing of her family's fate, kept interfering. After instructing Salma and several of the women on the rivets, the women followed Sam into the warehouse. Confidence Salma would gather the remaining items, Rex jogged over to the Mischief. He paused to check on the loading and then went to find Amy.

David C. Brown

Chapter 8

Purnell's ruse appeared to be working. The abandonment of fort at Port Delta by the Prussian battalion was complete. The task accomplished with their usual efficiency and dispatch. Waiting on the Kura, General Paget had watched about fifty of the remaining troopers board the armored sidewheeler, Rhineland, docked in front of the Kura.

The general knew the bogus Prussian orders told the Rhineland to proceed to River Point and complete the investigation of the Hendrick sinking. Purnell's fast steamboat would easily catch and pass the heavy warship, and deliver to the commander at Hickory Ridge new orders informing him that the Erie River truce was over. The garrison was to sink the Prussian warship.

The rest of the Prussian battalion had earlier re-boarded HMS Rhine Mar and departed. To Paget's delight, looking across the harbor, he realized in another fifteen minutes there wouldn't be a Prussian warship in sight. The Ichneumon army would be back in control of Port Delta, thanks to the businessman's clever gambit.

Paget wondered if the information that his friend, Colonel Xavier, had survived was correct. He hoped not, for there could be no explanation that could justify allowing Port Delta to fall into Prussian hands.

First, before worrying over who was responsible, the army needed to reestablish Ichneumon control over the damaged fort, and then the port. But with caution, he did not trust that Prussian, Colonel Markel, and held back the impatient troopers from rushing into the fort. The snapper platoon needed time to check for booby-traps. He was waiting for word from the snapper lieutenant when the Kura captain sent word that a Herr Erdogam wished to speak with Purnell.

"Your chief weasel wants to talk."

"Erdogam wants to tell me that the loss of my thirty prime Zamia slaves wasn't his fault. If they got killed because of Xavier's carelessness, I expect to be reimbursed."

A moment later, Erdogam entered the Kura conference room. The slaver kowtowed to them. Paget wasn't sure where the mongrel's loyalties lay, most likely to the D-mark. The general knew Xavier had never liked or trusted the slaver.

"Was my property harmed?"

"Herr Purnell, I have not been allowed in the fort to check," Erdogam said. "The Prussians did threaten to free any slaves that they found in the fort. I heard the slave cells collapsed and some of the slaves died, and others escaped."

"So what, why didn't you just round them back up? Or when the Prussians released them, grab them? You didn't just stand around and let other people hijack our property."

"I tried. Right after the explosion, I saw Salma and a couple of naked Zamia men," the slaver said. "Before I could catch them, Prussian soldiers detained the Ichneumon guards and me. The Prussians released me the following morning and I organized a search, but there was no trace of Salma and the Zamia men. They must have got on one of the ships that fled after the explosion and the invasion."

The general asked who Salma was.

"She's one of the few Zamians that understands and speaks our language," Purnell said. "She's smart for a savage and valuable. I told you to lock her in a cell, so how'd you see her in the market? Or were you selling her sexual favors and she escaped?"

The general watched large beads of sweat pop out on the mongrel's forehead.

"Sir, please, I would never do that, but the Ichneumon guards might have. I need to get in the fort. It's been three days and if the prisoners haven't received water . . .'"

The lieutenant from the snapper company rushed into the General Paget's room holding two Prussian detonators.

"General, these devices were in the main magazine powder barrels. We searched and didn't find any more."

General Paget recognized the devices were two-hour delay detonators. The lieutenant saw Herr Purnell had turned pale and added.

"They're safe. I put the safety pin back in the striker so when the acid finishes eating through the restraining wire, nothing will go off," the lieutenant said. "I also brought Colonel Xavier back to the ship. He's in terrible pain."

General Paget thanked the lieutenant for frustrating the dishonorable Prussian plot.

"We'll return the favor. I'll have our new rifled cannons blow the Rhineland apart if it returns. Teach those Prussians not to trifle with the Ichneumon army. Now return to the fort and check everything twice, make sure your men examine every barrel. Take Herr Erdogam with you so he can check on his property."

The Ichneumon snapper lieutenant hadn't exaggerated. The fort commander had suffered terrible injuries: loss of an eye, the other eye lens cut so bad he might never see well enough to read again, a missing foot, and a smashed purulent hand. The man smelled terrible. Paget knew that smell and reckoned gangrene was rampant in both of Xavier's wounds.

Purnell and the general realized the colonel had no idea what had caused the explosion. He even thought the Prussians had entered the fort to help the garrison with the injured. General Paget didn't enlighten the colonel to the fact that the Prussians had seized the fort.

"He's a useless cripple and will turn bitter," Purnell said. They were in the hallway. "More important, Xavier knows too much about our business to allow him back in Cusco. Do you want the sorry wreck talking with the emperor's investigators? I think it is better the colonel dies a hero."

"I'll deal with it," Paget said. Colonel Xavier was a longtime friend, but the Orleans businessman was correct.

"I will make certain that Emperor Ratakonda learns of your brilliant deception," the general added. "Go check on your slaves and property while I reassure the colonel. And thank you for your help with my family and getting those new orders to Hickory Ridge."

Purnell studied him for a moment and then left. General Paget told the doctor and orderly to leave and close the door. Colonel Xavier recognized Paget's voice and turned his sightless eyes toward him.

"The rot has set in," the colonel whispered. "Please end this, but before you do, know that I have Rex Knight locked in the dungeon."

"You're serious, how?" Paget asked. That was terrific news, if true. It would go a long way toward placating the emperor.

"The bastard was selling nuts to the tobacco company. The warehouse manager, Alpha, told me. He claimed to work for Purnell and that his name was Friedrich Burgdorf. But I'm sure he's the man the prince wants."

"If it proves out, you will get full credit. Regardless, my friend, I'll look after your family."

The general shot the trembling colonel in the head. The sound of the shot was still ringing in his ears when the boat lurched. Confused as to the cause, Paget wondered if the Aruba had bumped the Kura. A loud boom a moment later clarified the cause, a missed detonator.

A massive cloud of debris and dust was bellowing upward into the clear blue sky from the north end of the fort. The main gate, which had survived the earlier explosion, was gone. Pieces of rock were still raining down on the hillside below the fort when Paget reached the deck to watch. Some large chunks of the fort's stonework landed as far as the Erie River, their impacts causing huge geysers of muddy water, death, and destruction along the waterfront.

The explosion had caught two of the Ichneumon troop companies marching in column formation between the main gate and the Kura. Dead Ichneumon troopers laid scattered about the road. A few of the less seriously injured crawled or wandered in a daze toward the waterfront. Colonel Markel was a dead man. One-way or another, Paget would pay back that Prussian colonel for his treachery.

The explosion stunned Benjamin Purnell and whipped away his smug feeling from playing the Prussians for fools. The Ichneumons might think him clever, but as the sabotage just reminded him, the Prussians would be back. Time was critical. Purnell now knew the false orders had sent the Zamia blockade fleet to another station along the coast to delay discover of Harlem's ruse by Berlin. But when the General Staff did become aware of that fraud, along with the Delta con, they would move immediately to find and eliminate the source.

Rex found Amy in the pilothouse checking off items of her list.

"Hey, big boy, we're about done," She said, in a good mood. "Are you ready to . . .?" Something in his face warned her, for she asked, "What?"

"Your mother and sister are dead. Purnell had them killed."

Amy's face crumbled into anguish as she asked why. He explained what Sam had told him and why he hadn't asked the man to meet her. He couldn't endanger his family. If the machinist was to learn of her involvement in the equipment rip-off, and failed to report it, Purnell might hang the worker and his family.

"They were innocents," Amy whispered. "Camille was thirteen." She burst into heart-wrenching sobs and tears and hugged Rex. Captain Malik charged into the pilothouse and stopped on seeing them.

"We have a problem," Malik said. He realized Amy was crying and raised an eyebrow in question, before adding. "Razo and several patrolmen have arrested five of the Zamia men and taken them to the whipping blocks. Claim they were hassling the boatyard workers' wives that had arrived to protest the nude slaves. It'll cause a riot."

"I hate that evil man," Amy said, whipping her eyes. Neither Rex nor Malik knew what to say to comfort her. After a brief silence, she tossed her handkerchief on the counter and asked. "Is everything loaded and secured?"

"The Heron's loaded," the captain said as Rex watched her. "Kyle is still loading pipe and plates in the starboard rear barge."

"Wrap it up. We have enough," she told Malik. "We're departing in a few minutes. Rex, loan me one of your revolvers and come with me." He did. Not waiting on any acknowledgement, she then hurried to the whipping post area, checking on the way that the revolver was loaded. Slim went with them while Malik readied the boats for departure.

Amy was acting strange. Not that she lacked a good reason, but Rex feared she was about to kick the hornet's nest. He whistled for Andy and waved for several of the armed Wapiti to join them. They caught up with her as she arrived by the whipping post.

Razo was restraining Salma who was arguing with the police corporal and trading glares and insults with two stout middle-aged women in long indigo dresses, white lace caps, and gray aprons. With Salma's sole article of clothing consisting of that miniscule leather thong, Rex figured the difference in the quarreling women's outfits was a good proxy for the difference in their mindsets.

One of the Zamia men was fastened to the whipping post and bleeding from several lashes of a whip. The shirtless thug holding the whip stopped as they arrived.

"These slaves belong to Captain Malik. Release that man," Rex ordered.

The wives who had been trading insults with Salma went mute. The policemen and the thug with the whip appeared uncertain, and they looked to the battered Razo who had recovered his aggressive nature after the earlier beating.

"Razo, unhand my interpreter," he added, and then addressed the wives. "Ladies, please accept my and the captain's apology for any misunderstanding. The Zamia slaves are new and haven't learned our culture. The captain will deal with that problem."

The corporal looked toward the wives, evidently trying to discern if they were satisfied with Rex's offer. The wives appeared to have realized their complaints had attracted an angry group of armed people and events were in danger of turning lethal.

"As long as the immoral savages leave immediately," the older wife answered. She gave Salma a final scowl and walked away.

"Hold up until this is resolved," the corporal said. The thug with the whip, who had been lashing the man, looked to Razo for his orders.

"Release her, or I'll finish the earlier beating."

Instead, Razo grabbed Salma by the neck and pulled his revolver, an older cap-and-ball relict. The action stopped Rex from reaching for Razo's arm around Salma neck.

"Are you still Purnell's executioner?" Amy asked.

"What's it to you, bitch?" Razo asked, shoving Salma away and pointed the revolver at Amy. "Who gave you permission to have a gun?"

With Razo's attention on Amy, Slim, the Wapiti hunter, was creeping closer to Razo, clearly planning to grab the revolver. Rex caught the warrior's attention and motioned for him not to try grabbing the gun.

"I just wanted to meet the brave man that kills women and girls," Amy said. The man with the whip started to ease away from the whipping post and toward the warehouse.

"Hold it, pal, don't leave," she said. That simple request spiked the tension among the Wapiti, policeman, and Rex. Razo, fool that he was, looked haughty.

"Are you talking about those wailing women that Purnell hung for spying?" Razo asked. Amy's tears seemed to encourage him, for he added. "The little Caroom girl was so light, she twitched for an hour. You should have been there, great entertainment. If her traitorous sister, Amy, is alive and we capture the bitch, Purnell promised we can burn the witch at the stake."

The police corporal looked aghast. The two wives had stopped. They had heard Razo cruel remarks, for they appeared horrified along with Salma.

"That what happened?" the corporal asked. "I was told they were visiting the islands. Are you joking, you murdered Camille?"

"I didn't murder anyone, just doing my job. Our boss ordered it. I handled it. Corporal, now do your job and arrested these people for interfering in police matters."

The murderous creep had decided Rex was the greater threat and pointed his revolver at him. A gunshot, Slim had tried to grab Razo's revolver and instead been shot. Amy shot Razo, twice, and then without a moment of hesitation, turned and shot the whip man who had broken into a run toward the warehouse. Purnell's two executioners laid sprawled on the lot and appeared dead. The only sound was Salma crying over Slim.

"They murdered my family. Do you wish to make an issue of this?"

The policeman, seeing several revolvers and more rifles pointed at him, shook his head.

"Here, keep an eye on him," Amy said, handing back to Rex his smoking revolver. She then proceeded to strip off her disguise. Everyone watched the transformation. The two middle-aged women gasped on recognizing her.

"Tell my father that I'll find him."

The scene was ominous. Not at all what Rex and the Wapiti had expected to find on their return to Port Delta. The Prussian fleet had sailed off, replaced by two Ichneumon warships and half dozen smaller sail ships. Dozens of large Ichneumon's double-headed snake flags flew from the remains of the fort's walls, almost as if the flags were there as a substitution for the smashed cannons and toppled walls.

Rex had a hundred questions. Had the Ichneumons surprised and routed the Prussians? Was the mighty Prussian battleship, Schlesien, on the harbor's bottom? The fort had suffered additional damage since he last saw it.

The departure from Orleans had gone without a hitch. Even the trip along the coast had gone well, if slow. The loaded Heron sternwheeler could only maintain half of the Mischief's speed, even though the twin sidewheeler was pushing four barges. Both ships had consumed most of the hardwood from Orleans and needed their bunkers restocked at Delta. Rex wondered how much additional firewood would be required to overcome the river current. He also feared the slow Heron would prevent their convoy from reaching River Point before the Erie River froze over.

First Mate Saad had returned. He vowed revenge on Purnell and his henchmen for murdering his family and found a willing ally in Amy. Rex, no longer concerned about the first mate's loyalty, made him the Heron's captain. Kyle was back on the Mischief.

Amy had kept to herself. She spent hours on top of the pilothouse, watching the distant coast sail by. She would take no interest in conversations, or discuss her family, or her killing of those two men. When the subject was the boilers and engines, she would respond. She even ignored Hokee's efforts for a belly rub. The discovery that the Ichneumons controlled the fort at Delta snapped her despondency.

"We'll need firewood soon," Kyle said. "What are we going to do? I figure the Heron also needs firewood."

Rex, Malik, and Amy who had just joined them in the Mischief pilothouse, held a war council.

"Too late to switch flags," Rex said. "Dusk is near. Perhaps the Ichneumon watch won't notice us."

They all knew a miracle would have to occur for the Ichneumons not to see them steaming across the harbor. The bright white background of the Wapiti green star flag flapping in the breeze would aid in that discovery. Both steamships pushed heavy loads and were in no position to outrun those Ichneumon sidewheelers docked below the fort.

Bad luck, Rex thought, *what could of the Prussians been thinking to abandon such a strategic location?* The Wapiti boats had crossed the mighty river to reach Port Delta on the western shore for supplies. If only they had known. The Wapiti convoy could have stayed along the eastern shore in the slack water, and by now, been several kilometers up the river, the Ichneumon navy none the wiser.

"We're not stopping, right?" Amy asked. She was studying the Heron. It was about hundred meters starboard of the Mischief. He shook his head. She added, "You need to tell Salma."

Their translator and four other Zamia "slaves" were talking among themselves and gesturing towards the Ichneumon warships. Rex figured they were wondering if they had made a fatal mistake not going with the rest of the Zamia ex-slaves who had passed on the offer to join the Wapiti, primarily because of the cold weather. Those folks had disembarked at several points along the gulf coast.

"I think their boilers are cold," Captain Malik said.

"Switch flags, use the snake flag," Rex shouted, snapping out of his hesitation.

"But in Ichneumon harbors they usually have a couple of small sidewheelers for police checks. One of them usually has a hot boiler. If the harbor watch saw us, and we don't dock, they'll come out to investigate. With these barges we can't outrun them."

"We can't dock with those bastards back in control. And we can't allow the Ichneumons to board, so concentrate on getting out of range of the fort. It'll be dark in a half hour," Rex said. "Without stopping, maneuver close to the Heron, so I can yell at Saad."

A few minutes later, both Wapiti boats had Ichneumon flags snapping in the breeze. Captain Malik who had been watching the dock area with a telescope told them a police boat had pulled away from the dock.

"I figured they'd intercept the Mischief about dark. Oh, oh, there's a puff of black smoke from one of the armored sidewheelers," Malik added. "They're using oil to start a boiler. The chase is on."

The two Wapiti boats were slow, but far from impotent. Rex had Amy and six experienced soldiers armed with bolt-action rifles, four on the Mischief and two on the Heron. Zolfo and Helmick were now recovered enough to help. Salma had told Rex that she knew how to use a rifle and she would replace Slim who was recovering from Razo's bullet. And they had reinstalled the small brass canon on the Mischief's bow.

"Even using oil, the armored sidewheeler will need a half hour to bring the boiler pressure up," Amy said. "And the one firing its boilers is old and slow. Those old sidewheelers use two large slide-valve engines, one on each paddlewheel. They're even slower than the Heron."

"Hell, if they're that slow, why worry?" Rex asked, wondering for a moment what a slide-valve engine was. "Kyle, bring up two canister loads for the cannon."

"They carry a couple of rifled cannons that can reach out a couple of thousand meters. The Heron would never survive a hit from one of those exploding shells," Amy said. "And you never know when something will break, leaving the Mischief or Heron dead in the water."

"Let's try to be optimistic." Rex was tired of stewing about issues he had no control over. He wanted a fight.

The Ichneumon harbor police boat arrived abreast the Mischief just at dark. Rex and the crew were well aware the Ichneumons could see quite well in the dark. Judging from the lightning, an intense storm was brewing to the west but wouldn't arrive in time to help hide the Wapiti convoy.

Six Ichneumon sailors armed with single shot breech loading rifles waited on the deck as the captain yelled for the Mischief to stop. The policemen appeared irked, probably from having to go out in a storm at dinnertime, for sure, they didn't appear to Rex to be expecting any trouble.

The Mischief wasn't stopping. Rex stood beside the tarp covering the brass cannon looking puzzled over the Ichneumon's shouted orders. Zolfo, hidden under the tarp, was ready to pull the trigger on the fuse lighting device. The small cannon's charge consisted of a double load of canister shot. The Wapiti would have time for one shot, and he wanted to do maximum damage to exposed personnel on the harbor boat.

The mount of the Mischief's cannon was a wooden turntable. It allowed Rex to use his knee to swing the cannon barrel, though the tarp covering the cannon kept interfering. A crude method of aiming, but at less than ten meters, he couldn't miss as the police boat approached from the rear. The cannon's bow location did necessitate waiting until the police boat pulled alongside. The cannon barrel could only be swiveled so far toward the rear, and still avoid blowing a hole in the Mischief's pilothouse.

There, a perfect alignment, as the police boat edged past the center of the Mischief with the sailors lined along the handrail with their rifles at ready. Their captain was by then in a state of rage, yelling at Malik, who pretended confusion. Rex told Zolfo to fire. The cannon blast and canisters ripped the tarp from the cannon, upending Rex.

By the time he had gained his feet, the police boat was aside the barges. Everyone on the police boat appeared dead or at least incapacitated. The grapeshot had shredded the Ichneumon pilothouse walls. All the windows were broken. Of more concern, Rex could hear hissing and see steam leaking out of the deck hatch. Otherwise, the boat appeared undamaged as it steamed beside the Mischief. The bloody, shot-up hulk was edging closer to the port rear barge, threatening an imminent collision of its starboard paddlewheel with the Mischief's port side rear barge.

Captain Malik yelled from the pilot house to ask if they were okay as he was swinging the Mischief toward the east shore to avoid a collision. Rex's ears were ringing as he helped Zolfo to his feet. Amy arrived to check on them.

"Malik let the boats close," he yelled. "Kyle, think you can make the jump to the Ichneumon boat, get control of it?"

An eager Kyle nodded and in a moment, he was aboard the police boat with his brother John.

"Disarm them first," Rex yelled.

Amy made the jump with her tool bag as two gunshots rang out from the police boat engine room John and Kyle had just entered.

"Was that Kyle?" Malik asked, voicing Rex's worry.

A moment later, Kyle waved from the engine room door and Amy disappeared into the engine room.

"Well, that's a relief," Rex said. "Now we need to clear out of here. I figure the Ichneumons will expect us to flee up the east side of the river. What do you think about turning back toward the west side where they won't expect us?"

"You're right about the Ichneumons looking to the east, but when the captain of the armored sidewheeler doesn't find us, or the harbor police boat, he'll come back along the west shore looking," Captain Malik said. "And there's the firewood issue."

"I remember several bayous between here and the niter yard that might offer hiding spots come daylight," Rex said. "Not the best solution. If the Ichneumons discover us, then we're trapped."

"There are two large bayous still open to the main channel on the river's east side. The Ichneumons will want to examine them, before crossing back to check the west side. That should keep them busy tomorrow. Then tomorrow night, we can cross to the east side and head north. However, if the Ichneumon navy sends two sidewheelers . . ."

The Heron had caught up with the Mischief and was passing fifty meters off their starboard side. The Heron passengers gathered at the rail looking panicky. They had heard the cannon and now could see the police boat.

"Amy, Kyle, can the boat be salvaged, or is it sinking?" Rex asked.

Mischief's double load of grape shot had perforated the police boat's starboard superstructure with numerous jagged fist size holes. One or two such holes below the water line would sink the boat.

"The steam leak is stopped," Amy said on reemerging from the police boat deck hatch. "Want to keep the boat? I believe the boiler will hold to River Point."

"Yes, it might prove handy. What do you need to manage it?"

"We'll need a fireman to help feed the boiler. And it's low on firewood."

166

Rex sent one of the Wapiti troopers with a bolt-action rifle to help.

"Kyle, you're needed on the Mischief and Heron," Rex yelled as he felt the first drops on the storm. "John, you help Amy. Follow the Mischief."

Herr Saad, who was piloting the Heron, already knew to follow the Mischief.

Hokee leaped onto the police boat after Rex released his hold on the wolf's collar. He had kept Hokee from following Amy on to the police boat until they had secured it.

About twenty-five kilometers north of Port Delta the Wapiti found the bayou entrance along the west shore that Rex had remembered from the earlier trip. He was coming to appreciate the Erie River channel was ever shifting, nothing like the channeled Mississippi River he had known. River loops became oxbow lakes and a plantation that once was fronting on the river, after a flood, might find it was now several kilometers from the main river channel. The shifting river channel and landscape was a blessing for fugitives.

Especially when they were escaping on the shallow draft, twin sidewheelers like the Mischief and captured police boat. The Heron was a more fragile craft designed for the Prussian rivers with their dams and locks. Rex had never been on an Ichneumon armored sidewheeler, but figured its design was similar to the Prussian sidewheeler, HMS Hendrick, which required a water depth of about two or more meters to avoid grounding.

The Mischief and their hijacked harbor police boat needed less than a meter of water. Also helpful, both steamboats' hulls and paddles were stout enough to survive an encounter with a sandbar or river ice. The Heron was also shallow draft, but the timbers of its keel and hull were more fragile and a grounding might severely damage the boat.

The small Wapiti fleet closed together. Amy, Kyle Baler, Saad, Captain Malik, John Baler, Helmick, and Rex held a conference on the front barge of the Mischief's tow. The barges and Mischief were parked in the entrance of the bayou's drain way. Amy had tied off the Ichneumon's police boat to the Heron's stern. It was the farthest out in the river.

"Will the Heron clear the sandbar across the outlet with the heavy machines on board?" Rex asked, as dawn was just breaking. They needed off the river. The Ichneumon warship they thought was in pursuit could appear at any moment.

"Also, while I'm thinking of it, caution everyone not to disturb the vegetation along the inlet banks."

"It's a darn narrow and shallow channel," Kyle said. "The Heron keel may clear, but drag along the sides. I'm worried the Heron lacks the power to move if it does wedge in the inlet. Its timbers seem a bit flimsy on the bottom, and a grounding may cause a leak."

"The Mischief can pull it into the cove, bayou, if it grounds," Rex said. "But if it starts leaking, Saad, let Malik drag it around the corner." He pointed to the bend in front of the entrance. "It'll be out of sight of the river and we'll have time to figure out a repair."

"Captain Malik, bump the Mischief and her four barges across the sandbar," Rex ordered. A slight hump announced the starboard paddle wheel had made contact with the sandbar, but a moment later, the Mischief and her barge train floated into the tranquil water of the bayou-oxbow lake.

Next, Saad lined up the Heron with the inlet and eased into the entrance. The boat grounded gently and he gave full power to the stern-wheel paddles. The boat shuddered ahead another twenty meters and stopped with the paddles churning the water. No way could the Ichneumons miss seeing a boat stuck in the inlet. Then he heard Amy yelling to hurry.

"There's smoke down the river," She yelled from the Heron's pilothouse.

Rex and several Wapiti were busy dragging the Mischief's heavy towropes to the boat's stern where Saad's crew of Salma and the two Zamians from the boiler room were waiting to drag the ropes to the Heron bow. In a minute, they had two ropes tied to the front line bollards of the Heron. He saw Hokee on the shore, looking toward the river, then noticed the police boat backing out into the river.

"Who's on the police boat?" Rex asked the trooper he had sent to help Amy. The man was preparing to jump off the Heron and join Hokee. They were to watch for river traffic from the cove's inlet while the rest of them worked to free the Heron.

"Amy and John are on the police boat."

Good, Rex thought, *she'll have to realize they'll have the Heron clear of the inlet in another minute and the police boat can then zip into the bayou.* They'd better have all the boats hidden before the lumbering Ichneumon warship cleared the bend and could see the inlet.

He gave the signal for the Mischief and Heron captains to power up. The Heron shuddered and jerked ahead a bit, before stopping again. Both boats went to full power, threshing the water into brown foam. The wake from the Mischief paddles helped raise the Heron's bow. After more churning of the water, the steamboat slipped into the bayou. In a flash, the captains were reversing paddles and throttling back power to avoid a collision between the boats, and keep the Mischief from driving its barges into the far bank of the bayou. A minute later, the two ships were around the bayou bend and out of sight of the river.

The boats and barges drifted to stop, paddle wheels stopped. The crews slammed the dampers closed in the boiler fireboxes to stop the telltale smoke. In a minute, the bayou surface settled down, and the area turned quiet. The lone sound was the soft cyclic huffing and clanking of the police boat out on the river. The sunrise reddish glow reflecting off the river made seeing out into the river difficult.

Rex used a small rowboat to reach the bayou entrance. He found the wolf and trooper and located the police boat. It was far out in the river. Then two enormous geysers of water sprouted near the police boat, followed a heartbeat latter by two thunderous booms. The Ichneumon armored sidewheeler had spotted the police boat.

Chapter 9

General Paget thought the night watch had mistaken some local gulf trader's flag for the Wapiti flag on that small steamboat sighted the evening before. The one Wapiti crewed boat recently in Delta was that one with the winter sloe nut cargo. It had disappeared the night of the first explosion. Without doubt, it had bolted up the Erie to River Point and safety. But with the failure of the harbor police boat to return, now he wasn't sure what to think.

The watch had also reported hearing a cannon fire, but a storm had passed through about then, and Paget figured the watch had heard thunder. The Delta garrison was on edge from all the sabotage the fort had suffered in the past couple of weeks. The men were seeing threats where none existed. Still, caution was called for.

The Saukko had already embarked the afternoon before for Fenwick. Its mission was to guard his family. The Kura needed to remain at Delta. If a Prussian warship arrived, he didn't want to depend on the old Helot. The navy had refitted the out-of-date sternwheeler with new rifle cannons, but the warship still had the original low-pressure boilers and was slow. As consequence, the Helot was more like a monitor than a ship of the line. It wasn't the best choice for river patrol. The lumbering antiquated war ship could barely exceed the center river current. He had the Helot captain brought to the fort.

David C. Brown

"I want every boat encountered, boarded, and inspected," the general said. "Impound or sink all Wapiti and Prussian boats. This is in addition to your mission to stop all non-Ichneumon traffic on the Erie." Those orders caused the dour Helot captain to smile.

"Take Delta homing pigeons and send messages back to Port Delta if you encounter any circumstances I should know of," the general added.

After dealing with the Helot captain, General Paget had his orderly bring him a glass of wine. As he relaxed, his thoughts turned to Wilhelm's reception on arriving home. The Prussian fleet ought to arrive in the Baltic in two more days. That fool was in for a shock, maybe even a firing squad when Emperor Schnabel learned he abandoned the Port Delta fort. The unknown was the Prussian response on their discovery of the deception.

The Orleans trader believed the Prussian General Staff would hesitate to start another war while the eastern war remained unresolved and they no longer had the element of surprise at Port Delta. He didn't share that sanguine opinion. Colonel Markel, the Prussian infantry colonel, knew the two explosions had wrecked much of the fort's defenses. He would advocate for a quick assault to recapture the fort before the Ichneumon's could complete repairs.

Paget wasn't defenseless. He had at his command two armored sidewheelers armed with the new rifled cannons that fired shells that exploded on contact. Besides the hundred or so surviving garrison troops and dungeon guards, he still had six hundred Ichneumon marines. Well, maybe nearer four hundred marines after those losses from the second sabotage. And there was the promised convoy of a thousand more soldiers and two more armored sidewheelers due in a month.

Dark smoke from down the river meant the Ichneumon warship would be in sight of the bayou entrance in a few minutes and

Amy had to decide. She considered her options, dash for the inlet now that the Heron was free of the sandbar and had disappeared into the bayou or bolt. If Saad shut down the boiler and stopped the smoke, the trees would conceal the Heron from searchers out on the river. She decided to run. Trying to reach the inlet now would alert the Ichneumons where the Wapiti had hidden. The small police boat wasn't as fast as the Mischief, but it would have no problem outrunning the heavy Ichneumon boat. The problem was the lack of fuel.

John Baler and two of the Zamia men Amy had trained on the Heron boiler was her crew on the shot-up police boat. Two nearby explosions startled Amy. The Ichneumons had seen the police boat. Why the navy was trying to destroy it wasn't clear, how did they know the harbor police weren't still operating the boat? Amy had no illusion the little boat and her crew would survive a hit from an exploding fifty-kilogram cannon shell. Fleeing was their best option.

"John, you're a sniper. Try hitting their bridge with a few shots to slow them down," Amy said.

The warship was far out of the rifle's effective range, but even a spent bullet was dangerous. She yelled down to her fireman to stroke the boiler. She would worry about firewood after escaping the warship. Pointing the bow toward the east shore, she eased the damaged steam valve to full open. Now the Ichneumons would have to fire into the morning sun. In a couple of kilometers the river turned north, but by then they would be in the slack water near the shore and not fighting the current, which would increase their forward speed.

The Ichneumon captain would fear grounding, which should encourage him to stay in the deeper water where the river current was greater and would add to the difference between the boats' speed. Submerged trees caught in the shallows along the east shore were the main threat to the police boat. The ever-shifting river current constantly eroded the riverbanks and toppled large trees into the river. Amy's focus was on the river ahead, watching for the telltale ripples of a submerged snag. A collision with one of those trees would end their escape.

Several hundred meters ahead, a geyser of mud and vegetation erupted on the shore. She wondered what the gators thought of that while realizing the Ichneumons were either terrible marksmen or firing blind. John joined her in the pilothouse.

"I'm wasting ammo. The distance is too great," John said. "Do you have a plan?"

"Besides running?" Amy asked, smiling, but not taking her eyes off the water ahead. "How much firewood remains?"

"Enough for another hour," John said, watching the shore that they were racing past. "This boat is fast."

"Yeah, about as fast as the Mischief with the barges," Amy said. "Think we're out of range of their cannons?"

John nodded. After chancing a quick glance down the river, Amy resumed watching the water ahead and added, "We'll soon be concealed by that river bend coming up. One of those sulfur mine wharfs is not that far ahead, maybe another dozen kilometers."

"Ah, and they usually have firewood?" John asked. Rex had told her John was quick to understand.

"Yes, and a guard," Amy added. "John, do you know how to check the water level in the boiler?"

The police boat boiler lacked a condenser, and the engine's exhaust steam went to the stack. Running the boiler and engine flat out, the water that exhaust steam represented needed replaced or the boiler would soon go dry.

"I didn't but Nashi did. He added some river water," John said. The Zamians were proving to be fast learners.

"Are you game for raiding the sulfur mine's firewood?" Knowing that Nashi would keep the boiler safe, she focused back on the fuel problem.

"Yes, indeed, stealing beats having to cut it. Besides we're harbor police pursuing rum runners," John said, already guessing her plan.

"Then, let's pull one of Rex's tricks. There are two police uniform coats and hats in that cabinet."

The young Wapiti was positively gleeful at the idea of masquerading as an Ichneumon policeman. Amy wasn't sure what to make of that. John had always seemed the quiet Baler brother, but she didn't know him all that well. She hoped he realized the deadly seriousness of what she had proposed.

Since departing from Orleans, during introspective moments, Amy had been struggling to decide if she had forsaken any hope of being a moral person. Then she would imagine the horror her mother and Camille must have suffered and wondered if she was responsible. Should she have caved to her father's demands?

Rex, suspecting what was bothering her, had told her that she had no choice; it had been an act of self-defense. Razo had his revolver aimed at her and he had just shot Slim. Amy had disagreed. She had believed at the time, Razo shot Slim accidentally and he would have slithered off if given a choice, just as the thug with the whip had tried to escape her.

Her acts had been revenge killings, the very vengeance that the church warned led to evil. She had shot them for murdering her family, unlike the self-defense killings during her Orleans Queen escape. Rex told her that she was looking at it wrong. Her killing of those two murders was justified retribution.

Now she had just panicked, abandoning her friends on a sandbar. No thanks to her actions, they appeared safe for the moment. She was the one in peril.

"How's this going to work?" Amy asked, holding the black uniform with the Ichneumon unit patch and rank sewed on the sleeves. Gupta was the dead sergeant's name, she noticed, before adding. "No one would believe the Ichneumons would allow a female in their police ranks."

"Bind your breasts and stuff your hair in the hat," John said while pulling on the other set of coveralls. "Stay in the pilothouse and I'll handle the guard."

Most of the large Ichneumon flag had survived the Mischief's grapeshot and, though a bit shredded, it still flapped from the stern of the police boat. Her scarf subdued her breasts and with her hair hidden in the hat, no one would notice she was a woman if she remained in the pilothouse.

"I figure we'll have about fifteen minutes at the sulfur mine wharf before that warship comes into view," she said. "How much wood can we load?"

Not any, she feared, if the firewood wasn't stacked on or very near the wharf. John shrugged unworried, and studied the river ahead with a small brass telescope that he had discovered in the boat's pilothouse. Amy wished she could find such calmness.

"What are you looking for?" she asked after a minute.

"Checking out the fishing holes."

Rex had untied the barges from the Mischief and left them in the bayou. He had told the unhappy First Mate Saad and the Heron's crew to guard the cargo. Rex's plan was to follow the lumbering Ichneumon warship and find where Amy had gone. Unencumbered by the barges, Malik had the Mischief across the sandbar at the bayou's entrance and racing up the river within fifteen minutes.

"Do you agree, we can't allow the warship to spot us?" Malik asked.

Rex nodded, thinking of those rifled cannons.

"Then we'll run along the west bank and slow before each river bend to check the river section ahead," Malik said. "If the Ichneumons are clear of that section, then we'll dash to the next bend."

"Sounds like a good plan, Kyle, check the cannon is ready, but don't load it yet. I'm not sure if we'll need solid ball or canister."

The Mischief caught up with the Ichneumon warship after the second river bend and had to stop until it cleared the long straight river section ahead. Rex had spotted no new bayous along the section of the Erie River that they had just traveled, at least none with an inlet large enough that Amy might have slipped through to hide, nor did he see any sign of the police boat.

The sulfur mine wharf had no boats or barges tied to it, but several laborers were busy unloading wooden barrels from two freight wagons drawn by teams of four mules. Several large stacks of split firewood were on the riverbank near the wharf.

"Those are slaves," Amy said, "And look at that firewood by the dock."

John nodded, putting on the mirror glasses favored by the Ichneumons.

The laborers were Clovis men. The two men with shotguns appeared to be the typical Prussian brutes often found working as foremen supervising labor gangs and slaves. All the men at the wharf stopped to watch the police boat maneuver against the end of the dock with the bow pointed upriver.

"Who's in charge?" John shouted jumping on to the dock. "This is police business. Have your men stop the unloading and bring firewood. We're in pursuit of smugglers, rum runners."

Amy was impressed, the young Wapiti had the demeanor and voice most people expected from the typical haughty police sergeant, even if he didn't quite look the part.

"Our job is unloading wagons," the younger overseer said. "Load your own damn firewood."

Amy sneaked a look down river, while waiting to learn how John would respond to the thug's challenge. At least there was no sign of the warship, and then she saw John grab one of the heavy mauls by the firewood pile.

"What's in these barrels, rum? Are you in cahoots with those bastards we're chasing? That why you won't help?"

John swung the hammer, not waiting for a response from the guard. The hammer blow smashed in the top of the barrel and sent a cloud of yellow dust and pieces of splintered wood, into the air. The young Wapiti seemed surprised by the colored dust.

"Are you crazy," the older guard shouted, "That's yellow sulfur."

John delivered two additional hammer blows to the barrel's side that split it open, spilling out what Amy knew was a valuable commodity not to be wasted.

"Well that barrel didn't have rum, what about that one," John said pointing the maul at another barrel.

Both overseers had recovered from their surprise and had pointed their shotguns at John, threatening to shoot him if he damaged another barrel. Amy grabbed her rifle and aimed at the closest overseer, but she remembered at the last moment not to speak. Didn't matter for the older overseer had seen her and the aim of her rifle. He touched his partner's arm and nodded toward Amy.

"Tell those lazy menials to load the firewood, or I'll arrest you on suspicion of smuggling," John said. He appeared unconcerned about the shotguns. "Then I'll put those laborers to loading the firewood, so make your choice."

"Get the firewood," the older, seedy-looking overseer said. The young thug started to say something, but instead slung his shotgun over his right shoulder and yelled at the slaves to load the lazy bastard's firewood. The slaves jumped to hauling armloads of prime oak firewood to the police boat where Nashi and his partner then carried the firewood into the boiler room.

"That boat looks rough, shot up. What's your name, sergeant?" The now somewhat more cooperative older overseer asked and then added. "I'm Luke." He cast a baleful glance toward Amy who still had her rifle aimed towards the overseers.

"I'm Sergeant Gupta," John said, remembering the name on the Ichneumon police uniform. Noticing Luke's concern towards Amy, John added.

"The smugglers we're after ambushed us last night. We're not taking any chances, so Luke, tell your partner not to make any sudden moves. I figured those murderous rumrunners went by here an hour or so before sunrise. Did you hear or see anything?"

"No, but we were at the mine's tipple loading barrels," Luke said. "We couldn't have heard them. The Saukko went by yesterday and last week a Prussian warship went by, upriver. Then three days ago, the Aruba, stopped. The captain said they were headed to Fenwick Plantation to deliver a bunch of big shots from Delta, some celebration over two loads of Zamia slaves."

"They didn't invite you two?" John asked. Luke laughed at John's tease, the younger overseer just scowled.

"Apophis is always helpful. How far is his place?" John asked. He knew Amy was gunning for the monster.

"Helpful? Apophis, I'd figured he's where your rumrunners are headed," Luke said. John just laughed, as if he had been joking, to cover his mistake.

"His place is about twenty kilometers past Fenwick," Luke added.

The guard paused to check the progress of firewood loading, before asking. "Who is paying for the firewood?"

"The navy, there is an armored sidewheeler behind us. They'll be needing firewood and will pay for ours." The foreman looked down river.

"You're right. I can see the smoke. Looks like a big one."

"It's an impressive warship," John said. "The Prussians won't mess with it. Well, we'll get out of their way so they can dock." He hurried to the police boat.

"They're going to be around that bend in a minute," Amy said, anxious to go.

She handed John the rifle and engaged the paddles. Once free of the wharf, she hugged the west shore to keep the sulfur mine wharf between them and the Ichneumon warship.

"How much firewood did they load?" she asked, while easing open the damaged steam valve to full power.

"The bin's about full," John answered. "They told me a Prussian warship went up the river last week and the Saukko yesterday. Is that good or bad?"

"Let's hope we don't meet the Ichneumon warship," Amy said, looking back down the river. "I don't think they saw us."

"Luke told me Purnell's sternwheeler, the Aruba, went by several days ago to Fenwick and back by yesterday. He also told me that Apophis's plantation is not that far," John said. Amy's demeanor turned grave.

"Is Purnell on the Aruba?"

"They didn't say," John said. "Shouldn't we look for a place to hide before we're trapped between the two Ichneumon warships?"

"The Fenwick plantation is before Apophis's place," Amy said. After studying the river surface ahead, she turned the boat farther away from the shore. "I didn't like that ripple, could be a sunken tree. Anyways, there's a small bayou several kilometers below the Fenwick plantation. It curves around the backfields to where the niter yard is located. That sidewheeler chasing us couldn't fit through the narrow entrance of the bayou. We'll hide there."

"Yeah, but it could drop Ichneumon navy marines to search for us."

Amy shrugged. Her thoughts were on what would happen if by happenstance she ran into her father.

General von Moltke, head of the Prussian General Staff in Berlin, had been surprised to learn that Admiral Wilhelm and his fleet had returned to Port Baltic. The general assumed the Erie campaign must have gone quicker than anyone had dared hope. Then Berlin learned there had been no campaign. When asked why the 88th Battalion and the navy hadn't eliminated the Ichneumon forts in the Erie Valley, the admiral explained that the fleet had followed orders. Learning those orders were false left the shocked admiral with visions of being in front of a firing squad.

Emperor Wolfgang Schnabel, on hearing of the bogus orders, had been incredulous. That some unauthorized person could, and had, forged fleet orders in the current imperial code shocked him. Treason was afoot, though Admiral Wilhelm's behavior rather ruled him out as the culprit. Fortunately, for the admiral, the two warships blockading the slave trade had arrived in the Baltic the day after the Delta fleet, also with bogus orders, and again written using the current imperial code for fleet orders.

The emperor wasn't a man given to rage and hasty decisions, but he was determined to find answers and the traitor. He demanded an explanation from his uncle, Archduke Habsburg, as to the source of those orders.

The archduke supervised most of the empire's spies and the emperor reckoned that if anyone could discover the source of the treachery, his uncle could. However, the emperor was well aware that if a failure by the archduke's spies had allowed this fiasco to happen, then obtaining straight answers would be tricky.

"You knew Wilhelm's age was affecting his memory and wits, and he had the assignment because Admiral Scheer wanted a second-in-command who was biddable," the archduke said, pacing back and forth.

He's hedging and defensive already, the emperor realized.

The archduke was a tall, gangly, clean-shaven, humorless, old man who preferred moving to sitting when delivering distressing news. Consequently, Schnabel tolerated the irritating circling back and forth in front of his desk. It was a massive oak desk. His great grandfather had put it in the secured office where the Privy Council met over a century ago.

So far, his uncle's information hadn't helped solve the provenance of those orders. It was not much better than gossip.

"Then again, I shouldn't have recommended Admiral Scheer," Habsburg said. "He was an aggressive commander. He would have ignored those odd orders, demanded additional verification before giving up Fort Delta, but he was also a foolish man at times. He ignored the engineer on boiler pressure and got himself killed. His foolishness cost the navy a new steamship and the lives of eighteen sailors."

"Those orders had the proper code. Besides, I've heard a cannon ball might have caused the explosion." He thought Admiral Scheer had been their best admiral and didn't want to hear any more disparaging remarks or gossip. His uncle needed to understand he was serious about finding the traitor.

"General von Moltke wants to put Wilhelm before a firing squad. I'm thinking of signing the death warrant."

"No, Wolfgang, please don't! What will that accomplish other than tell the world that the Ichneumons made fools of us?" the archduke said, stopping dead. He realized no one ever told Emperor Schnabel no. "Please forgive me, I misspoke."

"It was your pal, Benjamin Purnell, who delivered the dying navy courier with those orders. How could he not be involved?"

Wolfgang Schnabel wondered if the critical bureau needed a younger man, or better yet, new blood. Lately, he had harbored the radical thought that a person's pedigree was no guarantee that they had any brains. Nepotism was fine if the person was talented, but Wolfgang suspected the rampant favoritism that existed in the empire's administration bureaus accounted for the incompetence he was encountering.

"He's not my pal," his uncle said. The man stopped the pacing and looked at him.

"Maybe Purnell is not your pal, but is he your banker?" His uncle shook his head.

Wolfgang knew his uncle had visited Purnell's resort on one of those exotic southern islands several times, without his family, never a good sign. He knew his uncle's love of high stakes gambling had gotten him into ruinous debt during his last visit, because he had asked Wolfgang to order the treasury to loan him five million D-marks. Since that had been his second such loan, the first one still unpaid, he had instructed the treasury not to loan any more funds to the Habsburg family.

"I settled my debt with Purnell and owe him nothing." The archduke said, resuming his pacing.

The new beads of sweat glistening on his uncle's forehead caused Wolfgang to doubt his claim of having paid off the Orleans businessman. However, last week, the emperor's spy in the Berlin IRS had advised him that the archduke had repaid part of the treasury notes and there was a rumor that the archduke had settled his vows with the casino resort. So perhaps his sweaty forehead wasn't from lying about owing Purnell, but from how he had obtained the funds to retire the debt. Which begs the question, where could his uncle have obtained that amount of money? The archduke had long ago mortgaged the Habsburg property and owed Berlin merchants embarrassing sums.

The Prussian blockade had hindered, maybe even closed, the lucrative transoceanic slave trade. *How much would those navy authentication codes be worth to a slave trader?* The emperor wondered. Could his uncle be that foolish? It would put Wolfgang Schnabel in an impossible position. With great fanfare, the empire had recently declared it would hang people caught engaging in the transoceanic slave trade. And treason had always been a hanging transgression.

Worse, if his uncle had been foolish enough to sell the codes, then Benjamin Purnell, who was a slippery character, would know of the treachery. Whether the Ichneumons owned the Orleans businessman, Emperor Schnabel didn't know, but he wouldn't discount the possibility, which meant the Ichneumons could also know the codes. And the Prussian empire didn't need its spymaster vulnerable to blackmail by a rival empire.

"Whoever blew up our mail boat is the probable culprit," the archduke added, interrupting the emperor's thoughts.

"You don't believe it was an accident?" He asked in a sarcastic voice, wishing he had asked Marshall Guderian and General von Moltke to attend the meeting.

"Well, everyone says it was, but I'm just saying if it wasn't, then whoever sabotaged the mail boat is the traitor. Or it was an accident and bootleggers, or pirates, discovered the wreckage and switched orders to prevent the Prussians from seizing the Erie and interfering with the winter sloe cocaine trade," the archduke said, and after delivering that nonsense, resumed pacing.

"You're suggesting a bunch of semiliterate bandits found and read the orders, then realizing a successful Prussian attack might interfere with their smuggling business, decided to craft new orders?" the emperor asked. "That's so farfetched I'm at a loss as to where to start. The paper, how do you explain them having the proper paper, navy parchment, where did they obtain that?"

"I'm working on that because those orders look like they were written by the General Staff," the archduke said, abandoning his pirate explanation. "There may be a traitor in Berlin. Anyone would have thought they were real orders."

"A traitor in the General Staff office, then the empire is in trouble," the emperor said. "On the other hand, your friend, Purnell, could have access to the parchment with all his connections." He hesitated to confront his uncle over the source of the funds used to pay off the gambling debt. Gentlemen didn't ask those questions.

His uncle appeared irritated by the suggestion and said. "Bah, I doubt any of them have parchment. It was an accident, the boiler exploded. Which is why I think those counterfeit orders came from your general staff. I never trusted von Moltke. You should have let me put spies in the general staff headquarters."

"I'm surprised you don't suspect Purnell's involvement," the emperor said, thankful he hadn't allowed Habsburg spies in the army. After receiving no response from his uncle, he added.

"It's interesting that you brought up bootleggers. The IRS has been chasing the source of bootleg cocaine in the western territories, and they now believe Purnell is the source. They even have several witnesses testifying in Roanoke about working for his cocaine operation."

"I'm aware of that. My understanding is the Wapiti captured and tortured all those supposed witnesses before bringing them to Roanoke. Most of the authorities in the territories suspect the Wapiti are the real bootleggers. Governor Bullard tells me the savages are after their own territory. The Ichneumons would love that."

"You think the Wapiti would help the Ichneumons?" the emperor asked, while wondering just how stupid his uncle was. "They're trying to become a Prussian territory."

"What a joke. Have you heard the proposed name for the Wapiti territory?" the archduke asked. Wolfgang shook his head. "Anarchy, you can't think those half-breeds and illiterate savages could manage a Prussian territory. Add their area to Guderian Territory."

Schnabel didn't encourage the prejudice that he knew was common in Prussia's upper classes toward the indigenous people of the empire's territories. The emperor knew he shared that bigotry, though he tried not to allow it to cloud his judgement, especially after several people he respected told him the Wapiti were capable people.

The man he was thinking about as a replacement for the archduke, Joachim Hansen, had asked him to meet with the Wapiti delegation. The best friend of his oldest daughter, Princess Erika, was Franciscka Weidman who had told him the Wapiti would make loyal productive citizens. Even Field Marshal Guderian had remarked on the Wapiti defeat of the Ichneumon army. The field marshal had told Wolfgang that he should seriously consider their request for a new territory. Keep them friendly was the marshal's advice.

"Uncle, where did you get the funds to pay off those gambling debts?" Wolfgang asked. *The hell with being a gentleman,* he thought. This issue needed settled. Had the archduke betrayed him and the empire?

The man aged before him. As his face drained of color, the archduke croaked, "What . . ., what debts? I . . . I sold the Lucifer match patent."

"That was last year. You even sold the sulfur and salt mines to Staedtler. I remember, because even with all that money, you chose not to pay back your treasury loans. Why'd you think I told the treasury not to make that loan last month? Your gambling is out of control." After a long silence, Wolfgang added, "I want your resignation on my desk by sunset."

Emperor Schnabel stood up and motioned for the guards to escort Archduke Habsburg from the room. The sputtering man was claiming he knew nothing about those Delta orders.

Taking two of the Imperial guards, the emperor walked across the Great Square to the Prussian General Staff headquarters. After all the salutes, greetings, and disruptions from an emperor's visit to the headquarters, Schnabel finally got General Von Moltke in his office alone.

"I'm aware you have an operation under way for securing River Point with the goal of supporting an attack on Hickory Ridge. However, since our orders to attack Delta went amiss, I want to secure Delta and block the Erie River, before worrying about Hickory Ridge. Send the 88th Battalion and General Markel back with orders to kick the Ichneumons out of the fort. Will the battleship Schlesien and a couple of armored sidewheelers be sufficient to provide support?"

General von Moltke nodded. "Then get with it. I want General Markel to strike before the Ichneumons can repair Delta's defenses."

The general staff assured him the assault force would sail within 24-hours.

Next, he would deal with Rudolf Habsburg, the archduke's oldest son. He would offer the man an opportunity to clear his family's name. Admiral Wilhelm could stay in the tower's VIP cell until his role in those bogus orders was determined.

David C. Brown

Chapter 10

Amy had wondered if the bayou they had ducked into to hide from the Ichneumons would reconnect to the river. She had hoped it would, but now, having encountered heavy algae growth in the water, she figured the bayou ended below the Fenwick fertilizer and acid operation.

The smell of burning sulfur hung over the river valley, but in the last kilometer up the bayou, Amy had detected another odor. An odor she recognized. She had once accidentally inhaled the fumes from a nitric acid retort at Heidelberg University. That whiff of the foul smelling reddish-gas, nitrogen dioxide, and the resulting severe choking had made a lasting impression on her.

The method used at Heidelberg University for making nitric acid involved boiling niter in concentrated sulfuric acid. The difficulty with the process was endeavoring to condense the corrosive fumes from the boiling niter-acid mix in a series of stoneware flasks that served as a condenser. The goal was to condense the noxious acid fumes and catch the liquids. The lab made less than a liter or so of nitric acid each batch, but the fumes that escaped were enough to stink up the lab for a day.

The burning sulfur odor was strong on the bayou, and Amy figured the sulfuric acid operation was near and running. The deteriorated wharf they had stopped by offered her a convenient spot to park the police boat. She didn't want to take a chance on grounding the boat in the ever-narrowing bayou ahead. John and she would scout the terrain ahead on foot.

"Nashi, cut fire wood while we check out the area," Amy said.

Nashi was the freed slave that Amy had trained to operate the boiler. He was learning a few Prussian words, but since Amy knew the Zamia language, she had no difficulty conveying her orders to Nashi and his friend, another Zamia freed from the Delta dungeon.

"John, bring your sniper rifle," Amy said, taking the double-barreled shotgun John had found on the boat.

Amy knew they should be backtracking to escape the cul-de-sac bayou and find Rex, not spying on an acid plant. Still, knowing the danger, she was eager to obtain a quantity of nitric acid.

Chemistry fascinated her. Understanding why certain waters when heated plugged boilers, or how a battery worked, or how to make explosives was valuable knowledge. However, making the precursor chemicals she didn't find so mesmerizing. It was grimy and dangerous work, especially in a near wilderness with few lab and safety supplies, no glassware, and almost no common chemicals such as ether, lye, or petroleum jelly.

In essence, what Amy needed to accomplish was to accumulate sufficient materials to stage a demonstration on her ideas for a new gunpowder and attract a financial backer. And that started with concentrated nitric acid, a substance she thought banned from the territories. Now, it seemed, there was a source of nitric acid nearby.

"Does the place have guards?" John asked. The path they were on showed signs of regular use.

"At the plant, but I don't think they patrol the area," Amy said. Smiling, she added, "Who would steal bulk acid?"

The Erie River was closer than Amy had thought, about hundred meters away through massive trees, heavy undergrowth, grapevines, and windrows of driftwood and other flood debris. Startled, she heard a steamboat on the river. By the time she reached the riverbank, it was out of sight. Worried, Amy returned to the path along the bayou. After about five minutes, the path forked, one path following the river north, the other path turning west and continuing to follow the bayou. Swarms of midges and mosquitoes provided shade as they jogged along the sunny path.

A kilometer after leaving the path's fork, they arrived at the edge of a large clearing. Amy recognized one of the structures was a lead chamber. The homely dark gray cubic structure caught the fumes from burning sulfur, part of the process to make sulfuric acid. It dominated the clearing and was operating, for malodourous steam was venting. The owner had fabricated his hundred cubic meter chamber from irregular-sized lead sheets. As lead-chambers went, it was small compared to the Bayer's unit she had visited near Berlin.

Another source of offensive odor was from the piles of bones with clinging pieces of rotten flesh and gristle. The Lucifer Match Company burned the bones and used the ash, along with sulfuric acid, to make crude phosphorus for their main factory in Prussia where it was refined into those matches that Rex liked.

Amy had inspected the phosphorus operation when the Orleans Queen had stopped during her trip to help Cinnabar's cocaine operation. The stoneware retorts and ovens used for that process were in the open sheds by the river. The phosphorus operation didn't appear to be running. North of the sulfuric acid lead chamber was a new set of brick furnaces and open sheds. Could that be the nitric acid unit?

"John, we're wearing Ichneumon Harbor police uniforms. I don't think those laborers will question our presence," Amy said. "Let's go check out that operation."

John nodded in answer and they walked into the clearing.

The laborers working at the lead chamber ignored them, though they appeared to work a bit faster. Amy walked around the lead chamber to inspect its construction. The chamber was an ugly thing, but appeared functional.

"We shouldn't linger," John said. Amy nodded.

A new yellow-brick furnace heated the retort holding the acid and niter mix. The engineer who built the unit had connected a dual string of stoneware flasks to the steaming retort. The setup reminded Amy of a scaled-up version of the university's unit used to make nitric acid. Nothing fancy, but the unit appeared to work.

The gray granular material piled under the shed, near the retort furnace was niter. Two laborers were unloading a wagon of charcoal beside several large piles of charcoal near the furnace. The acid operation would be making the charcoal locally, but Amy wondered who supplied the niter. She wanted to inspect the niter that the men were adding to the furnace, but feared getting any nearer and revealing that she was a woman.

"John," Amy whispered. "Ask what they're making."

He nodded and walked over to the furnace.

"What stinking crap are you cooking?" He asked the man who appeared to be the overseer, the only non-Zamia. He was holding a dipper, and appeared to be transferring the liquid in a lead-lined tub to a port on the retort part of the furnace.

The overseer's hands had numerous raw sores. The workers all had a wild look, with cotton rags wrapped around their head and mouths. Amy figured the rags were a desperate attempt at protection from the suffocating fumes leaking out the chain of stoneware pipes and flanks.

"Aqua Fortis, it's nasty stuff," the overseer said. He yelled at a slave to put two more scoops of niter in the furnace, before asking, "What are you doing here? I thought you were supposed to check the back bayou for that blockade runner."

"That's where we're headed," John said. He walked back to Amy. "He said it was aqua fortis, whatever that is. We need to get back. He also said the police are searching the bayou."

Jogging down the trail, they encountered a small two-wheel wagon heaped with yellow powdered sulfur. Two slaves were pulling it. The slaves avoided eye contact, and they stepped to the trail's edge as John and Amy hurried by.

"Where'd they come from?" John asked.

"The trail we didn't take probably goes to the sulfur stockpile. Do you remember the stack of yellow material we passed on the riverbank on the trip down-river? It must be nearby."

John didn't comment his attention was down the trail.

"Did he say how many policemen were searching the bayou?" a worried Amy asked.

He shook his head, as he brought his rifle up and aimed down the trail. A moment later Hokee came charging up the trail.

Kyle and Rex were at a fork in the narrow dirt trail they had followed north from the wharf where they had found the police boat. The mosquitoes they had encountered along the trail were a noticeable irritant, and Rex wondered what the flying scourge would be like after sunset. When they stopped at the fork to consider which fork to follow, biting bugs swarmed them.

After a moment, Hokee had gone left, and they jogged after the wolf. A couple of hundred meters up the left trail they had encountered Amy petting the wolf and John watching their back trail. Relief caused him to forget he was mad at her. Amy hugged him while describing what John and she had found.

"They have a nitric acid operation. We need to get several barrels and some of the sulfuric acid, too."

That damn we, Rex thought.

"Did you forget that Saad is waiting down the river with the Heron and those barges?" Rex said. "That the gold from the Wapiti winter sloe sales is on the Mischief. It's at risk, if that Ichneumon warship hunting for us finds us . . . And, by the way, two Ichneumon guards found your boat."

That her boat had been found seemed finally to alarm her and he added, "We have to escape this cul-de-sac."

"I know, but there's so much I could do with the acid," she said, pushing the wolf away to face Rex. The Baler brothers had walked down the trail a short distance. "There is no other source that I know of, besides the Bayer unit west of Berlin. Leave me several men and John. After dark, we'll raid the plant and meet you and the Heron on the east side of the river. I'll use the police boat to haul the barrels."

"Didn't you hear me?" Rex knew the woman tended to fixate on one issue, and it never seemed to be survival.

"The Ichneumon navy is hunting us. They could close the bayou exit at any moment," he yelled, getting aggravated. She looked hurt by his outburst, which silenced him.

"But I need it to make clean burning gunpowder," Amy said, trying a tenuous smile. "You're the one always griping about the dirty residue from black powder. Now we have a chance to fix the problem."

"You're serious?" She nodded.

It was hopeless. He couldn't refuse her. He knew from the full wattage smile she beamed at him that the witch realized she had won his interest. She had. Whether she could manage to make smokeless gunpowder was one thing, but Rex knew the stubborn female wasn't leaving without her acid.

"What's your plan?" Rex asked, resigned to another delay.

Amy's plan was workable, with a bit of luck, and Rex agreed to help, while wondering how she always managed to get her way.

"The sun is past its zenith, night will be on us in four or five hours," Rex said. "I can tell Malik to take the Mischief. He can reach

194

the barges before darkness and be back by midnight with the Heron and barges. That is, assuming they didn't encounter that pest of an Ichneumon warship."

"No, you and Kyle need to go with the Mischief. If you're not there, Saad and Malik will dither. Besides everyone knows about the gold and the temptation to steal it might be too much for one or more of the crew members without you and Kyle there to maintain order."

The trip across the bleak frozen mountains between Roanoke and Salt Furnace had taken an extra day. Fritz's cousin, Colonel Leibinger had suffered from the cold and harsh night camps, but the Berlin dandy hadn't complained. Both Prussian colonels were still reflecting on the message behind the orders that arrived in Roanoke from Berlin.

The emperor had ordered the IRS Roanoke office manager, Joachim Hansen, to Berlin, along with the Wapiti delegation. The emperor had threatened drastic action over the IRS and Hansen's failure to stop the illegal cocaine, but Fritz figured the arrest of Chief Cinnabar and exposure of Benjamin Purnell's involvement should have pleased Berlin.

The other rumor among the Guderian politicians was the emperor would hear the Wapiti petition for a new territory and then refuse it. That seemed to Fritz like a lot of trouble for the all-powerful Prussian emperor to go through. The other news was the sudden retirement of Archduke Habsburg and the assignment of his eldest son, Rudolf Habsburg, to the Volga frontier to head the armistice negotiations with the Mongols. Things were stirring in Berlin, how that might affect Tara and him, he didn't know.

How to accomplish General Moltke's order that Fritz ensure the Wapiti surrendered control of the River Point fort to General Markel, he had no idea. It wouldn't be an issue if Berlin approved the Wapiti request to become a Prussian territory, but he knew the

Guderian Territory politicians fought the request and stroked the emperor's well-known xenophobia at every opportunity.

Few of the people Fritz met in Roanoke had expected Berlin to even hear the Wapiti request, let alone grant it, but then the invitation from the emperor to Tara Smith and her delegation had arrived. Fritz figured acting like the territory request was a sure thing would be his best approach with Matt Brewer, the wily commander at River Point.

Their reception at the Wapiti capitol, Salt Furnace, had been friendly, though Fritz sensed most of the people he met were more concerned about the fate of the winter sloe nut cargo than the territory issue. There had been no recent river traffic from the south, and no news. Ice was forming in the areas of still water along the Southern and Erie Rivers. The freezing over of the rivers was one hard cold front away. Then all traffic on the river above Hickory Ridge would stop. Fritz and Colonel Leibinger had traveled by horse, so they weren't overly concerned about the river ice, but still they didn't delay and rode on to River Point the following morning.

Matt Brewer greeted the Prussian envoys at River Point. The retired hunter, who commanded River point, liked Fritz and congratulated him on his promotion to colonel. After welcoming the Prussians, Matt verified what they could see. The HMS Rhinelander hadn't arrived. The news, actually just rumors, wasn't good. Fishermen told of a fearsome battle at Hickory Ridge and the sinking of a Prussian warship.

The Prussian marine, Captain Beck, and a number of his surviving troopers from the ill-fated HMS Hendrick greeted them.

"What's with the stockade?" Fritz asked. Off the northeast corner of the River Point fort, the Imperial flag flew from a log wall surrounding a collection of wooden sheds and two barns.

"Matt's still leery of us and won't allow us in the fort with firearms," the captain said. "With winter about here, the men need shelter."

Matt just shrugged and said, "Council orders."

Nevertheless, the River Point scene was peaceful, gates open and Wapiti and Clovis families coming and going from the wharf areas, the new Prussian stockade, and the Wapiti stone fort. Fritz decided his orders to take control of River Point didn't activate until the Rhinelander arrived and that event appeared in doubt.

A dozen men, Clovis, Wapiti, and Prussians, working off two of Knight's wooden coal barges, were busy at the Hendrick's wreck salvaging iron plates. Captain Beck noticed their interest.

"I'm stripping the wreck before the spring floods bury it. The barn has the salvage items. The center boiler split along the starboard side riveted seam. No sign of a cannon ball strike," the captain said.

"That's very helpful. I want to examine the Hendrick boilers, and then I'll write a letter to my boss and copy the emperor," Colonel Leibinger said.

To Rex's pleasant surprise, the short trip down the Erie River to collect the Mischief's barges and the Heron went off without a hitch, a first on this star-crossed venture. Even better, on his return, Amy had been waiting along the east bank of the Erie across from the bayou where he had earlier found her with the captured harbor police boat. On seeing the Heron and Mischief, she had joined them. Rex wanted a conference and waved for the other boats to join the Mischief along the slack east shore water.

John and Amy still wore the Ichneumon police uniforms. Her comeliness undiminished by the grime and tattered enemy uniform. That they were in good spirits, cheered his.

"We were fortunate," Amy said. "The acid operation apparently hadn't missed those guards you captured. There were no guards at the warehouse, and we helped ourselves to six lead barrels of acid. I could have taken more, but feared overloading the boat."

"What happen to the guards?" Rex asked, remembering the prisoners.

"We took them for a boat ride," Amy said. Suddenly humorless, she studied him. "What did you expect us to do with them, free them?"

"I should have taken them and left them down the river," Rex said. He feared the murder of her family might turn her merciless, not that he could really blame her. "Well, it's war and I have no right to question your decision."

"Question my decision? What do you think I did with those Ichneumons?"

Rex was in no mood to play a game of questions. "That's why I asked, to find out."

"I released them a couple of kilometers down on the east shore." Amy waved toward near shore. "Most Ichneumons cannot swim. I'm surprise they didn't try to attract your attention. Maybe the gators got the bastards. Eels won't touch them." She laughed at his relief.

"Bless you," Rex hugged her, and remembering their audience, stopped with the hug.

Instead, Amy and Rex, holding hands, joined Kyle, Malik, Slim, and Saad on the Mischief to decide on a strategy. The goal was unchanged, to reach River Point before the river froze over and the ice stranded their cargo. Rex, thinking of all the unanticipated glitches and tribulations on what was to have been a simple trip down to Delta and back, was confident something would interfere with their steaming up the river and beating the ice. The unusually warm weather did make him a bit optimistic that all would turn out well.

The Wapiti convoy had to be beyond the Fenwick Plantation before sunrise since Amy was of the opinion that the Ichneumon warship would stop there for the night. Avoidance was the convoy's protection from a warship, and Rex wanted to use the night to slip past Fenwick. All had agreed with his opinion, and they set about readying the three boats for the hazardous night run.

Amy and John had completed the transfer of the acid barrels from the police boat to the front port barge with help from several crew members. The unloaded police boat was now the fastest boat in the Wapiti convoy. Rex planned to use it to scout ahead of the slower Mischief with her heavy barge train and the overloaded and unpowered Heron. If the police boat encountered an Ichneumon warship, Rex would attempt to lead it away from the convoy.

A brief, intense storm struck about an hour after the convoy started upriver. After the storm, a clear starry night had reappeared.

"The Fenwick Plantation is around this bend," Amy said, waking Rex. The rhythmic huffing of the steam engine exhaust had nearly put him to sleep.

"Then we'll be past the plantation while it's still dark," he said, though the eastern horizon was lightening. "Is the river still wide enough you can't see from shore to shore?"

Amy shook her head while studying the dark river.

"Dawn not far off but fog is starting to form. It'll protect us. By sunrise we'll be lucky to see ten meters."

The Mischief and Heron were plowing up the river at full power. Amy had throttled back the police boat's steam to half power to maintain the several hundred meters distance ahead of the Mischief. Still, in the dark, all the boats were risking a disastrous collision with one of those partially submerged trees that occasionally floated by.

"Will the fog slow us?" Rex asked, while wondering if the hot water in the boiler would be safe to use for coffee. None of them had had much sleep over the last two days.

"Look, there's a small boat in trouble," Amy yelled, pointing to the port.

The boat was a small single-mast skiff. The mast had broken. The sail was in the water, still attached to the swamped, though upright and floating, five-meter wooden boat. Two kids were waving to attract attention. Amy slowed and then guided the police boat over to the stricken vessel while Rex and John grabbed their rifles.

Both the boy and girl were similar in height with the same lanky build. They were young, maybe teenagers, with no business being out on this dangerous river in the dark. John in the police uniform helped the two wet teenagers onto the police boat.

"Are we glad to see you," the boy said. "I'm Hitesh and this is my sister, Aziza. A storm caught us." Hitesh looked at Rex. "You're a giant. Who are you?"

The lad appeared to be used to asking questions of adults. Rex figured them for children of one of the local aristocratic families.

"I'm hired help. Where are your parents?" He asked the boy.

He wished he had a decent light to examine their eyes. Could they be young Ichneumons, with that round shaped face and small nose? But then one of them was a female. Ichneumons never allowed their females to venture far from their capitol, Cusco. Both of the rescued boaters were dressed in soaked blue gray coveralls, the type of clothing popular on farms and among laborers. The girl was shivering.

"John, show Aziza the boiler room so she can get warm," Amy said. "Keep an eye on her. I don't want her to get sick." Then Amy engaged the paddle wheels and headed up the river, while Aziza stared at her.

"Hitesh, that policeman is a woman," the girl said. Then realizing they were leaving the swamped boat, she asked. "What about the boat?"

"Can't you tow it?" Hitesh asked. "My father will pay you."

"We're on a mission and will find it later," Rex said. He then asked again about their home.

"We're visitors at Fenwick Plantation," Hitesh said. He watched his skiff disappearing and then spotted the Mischief and barges. "There's another boat behind us, they may hit our boat. Do you have a flare to warn them?"

That damn Ichneumon night vision. The boy was an Ichneumon. He hoped the skiff didn't damage the Mischief paddles. Then again, Malik is an Ichneumon and he would see the skiff.

Rex had an inspiration. "Hitesh, is the armored paddle wheeler, Saukko, at Fenwick? We could ask them to recover your boat."

"Yes, that's a great idea," Hitesh said. "Captain Chetan and my father are friends. The Helot is also there, it arrived late yesterday. They're chasing smugglers."

Lord, two Ichneumon warships just across the river, Rex thought, nearly cursed on hearing the news and instead said. "Your father must be an important man?"

He'd seen the Saukko in Port Delta. It was a sternwheeler with a couple of small cannons, not the iron-plated monster chasing Amy yesterday. That must have been the Helot.

"Did you get to see those new rifled cannons?"

"Not yet, it just arrived. If you get us back to Fenwick in time, I'll get you a tour," Hitesh said. The boy walked over to look in the boiler-room, to apparently check on his sister and saw Nashi.

"I didn't know the harbor police used Zamia slaves." He looked again at Rex and then added, "Or Prussians. You are a Prussian?"

"Actually we're all Wapiti."

Tarun Apophis was returning from Fenwick Plantation in his old war canoe along with four other men, who were helping him to paddle against the river current. Their destination was his stockade and home about twelve kilometers up river, on the opposite bank from Fenwick. He was angry and broke. The five slaves Purnell owed him from the Zamia cargo had escaped or been killed in the fort explosion. Force majeure, the Orleans bastard had claimed, canceled their agreement. Dawn was breaking, and fog restricted visibility on the river to less than thirty meters when he heard an unmistakable sound.

"Did you hear that?" Apophis asked his foreman, Ojeda, an escaped Zamia slave turned pirate.

"Could it be those rumrunners that the Helot was pursuing?" The Zamia asked after pausing in his paddling. "Or do you think the captain relented and allowed the Saukko to search for Paget's brats before heading to Hickory Point?"

"He'd be a damn fool not to make an effort, after all Paget is the new commander at Delta," Apophis said. "But whatever this is, it doesn't sound like the Helot. I don't hear that pitman bearing clanking."

"You're right. It sounds like two boats," Ojeda said after listening some more.

"We'd better start paddling before the damn current takes us back to Fenwick," Apophis said, "Or the mystery boat runs over us."

Was it an opportunity? Apophis need a break. His canoe crew included three of his most trusted men and Burgdorf, a retired Prussian feldwebel, now working as a mercenary who had been at Fenwick on some mission for that weasel, Manual Prado. Burgdorf had wanted to catch passage on the Saukko to West Port, but the captain didn't want any Prussian soldier, ex or otherwise, on his warship with a war between the empires threatening. Apophis didn't trust the Prussian soldier, either, but gold was gold.

"Are you game for boarding the mystery boat?" Apophis asked while discreetly cocking the revolver hammer. His crew would do whatever he ordered, so his question was for Burgdorf, who nodded after a moment.

Apophis had been trying to find a steamboat to call his own. Maybe, if it was an unarmed merchant, he could seize the boat, kill the crew, and rename the boat with no one the wiser. Steamboats were the future and he wanted one.

The Ichneumon navy was switching out their older-style harbor police steamboats for the newer, faster boats with the high-pressure Caroom boilers and Apophis had offered Colonel Xavier a deal. In lieu of D-marks for his share of the Zamia slave shipment, he would take one of the old police boats in payment. The colonel liked the offer. Then the Prussian navy had somehow managed to detonate the fort's main powder magazine, killing Colonel Xavier and many of the slaves, including all of his, if Purnell was correct.

Now, with the war rumors, the Ichneumon navy was seizing all riverboats, which meant the approaching boat might be crewed with Ichneumon navy personnel, not some private merchant or rum running Wapiti gang. If it were crewed by the navy, they'd just wave and keep paddling.

The heavy fog covering the river was starting to lift. The sun was clear of the horizon, and visibility on the river was now about hundred meters. At first Apophis wasn't certain what he was seeing, and then realized he was looking at a train of coal barges. A moment later, the twin sidewheeler pushing it was visible. The barges were stacked with machine parts and barrels. Apophis even saw several Zamians on the barges looking at the war canoe. No sign of navy sailors. It was a fat target for plucking.

"That's not one of Purnell's boats, is it?" Burgdorf asked. They all knew Purnell's property wasn't to be touched.

"No, I'll bet that's those Wapiti nut traders the tobacco warehouse manager told us about," Apophis said. "He said it was a gold transaction. Colonel Xavier tried to arrest the Wapiti to recover the gold and impound the boat. I heard it didn't work out, and the colonel is dead."

"Get real, that's machinery from Purnell's boat yard. What would a bunch of savages do with that machinery? Hell, a better question is why would there be Zamians aboard. The Wapiti hate slavery."

"I don't know. Maybe they bought the junk with some of that tobacco gold Alpha claims he paid them," Apophis said. The damn Prussian tended to worry too much, forget his place, and ask too many questions. "By the same token, why would Purnell send machines up the Erie? We'll board and get some answers. I assume you're not afraid of a few Wapiti."

A prime opportunity was steaming toward him. Besides, he'd bet all of Purnell's slaves hadn't died. The fat bastard had used the explosion as an excuse not to honor their deal.

"We're boarding," the pirate said after a moment. "Are you okay with that?"

Burgdorf knew the discussion was over and nodded.

"If ownership comes up, we'll claim we thought it was a Wapiti boat, and those bastards are fair game. Our paddling days are over, boys. Hand me the scoped rifle and hold the canoe steady."

Apophis's shot at the man in the pusher's pilothouse sent the men on the barges scrambling for cover. The current helped them close the distance in less than a minute, limiting him to two shots. Ojeda expertly brought the canoe against the port side of the lead barge and the pirates leaped aboard.

Earlier they had put the Ichneumon children in the boiler room to dry out. Nashi had caught Hitesh, straining to close the boiler steam outlet valve and blow the boiler by spiking the steam pressure.

"We need to secure them," Rex said, "before they manage to sabotage the boat." The two young Ichneumon prisoners crouched against the rear bulkhead of the boiler room were glaring at him and Nashi.

"How are you going to do that, in slave collars?" Amy asked. Having heard Nashi's yelling, she had entered the boiler room to investigate. "I hate those things. What if the boat sinks?"

"Tough, the little bastard just tried to incapacitate the boiler. The jail cell door won't lock. A grapeshot ball struck and broke the latch. We can't let them run loose."

"Point taken," Amy said, glaring at Hitesh. "If Nashi hadn't thwarted you, the explosion would have killed you and your sister."

The Ichneumon boy looked unrepentant. After a moment, Amy said,

"Let's use the longer chains so the fools can at least go out on the deck for air. The chains are short enough to keep them from reaching the boiler controls."

Rex nodded okay and Amy went to drag the unwilling Aziza over to the slave collars. When she bent over to put the slave collar around Aziza's neck, the boy dashed across the room and leaped on Amy's back. The little rodent was fast and strong, and before Rex could swat Hitesh off her back, the boy had a knife out. When Amy felt it against her throat, she stopped struggling.

"I'll slice her throat if you don't release us," Hitesh screamed. The boy had one of those boot knives that Rex knew most Wapiti women carried. Girls, too, he remembered, thinking of his friend, Indira. Hitesh's grip on Amy's neck was causing her to turn red and the trembling knife in his left hand had already nicked her throat. The seep of blood removed any doubt the knife was razor sharp.

"Listen pal, if you hurt her, I'll kill you. Then I'll drop your sister overboard wearing a slave collar with the chain attached."

That prompted Aziza to start whimpering and the boy to study him. The little turd was trying to decide if Rex was serious about drowning his sister.

"You're all monsters. Maltreating prisoners, our father will see that you pay." He relaxed his grip on Amy's neck. In a flash, she released the girl, and had the boy's left wrist twisted away from her neck.

Amy was safe. She now had the knife, and the boy was rubbing his arm. She hadn't been gentle. He figured it was a good chance to learn who they and their father were.

"And who might that be, some ignoramus at Fenwick?"

"General Paget," Hitesh volunteered.

"Colonel Paget, he's your father?"

The boy, misunderstanding Rex's look, grinned. "Yes, and it's General Paget now. He's commander of Delta. He'll have the entire army and navy hunt you down, if you hurt us."

"I look forward to congratulating your father on his promotion," Rex said. "Now put on the collar."

Rex was inclined to believe the boy because Aziza's presence indicated they were the children of some high-ranking Ichneumon. The blue bloods, as a rule, didn't allow their scarce females to leave the safety of the homeland, but a commanding general could probably obtain permission to bring his family with him.

Amy finished securing Aziza, who was cute, if bedraggled. They were both attractive kids, if one overlooked those vertical slit pupils. Squatted by the jail cell, the girl looked woebegone with that large iron collar clamped on her neck, but it didn't stop her from glowering at them. Rex had just locked the collar around Hitesh's neck when they heard rifle shots from downriver.

Chapter 11

Fear seemed to be the one constant in Martin Johnson's life since those pirates captured him and Bill Hopkins two years earlier. The pirates had sold him at the Delta slave market to a contractor whose business was constructing and refurbishing wells. Along with his many other defects, Martin suffered from claustrophobia, a serious handicap for a well digger. After his second escape attempt, his owner had him arrested and tossed in the Delta Fort dungeon to receive fifty lashes as punishment. It would have killed him.

Martin had escaped during the prison break. Instead of doing the sensible thing and disappearing until he could find a ride to River Point and safety, he went with the Wapiti pirates to Orleans and helped them steal Herr Purnell's equipment. Now they were playing cat and mouse with the Ichneumon navy and death. Still, Martin reckoned the Mischief was ahead of the Ichneumon warship, and barring mechanical problems, they should be safe.

The gunfire out of the fog shattered the Mischief's windshield, along with Martin's composure, and wounded Captain Malik.

"What the hell, who shot?" the captain asked from the pilothouse floor.

Another heavy bullet ripped through the pilothouse, not striking either of them. Then Martin saw the canoe and several rough-looking men grab the lead barge and climb aboard.

"Pirates, they're boarding the portside front barge." He felt faint but knew passing out would be a fatal move and croaked out, "What should we do?"

"Find Kyle and see if he needs help," Captain Malik said.

"What about you?" Martin asked, at a loss on how to help.

"Don't worry about me, now go, before they see you." The captain's order sent Martin running down the stairs for the boiler room. More gunshots sounded.

Kyle was dead, a bloody bullet wound to the head. The two Zamia laborers appeared stunned by the violence. They had been in the act of throwing more firewood into the boiler's firebox.

"Pirates, just lay down and don't resist them. You'll be okay."

The laborers remained standing, looking as lost as Martin felt. He concluded that they hadn't understood him. Hearing the pirates screaming curses at the laborers in the barges, and more gunshots, got him moving again. He grabbed Kyle's revolver and ran into the engine room looking for a hiding place.

The place that offered concealment was the space on the outside of the leather seal of the driveshaft that turned the starboard paddle wheel. The leather skin protected the large inner shaft bearing from the water dripping off the paddles. The housing enclosing the paddlewheel blocked any view of the area from outside. Reaching the space would require cutting a small slit in the leather skin to allow him to squirm through and reach the framework of the housing. It would be a cold, wet, perilous refuge; lean out too far and the paddlewheel would tear him apart.

Martin had just slipped through the leather membrane when he heard the engine room slam open. His grip on the frame was precarious, but still he chanced a look through the slit to see who had entered the engine room. An older Prussian, the man had led a harsh life. He was missing his left ear and several fingers on the hand holding the shotgun.

Someone yelling, "Jake!" and the man in the engine room left. *Was that man Jake?* He wondered, along with how many pirates had boarded. Then, maybe a minute later, rifle shots started and he heard someone asking who was shooting. Martin couldn't hear the answer, but figured it was the police boat crew, Rex, and Amy.

The dripping cold river water from the rotating paddle was freezing. Martin had to act. Reentering the engine room ran the risk of Jake returning and finding him. He decided to climb up the paddlewheel enclosure frame and try to fit through the latticework that formed the enclosure's wall alone the upper walkway.

A soaked shivering Martin had just reached the top of the latticework when one of the pirates quietly passed on the upper walkway. He was a big blond Prussian, shirtless, with massive muscles, and missing an ear. *Maybe losing an ear was an initiation ritual for the gang*, Martin thought. The pirate was holding a revolver and appeared to be inspecting the upper cabin. More gunshots and the man hurried towards the prow.

Rex dashed to the rail to look, but the morning fog hid the Mischief and Heron. Nothing but fog was visible, but he knew the shots had to involve them.

"Has Dad found us?" Aziza asked her brother.

Both prisoners rushed out the boiler room door, dragging their chains to stand by Rex. They ignored him and eagerly peered down the river in the direction of the gunshots. The chains allowed the Ichneumon kids enough slack to reach the port handrail. The gunfire had given the two Paget children hope of a rescue. Rex figured they were too young to realize that rescue attempts often end in the hostages' deaths.

"John, swing around and find the Mischief and don't have a collision with it," Rex yelled as he rushed to get his rifle.

"I'll pilot the boat," Amy said. "John has a scoped rifle and can help you." She headed to the pilothouse after telling Nashi to handle the boiler room and keep an eye on the brats.

She had just managed to turn the police boat around and headed down the river when the barges appeared out of the fog. She had to reverse the paddles to keep from over shooting the Mischief, which was still plowing up river at full steam.

"Whose canoe is that?" Rex asked. The port front barge was dragging a large, tied-off canoe.

Three of the Zamia laborers were standing on the Mischief's bow with their hands in the air. A stranger, another Zamia, had his rifle pointed at them. Malik was lying on the stairs.

"River pirates," Amy said. "God, I hope Kyle and Malik are okay." Malik didn't look okay. Rex was wondering if Kyle was safe when bullets tore through the pilot cabin. Amy's grunt followed by a curse meant something had hit her, a slug or a wall fragment.

"Damn, it nicked my leg," she said, adding, "Shot back, don't stand there. Who's shooting?"

"Are you okay?" Rex asked. He couldn't see any wounds, but the scattered wood splinters from the several heavy slugs that had struck the pilothouse now dusted both their legs and boots. Then two tough-looking men had stepped from the Mischief's cabin and shot again at the police boat. The glass windshield shattered and sprayed glass on them.

"Do something, before they kill us," Amy snapped. She was busy working the steam valve and linkage to slow and reverse the speed of the police boat to match the Mischief's speed without over straining the drive linkage. Hitesh's yelling for Apophis to save them added to the confusion.

"You need to get control of the Mischief," Amy said, "I can't control this boat. It isn't stable traveling backwards."

The gray smoke indicated the shooters were in the main cabin and the pilothouse. Kyle's location was their concern. But when the pirates reappeared to fire another volley at the police boat, Rex told John to aim high and they returned shots. He hoped Kyle remembered to stay on the floor. For sure, he wasn't operating the Mischief.

"Apophis, Apophis, help us," both Paget children were now shouting. Their hollering caused a large Prussian man to look out the Mischief's cabin door toward the children, presenting Rex with a perfect target. His shot knocked the pirate back into the cabin. A moment later, John shot. The man on the bow, who had been guarding the Zamians while staring at the approaching police boat, tumbled off the Mischief. The starboard paddle wheel ran over him.

"Bring the boats together so I can jump, then back away," Rex said. "John, cover me." He handed his rifle to John and then raced down the stairs and leaped to the barge just as the police boat swerved against the canoe, smashing it and tossing him along with pieces of the canoe into the barge.

He landed among the acid barrels. The containers hid him from anyone in the pilothouse, but the barrels' protection was an illusion. The concentrated acid was just as dangerous as a bullet, and a rifle bullet could easy penetrate a barrel, spraying acid on him. No one had shot at him and he dashed on across the barge into the front starboard barge loaded with the large milling machine parts. The machine's cast iron frame offered protection from bullets.

Amy had managed to disentangle the police boat from the canoe and barge, and now fifty-sixty meters separated the boats. He heard John's rifle fire twice more before the police boat disappeared into the fog.

The Mischief slow and Rex wondered if whoever was in the pilothouse was dead, or preparing to turn down river to head back to Fenwick and the protection of the Ichneumon warship. He couldn't allow that, all the gold from the winter sloe sales was on the Mischief.

A lead slug slamming into the heavy iron base of the milling machine meant at least one pirate remained active.

After a quick check to verify his revolver had five live rounds, Rex dashed to the rear of the barge. He paused by the drill press. No shots from the pilothouse, so he ran across the stacked iron pipe cargo of the rear starboard barge to reach the Mischief's bow. He leaped over two of the Zamia laborers huddled on the barge floor for protection from the gunmen in the pilothouse. After landing on the wet bow deck, Rex slid to a stop against the front cabin wall. The thin wood wall offered some protection and prevented a gunman in the pilothouse from seeing him.

Captain Malik was lying face down on the upper deck outside the pilothouse entrance. His condition wasn't clear, but any aid would have to wait until the pirates were disarmed or dead.

A movement of the lower cabin door caught his attention. An unkempt-looking thug, a Prussian, had leaned out of the cabin entrance to aim a double-barreled shotgun towards Rex, who was crouching under the stairs to the pilothouse. The man was quick, but Rex was faster. His shot struck the thug's head, dropping him and causing the blast of buckshot to hit the river. The shotgun clattered onto the deck and then rolled overboard.

"Sid, did you get the bastard?" a man in the pilothouse yelled.

Rex, unclear if Sid was whom he had just shot, watched the thug stumble into the handrail and flip overboard. Should he storm the pilothouse or check the cabin? If another pirate were lurking in the cabin, being on the stairs to the pilothouse would be a precarious spot. He decided on the cabin and dashed from under the stairs and into the cabin.

Kyle was on the floor. A quick glance round the engine room verified that two Zamia laborers were present. Sensible fellows, they were on the floor in front of the boiler firebox using pieces of split logs from the fire woodbin for additional protection from stray bullets. There was no sign of Martin, the dwarf who served as Malik's gofer.

Distant gunfire and the sound of a bullet impact sent Rex racing to the cabin's portside door. The one vessel visible was the police boat, so John was the shooter.

"John, stop shooting," Rex yelled across the water.

"Herr Knight, is that you?" the pirate in the pilothouse yelled.

Rex had stayed in the cabin's doorway for the protection it offered from whoever was in the pilothouse. The man in the pilothouse sounded familiar.

"Who's asking?"

"Friedrich Burgdorf, I helped you recover those Wapiti women. Listen, I'm not involved with Apophis's gang. I hired him to take me up river, but he couldn't resist raiding this merchant vessel. He would have killed me if I had refused. He's dead now and I'm trying to steer the boat, not hit a sandbar. Come up and take the helm."

Burgdorf had a history of switching allegiance to the winning side. In other words, his trustworthiness was problematic. Instead of answering, Rex went to check on Kyle, who was now sitting up.

"Did you hear me?" the pirate yelled.

"What happened?" Kyle asked, looking at his bloody hand. "I was checking the boiler." Rex examined the wound, a furrow across the young Wapiti's head, just above his right ear.

"One of the bullets grazed your head." The information had Kyle looking wildly about and trying to stand. "You're lucky to be alive."

The Mischief was turning down river.

"Burgdorf, turn the boat up river," he yelled. He then whispered to Kyle, "Ready to reclaim our boat?" Kyle nodded, and after a couple of tries, was unsteadily on his feet and discovered his revolver was missing.

"It's the fog. I don't know which way is upriver," Burgdorf yelled. "Come and show me."

"Where's Martin?"

"He was in the pilothouse with Malik," Kyle quietly answered. "Is that thug the same one who worked for Donnelly?" Rex nodded. "Then don't go up there, it's an ambush."

Time wasn't on the fleeing Wapiti side. They weren't that far up river from Fenwick Plantation where they had last seen the Ichneumon warship, Helot. In an hour, with the added boost of the river current, they would be back at Fenwick. By then, the sun would have burned off the fog, exposing the Mischief to the warship's rifled cannons.

Breaking the latticework proved tougher than Martin had expected. While he struggled with enlarging the opening to gain the upper walkway, a raging gunfight erupted from the front area of the steamboat. By the time the wet and frozen Martin crawled onto the walkway from the paddlewheel enclosure, the gunfire had stopped. He heard Rex yell for John to stop shooting.

With Rex aboard, Martin's hopes of surviving the pirates soared. He started to hurry to the stairs that went down to the boiler room to find Rex, and then stopped. Where had that pale one-eared pirate gone? He could hear Rex talking with the pirate in the pilothouse.

"Burgdorf, no more talk. Turn the boat up river, or I'll have the police boat start shooting up the pilothouse."

Martin tiptoed to the stairs. Looking down, he spotted the blonde pirate ahead on the main deck, edging to the boiler room door. The man had a revolver. Burgdorf was promising to change direction. In fact, he could feel the Mischief swing back up river. The pirate in the pilothouse was trying to distract them so his partner could bushwhack Rex. Martin aimed Kyle's revolver, made a brief prayer, and shot the pirate in his back.

By noon, the harbor police boat was again steaming up the Erie River with John as the skipper and Helmick as his helper. A beautiful clear late autumn day had replaced the fog. Rex, standing on top of the Ichneumon patrol boat pilothouse stairs, could see the Mischief with her barges down the river. Amy now piloted the Mischief. Kyle and Malik were recovering from wounds suffered during the river pirate attack. Saad piloted the Heron, which followed a couple of hundred meters behind the Mischief, forming the rear of their fragile convoy.

The blond headed pirate was Tarun Apophis, a merciless slave catcher who contracted with plantation owners to recover their property, runaway slaves. The man's death had cheered Amy for he had been one of the thugs that had raped and almost killed her friend. The two Paget teenagers, Hitesh and Aziza, thought the gang had been trying to rescue them. They huddled in the back of the police boat cabin, resentful and sullen.

Friedrich Burgdorf, the former Prussian feldwebel turned mercenary, had surrendered control of the Mischief on realizing Apophis was dead and their planned ambush of Rex wouldn't work. The Wapiti had chained Burgdorf to the police boat rear anchor. Release of the winch claw would send the anchor to the river's bottom along with the pirate. Rex figured the precarious position would motivate the mercenary to cooperate.

"I had no choice. Apophis would have killed me," Burgdorf said for the tenth time. He was sitting on the rusty iron block that severed as the anchor, eyeing the ratchet tooth that locked the anchor chain winch.

"Tell me something useful," Rex said. He was sitting on a stool by the winch with a pot of coffee and two tin mugs. "Like, where are those Ichneumon warships?"

"They were at Fenwick. The Saukko was to start a search this morning for Paget's brats, stopping at all the farms and fishing communities along the Erie between Fenwick and the sulfur mine. Since we know they won't find the missing children, I figure they'll search for a day or two, before heading to Hickory Ridge." Burgdorf studied the passing shore and then added as Rex handed him a cup of hot coffee, "How fast they finish and turn up the Erie will depend on the thoroughness of their search."

"Let's hope they're diligent in their search. Where's that large warship?"

"The Helot, it's headed to Westport to help finish the fort. I'd forgotten how good coffee is, thanks. The Helot is an old warship never intended for river duty. Its draft is deep. It's underpowered and slow. Unless you stop for a day, it will never catch you before Westport."

"Good to know, but I've seen its large rifled cannons. Those guns make the Helot dangerous, though the crew's marksmanship didn't appear to be good."

"One should never complain of his enemy's poor marksmanship," Burgdorf said. Rex laughed, agreeing.

"Your problem is Westport and Hickory Ridge garrisons," the prisoner said. "Their orders are to seize or sink all non-Ichneumon ships."

"The war has started for control of the Erie? Then why did the Prussians quit Delta?" That retreat made no sense to him.

"The rumor is someone changed the Prussian General Staff's orders to make Admiral Wilhelm believed the fleet was to return to the Baltic. If it's true, whoever did it had better hope the Ichneumons win."

"Well, I'm rooting for the Prussians," Rex said. "Tell me about the Saukko and its captain. Try to be truthful, for if the Saukko finds and sinks this boat, I can swim away, you can't."

"Captain Chetan and General Paget are close friends and both are competent officers. The navy captain just hasn't had a lucky break as you gave Paget on that prince's ransom negotiation. The Saukko is a smaller sternwheeler, similar to Dalporto's Clovis Belle. It has two small cannons, thin armor plating, and a decent power plant that makes it fast. Its real sting is provided by the twenty to thirty marines on board with bolt action rifles."

"So we're trapped if we stay on the Erie," Rex said. Burgdorf shrugged his shoulders. The mercenary offered no comment. "Damn war, we'll have to spend the winter up the Great Western River and hope the Prussians win."

"How's that going to help?" Burgdorf asked. "You'll just be trapped up the Great Western."

"Amy told me it's a long river, with over a thousand kilometers of navigable channels and countless lakes and swamps that offer plenty of places to hide. Ninety-five percent of the surrounding territory is uninhabited, except for a few Clovis tribes and gold camps. The area is lawless. It seems to me the perfect place to avoid the Ichneumons. Besides, they aren't sure we exist, don't know we have Paget's kids, and have a war to fight, so they're not going to waste time chasing ghost ships in hostile territory. No, the more I consider it; I think that's our best move. Maybe check out the gold strike while we wait for the Prussians to win. That's what I'll suggest."

"What about me?" Burgdorf asked. "I was just an innocent passenger that Apophis dragooned into his piracy."

"Maybe so, but you were Donnelly's main lieutenant on his last raids to wipe out the Hopkin tribe, and you provided those Wapiti women for Cinnabar's warriors to rape," Rex said. "The Wapiti want you drowned."

Burgdorf watched the Wapiti boats tie off together as Rex Knight held a brief meeting on the Mischief. He couldn't hear what they were discussing, but at one point during the meeting, Rex pointed at him. The Wapiti all looked his way and most nodded, no one looked friendly. He figured the bastards had approved his drowning.

Rex had visited him after the meeting and verified the verdict and death sentence. The sentence would occur at tomorrow's sunrise. Sunset was an hour away as Burgdorf studied the passing east riverbank while trying to open the chain lock with a bent nail. He estimated the convoy would pass the rock quarry an hour after sunset. Westport and the confluence of the Great Western River with the Erie were four hours up river at the convoy's current speed.

At sunset, the elderly Zamia who fed firewood to the police boat's boiler had a break, and walked over. The ex-slave, who Burgdorf remembered, had been on one of Purnell's labor gangs he had supervised, stopped to visit. The ex-slave probably wanted to see how the condemned foreman, who once lorded it over them, was taking his pending death.

"These people are crazy," the ex-slave said, looking to see if anyone was nearby. "Are you still tight with Purnell?"

"Yeah, I'm one of his main foremen," Burgdorf answered. He had no idea what the Zamia was getting at, but decided to go out defiant.

"Some of us are afraid the Ichneumon navy will catch and sink these Wapiti boats. If we don't drown, the Ichneumons will consider us runaways and cut our tendon."

Burgdorf knew the old man was referring to the Achilles tendon.

"Or they'll send us to the mines. If I was to drop a key by you, will you tell the navy and Purnell we didn't run away, we were stolen?"

Burgdorf knew he had agreed too fast. His potential savior turned cagy. "Bah, it was a foolish idea. I'll get in trouble with that big Prussian."

"Wait," Burgdorf pleaded, "I will put in a good word for you. I promise. Don't leave."

"What about the eels, the cold water, you'll never reach shore and I'll be in trouble," the laborer said, shaking his head.

"I have eight hundred D-marks. They're yours for the key," Burgdorf pleaded.

One halfhearted eel bite occurred during his precarious swim from the police boat to the quarry's south dock. Burgdorf's left leather boot had several punctures, but the fangs hadn't broken his skin. That the wound hadn't bleed probably saved his life.

The Wapiti convoy was nearing Hickory Ridge and Rex had no certainty of the reception to expect from the Ichneumon garrison. He hoped the rampant rumors of war and a river blockade were overblown. He needed the latest news and was relieved to spot the Clovis Belle docked at a timber yard wharf a half-day's travel below Hickory Ridge.

Occasional pieces of thin ice flowed past the Wapiti convoy as they maneuvered to drop anchor by Dalporto's steamboat. John, who was now the pilot for the police boat, maneuvered the boat beside the Clovis Belle while Rex attached the lines. Amy then parked the front barges against the stern of the police boat, trapping the Clovis Belle against the wooden wharf. Saad parked the Heron along the riverside of the police boat.

The captain crossed to the police boat and greeted them. The rotund, middle-aged, white-haired, bearded river man, an alleged reformed slave trader and Rex hoped, still an ex-pirate, had always reminded him of Santa Claus. Today the man looked morose.

Hokee interrupted their greetings. The wolf had leaped from the front Mischief barge and snatched a brown chicken from the flock perched on Dalporto's Clovis Queen front handrail. The cloud of feathers and squawking scattered the other chickens. The birds flew every direction, a couple of hens even ended up on top of the police boat pilothouse. Since Hokee had already killed the unfortunate bird, Rex figured he'd better offer to pay the owner. He asked the captain whose chicken the wolf was eating, while wondering what was the cause of his friend's gloominess.

"They're your hens." The captain, on seeing Rex's baffled look, smiled. He explained, "A lady and two girls stopped the night of the Delta explosion and said you wanted a dozen Ridge Browns for eggs, but they only had ten. I paid eighty bags of nuts for those ten chickens, which you owe me now."

Had to be the Yoon girls from the Delta market, Rex decided. The young sharpies had charged him twice the price they'd discussed. "Are the eggs any good?"

"Sure, they're fresh, but if you don't control the wolf, the hens will fly off. As it is, they won't lay for a week after the trauma of your mutt's vicious assault."

"I'll have Amy speak to Hokee concerning his unsocial behavior," Rex said. They both laughed knowing she'd do no such thing. "We have bigger concerns, though before I get in those items, you owe me for at least two weeks of eggs."

"As you're totaling up what I owe, remember feed cost and delivery charges," Dalporto said, acting more like his old self. Smiling, he asked, "Where are Amy and Captain Malik?"

Rex bought the river man up to date, skipping any mention of Burgdorf and the Great Western. So far, there had been no sign of an Ichneumon warship.

"I also have a dilemma," the captain said. No longer the pleasant grandfather, the worried man closed the pilothouse door after checking if anyone was in the hall or on the walkway. "General Mehta impounded my boat when I stopped at Hickory Ridge. He reminded me of Colonel Xavier's warning in Port Delta. Only Ichneumon-flagged vessels are now allowed on the Erie River and must operate under their control."

"What's the problem, change your flags."

"You ask what the problem is, besides the outrageous fees and that the Prussians won't use my boat," Dalporto said. "As if that's not bad enough, he wants me to haul all the prisoners at Hickory Ridge to Port Delta. That garrison needs slaves to rebuild the fort, and I know those bastards will work the prisoners to death. If I'm a party to that, the Wapiti and Prussians will never forgive me. Hell, he even has Tom and Fritz imprisoned."

"Christ, why'd he arrest Tom? And why isn't your boat still impounded?"

The captain shrugged. "General Mehta told me, because of our past dealings, that I was free to return down the river, but I shouldn't try and pass back by the fort. I think he released me to warn other boats. He said he would blow the Clovis Belle out of the river the next time they sighted me unless I agreed to haul the prisoners."

Apophis bullet had shattered Captain Malik's knee, leaving Amy no choice but to amputate the Ichneumon's leg. He had survived the rough surgery, but would need help with baths, learning to walk, dressing changes, and other nursing duties. She considered who to assign the task. Salma would be good, but she was busy with supervising the Zamia laborers. Amy was aware Aziza Paget and the captain being acquainted because of his prior dealings with her father.

After the failed pirate raid, Rex had the two Paget teenagers separated. The girl, Aziza was on the Heron. Her brother, Hitesh, remained on the police boat.

"Are you tired of watching spiders weave webs?" Amy asked.

Sitting on a piece of log that served as a chair, the girl looked sullen. The smell confirmed what Amy had feared. The Heron crew was neglecting the prisoner's basic sanitary needs.

"Is my brother all right?"

"Yes, but who isn't, is Captain Malik. He lost a leg and needs help with his baths, laundry, and other minor nursing duties."

"He's a traitor and deserves what happens," the girl said.

"The captain is the one person in this convoy who cares whether you and your brother survive," Amy said, though she suspected Rex cared. "He needs help, will you help him?"

The Ichneumon girl nodded, "Better than watching that spider."

The Slater brothers ran a timber operation and owned the wharf where the Clovis Belle and Wapiti convoy had docked. Captain Dalporto had introduced them to Rex and Amy. The machinery in the barges fascinated Jeremy, the oldest of the three brothers. The brothers' business was hand-sawed hardwood timber. The middle brother was Andrew, who along with his brothers, were typical frontier mutts, part Clovis, part Prussian, part who knows. If they had lived along the Southern River, people would consider them Wapiti. They were large strongly built men with full beards, long brown hair in a queue, and cheerful natures.

"We'd like to find a steam engine to run our mill," Jeremy said. "Like that one in the barge. Would you sell it?"

"Not that one, I need it to run my machine shop. If we can make Smithtown before the ice and set up the shop, I can make you one."

The revelation that Amy planned to build brand new engines from scratch startled the Slater brothers. If she had walked on water, Rex doubted the brothers would have been more surprised. They went off to inspect the Mischief engine room with Jeremy trying to get a firm price and promise out of her for the first steam engine built at Smithtown.

Amy declined to commit and instead said. "I'd like to see your sawmill. The blockade at Hickory Ridge has wrecked my plans, has it hurt your business."

"It's certainly complicated things," Jeremy said.

"It did for the Prussians," Andrew said. "Our younger brother, Gary, hitched a ride on the Prussian ship that the garrison sank."

Andrew paused to relight a small clay pipe, similar to the ones that Rex had first encountered in the Jarrell River backcountry. The timberman was a tobacco smoker.

"Gary's a prisoner," Andrew said, releasing a cloud of tobacco smoke, "Along with the Prussian survivors. We've heard the prisoners may be shipped to Delta and sold into slavery, or used for their evil sunrise sacrifice."

"What have you got in mind to free your brother?" Rex asked as Aziza came out of the Mischief lower cabin and dumped a chamber pot.

"Is that an Ichneumon girl?" The timberman appeared alarmed.

"Relax Andrew, we're not Ichneumon allies. She's no one important, a slave we freed."

"I've heard their females are never allowed out of Cusco. Were you in Cusco? Did you kidnapper her?" The man was dubious of Rex's explanation as he watched her rinse the chamber pot and then saunter into the cabin.

The very problem Rex had feared when he learned what Amy had done. The girl might not run off because of her brother, but other people would see her, realize Aziza's value, and try to grab her. Andrew had probably already realized the Ichneumon garrison would willingly trade his brother, Gray, for Aziza.

"Does your operation use slaves?" Rex asked. Andrew shook his head, his attention back on Rex. "That is good, because the Wapiti and I will not do business with people who use slaves."

Andrew looked back at the door Aziza had disappeared into and pointed at it. "Is she part of your passage fee by Hickory Ridge?"

"I'm after more than being allowed to pass Hickory Ridge. Do you know where your brother and the prisoners are being held?"

Andrew nodded, looking intrigued.

"Can you get a message into Hickory Ridge?" Rex asked. "I need to contact Sam McCoy, the manager of the coal yard."

Matt Brewer, commander of River Point, and Colonel Leibinger, the visiting Berlin diplomat, had discovered they rather liked each other, though they had no common interests, except horses and a desire to avoid more war. After two days with no message from Colonel Fritz Caprivi and his men, they were both worried.

Matt and Leibinger were in the mess hall having their breakfast when Chief Red Fox barged into the mess hall with a small war party of several warriors from the Beaver tribe.

"The Ichneumons seized them," the chief announced without preamble.

Matt feared he knew who as the chief yelled at the Walker boy to get his attention. When not waiting on the tables, Billy was helping his mother in the kitchen.

"Bring me a mug of tea and feed them," Red Fox ordered. He indicated his warriors with a wave of his hand while he pulled out a chair and joined Matt and the Prussian diplomat.

You're shocking bossy for a guest," Matt said, smiling. The chief and him were old friends who knew they could depend on the other, no matter how perilous the situation.

"What, you don't want my news, or my help?" The chief said, looking at the fort's commander with a perplex expression, before grinning. "Of course it was mostly Prussians they arrested, but I thought you liked Tom Jarrell."

"Why?" the colonel asked the chief who shrugged. "It'll start a war."

Matt nodded and Leibinger added, "I need to alert Berlin and Roanoke. We have to free them."

"Send your message," Matt said. "But it'll be a month before any trooper can make it to River Point, assuming the Roanoke authorities even acknowledge your request."

Billy arrived with the tea and freshened their mugs. Colonel Leibinger, who appeared shaken, waved off the tea refill. Matt asked if they could count on the chief for help.

"We'll help you and the Wapiti," the chief said. "But the tribe can't afford to offend the Ichneumons, so our help can't be obvious. We have to live with the bastards, and so far, the Prussians appear toothless, useless as an ally. No offence colonel."

Matt was relieved the chief's blunt remarks appeared to snap the Prussian colonel out of his distressed appearance.

"Your opinion is understandable, but I can assure you the Prussian Empire will prevail in kicking the Ichneumons out of the Erie," Leibinger said. "It would be a great help if you could discover where the prisoners are being held."

"I can do that, but don't delay mounting a rescue. I fear the Ichneumons will send the prisoners to Delta on the first boat headed down the Erie."

Matt agreed with chief on the need for prompt action. He sent word to the council at Salt Furnace that he needed Larry Hopkins and his group of policemen.

David C. Brown

Chapter 12

A clear day was breaking and the rising sun would be in the Ichneumon gunners' faces as the expected battle for control of Delta's fort unfolded. The Prussian navy was maneuvering to retake the fort that Admiral Wilhelm had abandon because of Purnell's counterfeit orders. General Paget needed a year to repair the fort's defenses. He had gotten three weeks. His men had time to install the two new breech loading rifle cannons. One of the revolutionary weapons had gone in the north turret, the other one in the south gun turret where he waited for the mighty Prussian battleship, Schlesien. The ship was steaming toward the fort from across the Delta bay where it had waited after arriving the prior evening out of the fort's cannon range.

As invading naval convoys went, the Prussian one sent to recapture Delta was small. One battleship, two armored side-wheelers, and a couple of unarmed ocean going sternwheelers, which meant the Prussians had rushed the attack preparations. They were gambling that the Ichneumons couldn't repair Delta's defenses in a few weeks. It might be a small naval force, but the Prussian battleship was the largest in the world with the thickest armor and largest guns.

For two weeks, Paget had driven the four-hundred-man garrison and contractors without a break. Over a hundred slaves and troopers had died from various accidents during the effort to install the new breech loading guns. He had postponed repair of the fort's walls to the distress of his staff officers and General Bezdek. Success, he told them, depended on a good offense, not hiding behind stonewalls. The new rifled cannons would protect them, if they were in place. He drove the men harder.

The Ichneumon general knew the men were right to be worried, for the Schlesien was maneuvering to a make a close pass parallel to the fort's damaged and down walls facing the bay. Whoever the new Prussian admiral was, he didn't appear to be aware of the new weapons and believed he dueling with Delta's old smooth bore cannons and solid iron shot. At five-hundred meters, Paget figured the Schlesien's commander intended to deliver a bombardment of heavy canister loads. The battleship had to maneuver close ashore because the canister's fist size iron balls lost their effectiveness after a thousand meters. At this close range, the shot would slaughter any defenders that exposed themselves trying to stop the two side-wheelers that hoovered behind the battleship from disembarking their load of a thousand Prussian marines.

Those marines, if they reach shore, would quickly overwhelm the outnumbered and exhausted garrison troops. The new cannons would be useless against the marines if they landed. Instead of the temping battleship target, Paget had the first shots aimed at the side-wheelers. Emperor Ratakonda had told Paget the two artillery captains assigned to new rifles, were the best in the world.

"Just tell Captain Jain and Captain Ansha the targets," the emperor had said.

After dealing with the two captains during the weapon installation, Paget had to agree with the emperor. They were competent and he followed the emperor advice.

"Sink the side-wheelers first," the general told Captain Jain.

A flag signal sent Paget's order to Captain Ansha in the north turret. Moments later, the massive rifles fired. One of the side-wheelers exploded throwing debris and men into the air. The other side-wheeler, the Rhine Mar, took a hit in the rear of the port paddle wheel cover, but the shell failed to explode. Reloading the new breech-loading rifles required about a minute. The Ichneumon turret crews learned the Schlesien crew didn't need that much time to recognize the danger. A canister load slammed into the face of the south turret. The metal shield, an iron plate that fastened around the rifle barrel, to block the entry of bullets through the turret's dome slot, the opening that permitted the rifle barrel to traverse vertically, was not adequate to stop canister shot.

Two egg size iron balls ricocheted around the inside of the iron dome killing one of the gunner-loaders and smashing a couple of fingers on Captain Jain's left hand. Enraged the captain threw the dead gunner out of the control seat, taking charge of the gun. He rapidly traversed the massive gun barrel toward the battleship while cursing and slinging drops of blue blood over the gun machinery and controls. Paget just watched, not wanting to distract a man on a mission. The captain had apparently decided the battleship was too dangerous to ignore.

"Load the green shell, double powder bags," the captain yelled as more canister shot pounded the turret.

"Breech is locked," the loader shouted.

Boom the south gun fired, jarring Paget. He knew the green shell the captain ordered loaded was some type of experimental delayed fuse shell for piercing armor plate. He heard the north gun fire, followed a moment later by a loud explosion. The turret seemed to sway, but the general knew that wasn't possible. The captain was now rapidly traversing the gun barrel back toward the second sidewheeler while yelling for a brown shell and one bag of powder. A look out the port showed a huge column of black smoke, and a violent wave tossed field of floating debris where the Schlesien had been.

Amy Caroom hadn't had the luxury of a real bed and hot shower in a month. Captain Dalporto had offered her the first-class suite on the upper deck of the Clovis Belle in exchange for her help repairing the port side steam valve. The Gooch oscillating linkage used to change the direction of the Clovis Belle engine had come apart, and the crew couldn't figure out how to fix it. She had walked the operator through the proper steps to reassemble and adjust the valve.

The squawking of the chickens woke Amy. Hokee was growling at the room door. She grabbed her revolver and hurried outside to the upper walkway. It was still dark. Hokee leaped off the police boat and ran to the Mischief where Captain Malik was recovering from his wounds. Arriving a few moments behind Hokee, she saw the wolf hurdled off the Mischief onto the wharf where two men were struggling with a bundle.

"They have Aziza," Malik yelled from the pilothouse.

A shot and Hokee cried out with a yelp. A third man had joined the two with the bundle. Amy figured that bundle was Aziza wrapped in a blanket. She couldn't allow the kidnapping to succeed for Rex's plan depended on the Paget children.

The third man remained at the end of the wharf. As Amy ran onto the wharf, he shot at her as his two partners disappeared into the woods. The gunman's second shot also missed. She remembered Rex's instructions and paused the necessary instant to acquire a proper sight pattern with the revolver before firing. Her shot ripped a piece of his skull away and the kidnapper collapsed on the wharf. Then Kyle had arrived with a shotgun. In the distance, she could hear residents of the timber yard shouting questions.

Though Amy was virtually naked, wearing only a white cotton nightgown and no boots, she ran off the wharf in pursuit with Kyle following. The rough ground was painful on her feet, but her sprint bought her to a farm lane. The kidnappers, already mounted on two horses, were in the process of turning their mounts to gallop away down the farm lane when Amy arrived. The bundle was across the larger man's saddle in front on him. A shot at that man would endanger the Ichneumon girl. Amy instead shot the man's horse twice in its rear legs while Kyle blasted the second man off his mount.

The twice-shot horse fell, throwing the bundle off to the side and pinning the man. Amy saw his revolver fly into the brush when his horse collapsed.

"Deal with the bastard," she ordered while unwrapping the blanket to free a nearly naked and hysterical Aziza.

"Find out who he is, before a bunch of spectators arrive. Run, Aziza. We can't be seen with no clothes," Amy said while trying to calm the Ichneumon girl. She could see torches approaching down the farm lane from the encampment.

Salma met them at the wharf. She had been rifling the dead man's pockets.

"He's an Ichneumon, might be one of those deserters that plague the river," Salma said. "No ID, no money on him."

"Help Aziza while I attend to Hokee," Amy said.

The wolf licked her hand, but wouldn't stand or open its eyes. The wound in the front center of the wolf's chest probably occurred during his leap at the man's throat. The man had used an old ball-and-cap single action revolver. The seriousness of Hokee's wound would depend on the amount and condition of the gunpowder charge. The old guns were slow and difficult to load, and people tended to leave them loaded, which allowed the gunpowder to become damp and fire poorly. That might explain how he managed to miss her twice. A laborer helped her carry Hokee to the Mischief's warm boiler room.

Jeremy Slater arrived a few minutes later from the village. Amy by then had dressed and joined Salma, Kyle, and Aziza on the Mischief.

"The Orr brothers are part of a whiskey bootlegger family from down the river," Jeremy said. "The dead Ichneumon was a stranger who arrived last week. I think they were just after a female to take back to their hideout."

Amy could tell Malik shared her skepticism of that neat explanation, but Salma thought it likely. So far, none of the timbermen had mentioned the children's connection to the Ichneumon commander, so she didn't. Instead, she asked Kyle what became of the bootlegger. He died.

The note had said go to the southwest service entrance at midnight. A stout cut stone barbican sheltered the wood gate located there. A small smoky oil lamp illuminated the gate that Rex banged. An Ichneumon sergeant, with four armed soldiers behind him, opened the gate.

"I'm here to see Ares," Rex said.

The sergeant nodded and told him to put his weapons on the small shelf built in the wall of the passageway. The guard didn't bother to search him, but seemed satisfied he was weaponless and led Rex off to General Mehta's private quarters.

"I had fresh coffee made," the general asked, "Would you care for a cup?" They were by themselves in what to Rex appeared to be a small library off the main room.

"Yes, coffee would be good. Are we alone?"

"I would have a difficult time explaining why I met secretly with a man on whom our prince had placed a fifty thousand D-mark reward, so yes we're by ourselves," General Mehta said. He handed Rex the cup.

"I had hoped to complete my business before the war started, but I was delayed. I understand you have closed the Erie to non-Ichneumon traffic. The reason I requested this meeting was to learn if an arrangement could be made for a one-time passage of my small convoy."

"The garrison closed the Erie on orders from General Paget," the Hickory Ridge commander said. "His order was clear. I am to sink or seize all non-Ichneumon traffic, no exceptions, even for the Clovis Belle. I did intervene to prevent the seizure of Captain Dalporto's boat. I can't grant your wish. Paget has sent a minder, Captain Bezel, along with a squad of soldiers from Delta. And please don't suggest a bribe."

"With a war flaring up between the empires, I can understand stopping Prussian traffic, but why hassle other commercial river traffic?"

"General Paget didn't explain the reasons behind his order. Normally, I'd ask for an explanation, but after the disaster at Delta and learning of his children drowning, I didn't bother the man. It's getting late, was there anything else?" General Mehta asked.

"Yes, what is the status of the Prussians who were on the Rhinelander?"

"Interesting you should ask. Two nights ago, the guards caught your partner, Tom Jarrell, with two Prussian army officers. Have you cast your lot with the Prussians?"

That Tom Jarrell was a prisoner surprised him. At least General Mehta didn't appear offended.

"I reckon the Prussians asked him to help them check on the Hendrick crew." The general shrugged. Rex added. "Along with Tom, your men have another civilian, Gary Slater, one of the timbermen I deal with. He was hitching a ride on the Hendrick."

"If you're asking for their release, it's out of my hands. Captain Bezel has control of them."

"The last thing this valley needs is another war. I understand we have no say in the madness of emperors, but perhaps we can avoid some of the damage. I want to trade the Paget children for a one-time passage and your prisoners."

"You're talking about the drowned children, Aziza and Hitesh?" the general asked. "You have their bodies?"

Rex told him the story.

"Do you appreciate what danger you're in?" the general asked. "If I don't seize you and torture their location out of you, Paget will have my head."

"They're in my convoy. No need for threats. Aziza is nursing Captain Malik back to health from losing a leg during a battle with river pirates."

"Are they alright, unharmed?" the general asked. "Will Malik recover?"

Rex nodded and got up to refill their coffee cups.

"They are in danger if an Ichneumon warship catches the Wapiti convoy." Rex said, holding the expensive silver teapot the general used for coffee. He was waiting to refill the general's cup after the man finished the last dregs of his earlier cup.

"That could happen at any moment and it would be a shame since their transfer is easy."

General Mehta looked skeptical and Rex explained.

"I tell you that we'll kill the kids if the fort fires on our convoy. That's the first you'd heard about the Paget kids and have no choice but to agree. Wait, do you think that Captain Bezel would interfere, object?"

"That I wouldn't allow, besides they're Paget's family, he wouldn't dare."

"After we're out of cannon range," Rex continued, "we give them to your man in a small row boat and go on our way. The harder transfer to arrange, without endangering you, will be the prisoners."

"Forget that, it will not happen. The one-time passage I'll agree to."

"I'd bet Paget would for those kids," Rex said. "How many prisoners do you have?"

"Six of the Prussian sailors are not ambulatory, twenty-two of them are," the general said. "I'm not sure how many of the 88th troopers escaped, but 32 bodies were recovered, so not many, if any, escaped. I will ship all the able-bodied prisoners to Delta to help repair the damage the Prussians did. You should also know the Saukko is expected."

"Then you need to decide," Rex said.

"I have. Have your lead boat stop at noon tomorrow and take the rowboat with my men under tow. I'll trust you to honor our exchange up-river when you're out of cannon range. The prisoners are headed to Delta, either by the Clovis Belle, or the Saukko, depending on who arrives first," General Mehta said.

"What happens to the wounded men?" he asked. With Paget's spy now at Hickory Ridge and in charge of the prisoners, Rex accepted the matter was out of his friend's control.

"All prisoners will be loaded aboard," General Mehta said. "What happens to them is on Captain Bezel and the boat captain's conscience."

They spent several minutes working out the exchange of the Paget children. Satisfied, General Mehta stood up and said, "Take these, you may find them of use. Good night, and until the war is settled, don't come back." He called for the sergeant.

Back on the horse with the Slater brothers, Rex opened the leather purse and found a small ring of keys.

Purnell was at his casino on the Southern Island. The island was neutral territory. Neither the Prussians nor the Ichneumons claimed the island. Levi Ottoman found him there. It had been sixteen days since they had parted at Fenwick Plantation.

"I was lucky," Levi said. "The archduke was still the spy master when I delivered your message. Since then, the emperor has fired the archduke."

"What?" Emperor Schnabel unexpected response to the bogus naval orders shocked the Orleans businessman. "The emperor had always deferred to the archduke in the past."

"You heard right. He arrested his own uncle. The former director of the Imperial Intelligence Service and your main spy in Berlin is in prison."

He had made a significant investment in the archduke. In the last several years, Purnell had advanced the fool several million D-marks to cover various gambling markers. In return, the archduke kept him appraised of the emperor's plans and ensured Berlin treated the Orleans Boatyard bids for navy work favorably. The arrangement had been a sweet deal, since most of the archduke's gambling had occurred in casinos where Purnell had a major ownership interest.

"That's not the most amazing part, he replaced him with a commoner, the former head of the Roanoke IRS," The acid trader said. A commoner himself, he was enjoying delivering the stunning news. "The Berlin aristocrats are in an uproar over that breach of protocol and no one's happy over yet another war. Just as the eastern war is winding down, the emperor has started a war with the Ichneumons."

"Did he get word to the traitor?" Purnell asked. He couldn't care less about the Prussian upper class concerns. "Do we have a deal?" He knew the IRS manager Joachim Hansen was no friend.

"I believe so, but with the sudden arrest, I couldn't verify it," Levi said. "The scuttlebutt at the Hamburg docks when I left was that Major Lyons had confessed that an Ichneumon agent, Sanita Chopra paid him fifteen thousand D-marks to switch the navy orders."

"Chopra was involved?" He asked to be sure that he had heard correctly. Levi just shrugged but Purnell knew having a known Ichneumon spy involved, if true, would help throw the Prussian investigators off him.

"The Ichneumon escaped or was never there," Levi said. "No one in Hamburg knew what orders the traitor changed, but with the

Zamia blockade and Delta fleets both unexpectedly returning to the Baltic, everyone assumed those orders had been involved."

"I'd better get back to Orleans, wouldn't want to appear I'm hiding. Levi thanks for your help and news."

Late the next day, the Wapiti convoy steamed into the range of the Hickory Ridge cannons. *Word must have spread swiftly about a strange convoy on the Erie River,* Amy thought. Hundreds of people were hurrying to the waterfront. It appears that the chance to watch steamboats pass by flying the green star Wapiti flag and pushing barges loaded with heavy unfamiliar machines had caught the inhabitants' interest. The convoy was the first traffic up the Erie since the blockade and war had started. Amy figured rumors were rampant among the gathering spectators as to what the convoy signified.

John Baler was in the pilothouse of the police boat. Holding her revolver, Amy was standing on the walkway by the pilothouse, in clear view of the crowd. She was beside an anxious Aziza. Amy wondered how many in the crowd knew who the girl was and about the agreement, that if the fort fired on the Wapiti convoy, she was to kill Aziza. Nashi, also with a revolver, had Aziza's brother, Hitesh, in the boiler room with three other armed Wapiti.

Neither Nashi nor Amy would kill the Ichneumon teenagers. The threat was to stay the hand of some overzealous Ichneumon officer ignoring General Mehta's order not to engage the passing convoy.

At the end of the coal yard wharf, an Ichneumon lieutenant, a large rowboat, and four sailors waited. Amy was well aware that she presented an easy target for a sniper as John brought the boat against the wharf to allow the Ichneumons to board. She wondered if any of the Ichneumons or the waterfront audience recognized the Delta harbor police boat. Rex had painted it flat black to match the Mischief's color.

"Let's get this spectacle over," the officer said, addressing Amy, but studying Aziza, who seemed to wilt.

"Is your boat secure, officer?" Amy asked. The lieutenant checked the rope fastening their rowboat to the police boat, and then the location of his men, before nodding. John then engaged the paddlewheels and the steamboat pulled away from the wharf.

"Tell your men to stay at the stern," Amy added.

Recognizing General Mehta in the group of Ichneumon officers standing by the coal stockpile, she gave him a friendly wave as the boat pulled away from the wharf. To her surprise, the general saluted her, before turning and walking toward the fort.

"Where is the boy?" the lieutenant asked. A loud steam whistle sounded causing everyone to look down the river and see the Clovis Belle approaching.

"Hitesh is in the engine room. Whose boat is that?" Amy asked, feigning ignorance.

"The Clovis Belle," the lieutenant said. He looked pleased. "It's here to haul the prisoners to Delta where the animals can earn their keep."

No one was quite sure what to expect around the river bend that would shield the convoy from the fort's cannons. Amy worried about an Ichneumon ambush, and for that reason, she had told the Mischief and Heron not to stop, but continue at full power up the river while she made the transfer. She couldn't detect any threats looking around the river ahead and the forested riverbanks.

"Is this spot satisfactory for the transfer, lieutenant?" She asked. He also had been studying the area and nodded. "John, stop and hold against the current. Lieutenant, you and your men get in the boat. Nashi bring out Hitesh."

"I don't want to leave," Aziza said. She started crying. "They'll just lock me in a cage."

Amy hadn't expected this twist.

"Aziza, sadly, you and I have no choice. I'll miss you and wish you well, but you have to get in that boat." She felt like a monster forcing the young girl back to that closeted life that awaited all Ichneumon women.

The lieutenant helped settle the sobbing Aziza in the rowboat by her morose brother. The Ichneumon officer gave Amy a last hostile look and then told his crew to cast off.

A half hour later, the harbor rowboat returned with the Ichneumon lieutenant, the four sailors, and the two Paget children. By then the crowd knew what had occurred and cheered the lieutenant and his passengers. Most people assumed the girl was crying for joy after the brave lieutenant had recused them from the savages.

Rex watched the return of the rowboat and the cheering people gathered along the waterfront from the Clovis Belle upper walkway. Relieved at the apparent success of that scheme and the escape of the Wapiti convoy and Amy, he relaxed a bit and went to make a final check on his men. The Clovis Belle, flying the blue and gold double-headed snake flag of the Ichneumon Empire, would dock at Hickory Ridge coal wharf in a few moments. Captain Dalporto had cautioned them to expect a thorough inspection from the authorities prior to any transfer of prisoners.

"All crew members on the wharf," the sergeant ordered as the crew finished securing the Clovis Belle to the wharf.

The sergeant and several Ichneumon soldiers in their black uniform with the double-headed snake patch on their left should and the red skull and cross-bone patch on the right shoulder were all business. As Rex and the crew disembarked from the Clovis Belle, several soldiers boarded to verify everyone was off. They then relieved the crew of all weapons, including knives and the various slave collar keys the crew had in their custody.

A corporal asked each crew member his name, which the sergeant checked against his list. One of the boiler room laborers' name caused the sergeant to order the laborer seized. Captain Dalporto watched from the upper walkway outside the door to the pilothouse.

The heredity of the skinny laborer was a mix of Clovis-Prussian. Rex knew he was a Clovis Belle employee, but otherwise knew nothing about him. The man was protesting strongly that they had the wrong Cisman. He was Art, not his thieving cousin, Ray. A loud gunshot ended laborer's protest. One of the Ichneumon soldiers, stationed behind the lined-up crew, had stepped up and shot Art in the back of his head. As he collapsed on the wharf, the sergeant with the list nodded his head. The corporal then asked Rex his name.

"Ron Wilhelm," Rex answered, hoping there was no Ron Wilhelm on the list. His ears ringing from the gunshot, he shuffled to the left to avoid Art's pooling blood. The sergeant checked his list, pausing to study him for a moment, before telling the corporal to move on. Kyle Baler was next and his name wasn't on the list.

The prisoners arrived a few minutes later as the sergeant finished with his list. Twelve of the uninjured Prussian prisoners carried six stretchers with the badly injured prisoners. One of the prisoners carrying a stretcher was Tom Jarrell. Rex needed to get one of the collar keys to Tom and warn him.

Rex figured the Ichneumon officer's plan was to chain the men carrying the stretchers together as soon as they laid down their burden. The Ichneumons had already formed the other ten prisoners into two groups of five prisoners chained together by two-meter lengths of chain hooked to their neck collars. Those prisoners also had their hands tied behind their back and had shuffled along behind the group with the stretchers. Gray Slater and Colonel Fritz were in the last group of five prisoners.

The Ichneumon captain's nametag said Bezel. He watched the crew as the prisoners limped by and stopped at the gangway. Rex figured the captain was checking for any sign of recognition between a crew member and a prisoner. Apparently satisfied, the captain asked the first mate to step forth. Rex stepped out of the lineup.

"First mate, tell two of your crew to carry those collars and chains to the deck. While they do that, show my men the lower front hole."

Rex assigned Kyle and Jeremy to that task before taking the smaller corporal to the front cargo hole. Both Kyle and Jeremy had one of the keys General Mehta had given Rex.

"Put the stretchers on the stern deck," Bezel ordered as Rex left with the corporal and two Ichneumon guards.

"The door doesn't have a lock." The Ichneumon corporal didn't like the cell setup.

"Captain Dalporto figured with the prisoner chains anchored to the timbers, there was no need for a costly lock," Rex said.

The fresh cut planking used to build the door and benches gave the hole a fragrant piney scent. The construction was solid, the eyebolt anchors for the chains unyielding. Still the difficult corporal didn't like the arrangement and went to discuss the matter with the sergeant. Rex hurried to the stern.

Captain Bezel and the sergeant were supervising the chaining of the stretcher-bearers together before marching them to the lower front cell. Rex heard the sergeant tell the corporal not to worry about the door lock and get busy putting the prisoners in the cell.

"First mate," the captain yelled, "Get those wagons unloaded before our bags get soaked." A misty cold drizzle had started. Kyle winked, which Rex hoped meant he had been successful in passing a key to Tom.

Three mule-drawn wagons had arrived, two with the Ichneumons' luggage and one stacked with rations. Rex had three of the crew help carry the wagon cargo aboard the Clovis Belle as the corporal and two soldiers yelled at the prisoners to get up.

241

Rex realized that unless the prisoners' hands were untied, a key wouldn't help. They needed a knife, which Rex didn't have on him.

"The crew's loading firewood. Can some of the prisoners help?" Rex asked. The captain looked to the sergeant, who nodded.

"Use that last group while we get the rest of them locked down," Captain Bezel said. He pointed at the group Fritz and Staler were in. "And get the bags first, I don't want my uniforms to get wet."

"You heard the captain, corporal," Rex said. "Free their hands so the lazy bastards can do some honest work."

A couple of the Prussian prisoners, marines from their looks, refused to get up for the corporal. Rex grabbed their collars and non-too gently jerked them to their feet so the corporal could cut the bindings. The Ichneumon captain had noticed their scuffle, so Rex smacked the two marines hard in the face to reduce Bezel's suspicion.

"Don't give me any of your guff," Rex screamed. The younger marine lunged at him, trying to reach his neck. He batted away the attempt and gut punched the man. As the Prussian gasped for breath, he added, "Now get to work, enough horsing around."

Fritz grabbed the largest bag and had trouble getting it on his shoulder. Rex helped position the heavy bag on Fritz's shoulder and then handed a bag to the still woozy marine.

"Move it, get the bags to the upper deck. The corporal will show you which cabin the bag goes in."

The Ichneumon guards had commandeered all the upper cabins for their use during the trip to Port Delta. Afterward, Rex used the prisoners to load the rations, for the most part, bags of ground corn, rice, and brown beans. The bags went to the mess area in front of the boilers and over the front lower hole with the prisoners.

Sunset was about an hour away, and Rex knew Dalporto wanted to head down the river before dark. Topping off the coal and firewood bins would have been nice, but he decided not to take the time. The Ichneumon warship, Saukko, could arrive at any time. A bigger concern was the weather, a cold drizzle had set in and the prisoners on the stretchers had no protection. After finishing with the rations, Rex asked Captain Bezel where the crew should place the stretchers.

"They're not your concern," the Ichneumon said. "Your concern is getting the boat underway."

Rex was all for that and told the crew to bring the ramps in and went to the pilothouse. Worried about the weather, he asked Captain Dalporto his understanding concerning where the injured prisoners where to be kept.

"They're no use to the Ichneumons," Dalporto said. "I expect Bezel and his thugs plan to throw them over board tonight."

"You're serious. They'd do that?"

Dalporto nodded. "Look what the murderous bastards did to Art."

"Well then, here's what we're going to do . . . ."

Emperor Wolfgang Schnabel's morning had been uneventful and he was relaxing with Bishop Hildegard von Bingen in the secured office where the Privy Council met. No public ceremonies that required formal attire and wearing the royal jewels and crown were scheduled. One private meeting with his spymaster and a representative from the Wapiti tribe was scheduled.

After that meeting, Wolfgang planned to make a surprise visit to the warehouse district north of Berlin. With a new Ichneumon war flaring up in the western territories, he wanted to be certain the Empire's niter inventories were sufficient to meet both the agriculture and military needs. In the past, if he had even thought of the commonplace commodity, let alone been worried about the sufficiency of its inventory, he would have asked General Von Moltke of the Prussian General Staff. Today, he'd visit Bayer's powder works and see for himself.

The above-the-fray management style of Wolfgang's father wasn't working. As emperor, he needed no one's approval to issue a decree. However, he had learned a command without proper implementation and follow-up, often made the problem worse. The current antislavery law was an example. It had caused turmoil and erosion of support for the Imperial rule throughout the Guderian and Myrtle territories without ending slavery. He needed a new strategy that would address the concerns of the plantation owners without gutting his antislavery imperative. Perhaps his new spymaster would have a suggestion.

A more intractable issue was how to replace the compromised and incompetent department heads embedded throughout the vast bureaucracy of the Prussian Empire. They needed replaced with capable and honest people. The bogus navel order disaster was proof that a close blood tie to the royal family wasn't enough to ensure protection from malfeasance. Wolfgang knew the personnel problem was bigger than any emperor could ever hope to eliminate, but he intended to try.

Joachim Hansen, Prussia's new spymaster, was an example. A number of senators had asked him why he had chosen the commoner. Wolfgang had picked the man because he had no taint of corruption in a position notorious for bribery and favoritism. That the territorial governors and their henchmen hated the Roanoke IRS manager he had considered an additional endorsement.

"I'd like to stay and hear what the Wapiti lawyer has to say," Bishop Hildegard von Bingen said. The sergeant at arms had just announced Herr Hansen and Fraulein Smith. Wolfgang nodded as he stood and motioned for them to enter.

"Emperor Schnabel, may I present Tara Smith?" Joe Hansen asked. "She is the attorney representing the Wapiti tribe's request for a Prussian territory designation."

Wolfgang had heard stories about the beautiful Wapiti women and the one in front of his desk was a fine-looking lady. She was a lean tall woman with a dusty complexion, raven hair, and emerald eyes, a gift from her rebellious York ancestors. The attorney wore an attractive dark two-button pantsuit and looked professional. He introduced the bishop and then inquired if they'd like a cup of coffee, tea, or mineral water.

"You're very young, Fraulein. Where did you earn your law degree?" Bishop Hildegard von Bingen asked. An aide served refreshments.

Wolfgang was wondering the same thing. The Prussian bar association was resisting the licensing of female lawyers. That the territorial courts were already allowing women lawyers surprised him.

"My bachelor of arts degree was from the Jesuit School in Roanoke," the fräulein answered. "The Guderian license was from passing the bar exam."

"Several women have earned their law license in the territorial courts," Joe said. "Suzie Penton received her license just before we left for Berlin. She makes four female attorneys."

"Is she any relation to the Penton cotton interest in Myrtle?" Wolfgang asked.

"Yes, your majesty, her father is Harlem Penton." To the emperor's unasked question, Joe added. "She, like her father, is an opponent of your antislavery law."

"What about you, Fraulein Smith? Are you opposed to the antislavery law?" Wolfgang asked.

"Your majesty, I and most Wapiti support and approve of your efforts to eliminate slavery," she answered. "Our complaint is with the territorial authorities' tepid enforcement of the law."

"I know you're here on behalf of the Wapiti request to become a Prussian territory," the Emperor said. "Give me a brief summary of the key points in their request."

"Existing property deeds and contracts issued by the Wapiti Chief Council remain valid. Wapiti have the same rights and responsibilities as citizens in other Prussian territories. The western boundary of the new territory is the Erie River. The other boundaries are the current York, Guderian, and Myrtle territorial boundaries. All council property becomes the new territory's property. That's the request's key points your majesty," Tara said.

"The Wapiti understand their new responsibilities would include paying Prussian taxes and serving in the military?" Wolfgang asked. She answered yes.

Emperor Schnabel looked to Bishop Hildegard, who shrugged his shoulders, and Joe Hansen, who smiled.

"Fraulein Smith, I'm aware the Minister of Territories, von Siemen, has been stonewalling your request, and I will speak with him. Submit your request to him, two days from now, and then head home. A war is breaking out in the Erie Valley. I want you to give your chiefs' council a message. Their helpfulness to the Prussian army in the coming war against Ichneumons will be the main factor I use to decide on whether or not to accept their territory request."

"I understand perfectly and assure you the Wapiti will stand tall with the Prussians. Thank you for listening." Tara said. The Wapiti lawyer then curtseyed and walked out the office.

"Joe what have you learned on those Delta orders that caused the admiral to abandon Delta?" The emperor asked as he watched the handsome lawyer leave.

"There was an interesting development," Joe said. "Major Lyons has admitted taking money from a stranger to change the Zamia blockade orders. Said he would have done it for no money if he had thought of it. He hates Zamians."

The bishop asked why.

"No rational reason, he thinks they're animals and making them useful slaves is best for them, the usual racist nonsense," Joe said. "Lyons claimed no knowledge of the Delta orders until the day after the archduke paid him a visit."

"When was that visit?" The emperor asked.

"It was the evening prior to you sacking him. Now the major claims to have changed both the blockade and Delta navy orders for money paid by Sanita Chopra."

"Chopra, the Ichneumon agent?" Wolfgang asked. "How could a spy as notorious as Chopra operate in Berlin? Your department needs new blood."

"There was another visitor that I think explains the major's sudden remembrance of Chopra's involvement," Joe said. "Levi Ottoman spent an hour with the archduke that last afternoon and went with the archduke to visit Lyons."

"I know Ottoman," the emperor said. Joe looked surprised. Wolfgang had met Levi Ottoman at a Bayer conference on explosives. "The man is a business partner of Benjamin Purnell and trafficked in acids."

Joe nodded.

"So Purnell is involved?" the emperor asked.

"I believe so. No one expected that explosion of the fort's magazines or Colonel Markel's daring seizure."

"General Markel now," Wolfgang said. "If I've got the chronological order of events right, the Delta explosion occurred a few days after the slave ships had delivered those hundreds of Zamia slaves."

"Yes and Admiral Wilhelm believed our fleet had no legal right to interfere with the slavers disembarking their cargo of human misery," Joe said. The emperor shook his head as his new spymaster added. "The admiral knew about the blockade of the Zamia coast, you would have thought he would have realized something was a miss."

"For sure Wilhelm's alarm bells should have gone off on receiving new navy orders from a businessman with known Ichneumon dealings, no matter, how plausible the tale."

"Purnell and the cotton growers' big investments in slaves were worthless if Delta was under Prussian rule," Joe said. "That was the reason for those bogus Delta orders." The emperor and bishop both nodded.

An army messenger had been waiting at the Privy Council door. Wolfgang told his new spymaster to deal with the messenger and asked Bishop Hildegard for his opinion on whether Purnell was in league with the Ichneumons.

The messenger handed over the message and Joe signed for it. As the man left, Joe opened and read the message, *"My God, the Ichneumons sank the Schlesien!"*

Captain Dalporto had advised the Ichneumons would disarm the crew and Rex had arranged a weapon cache before docking. He told the Clovis Belle crew to hide their best weapons about the steamboat and carry the older ball-and-cap revolvers. Sound advice, the Ichneumons had been thorough in their disarming of the Clovis Belle crew. The soldiers had confiscated all their firearms, knives, and collar keys.

Between Kyle, Rex, and the two Slater brothers, they owned seven of the latest Walters five-shot revolvers chambered for the new waterproof 9x19mm brass cartridge. Rex had hidden those revolvers, along with sharp knives, in strategic locations around the Clovis Belle.

The front lower cargo hole of the Clovis Belle was a dark damp space used for barrel storage. Captain Dalporto believed the Ichneumon soldiers would approve use of the room for their prison if they added benches with eyebolts to anchor the prisoners' chains. The one opening to access the cell had a rough-cut wood frame. Rex added a door.

The beam forming the top of the doorframe created a dark ledge above the opening. One of the Walters revolvers was wedged in the space. The gun location whispered to Fritz when Rex passed him the collar key while helping him hoist the bag earlier.

Kyle and the two Slater brothers were in the boiler room waiting for the cook to finish the Ichneumon's meal. Jeremy and Andrew Slater would carry the food to the upper conference room that the Ichneumons planned to use for their mess hall.

"Where is everyone?" Rex asked as he went to the coal bin and recovered his two revolvers.

"The sergeant and three guards went upstairs to clean up for dinner," Kyle said. On seeing Rex retrieving his weapons, Kyle and the Slaters started pulled their guns from various hiding spots around the engine and boiler rooms. He added.

"The captain and another guard went to check on the injured prisoners."

"Where's that corporal?" Rex asked. No one knew, though Andrew thought he might have gone to the front prisoner cell.

"Dalporto thinks they're planning to throw the wounded overboard at dark," Rex said. They all looked out of the boiler room door and could see the sun was about set.

"At sunset, he'll reverse the portside drive to put the boat in a spin, which should distract the Ichneumons. He'll claim the linkage failed if we're not successful in winning the boat."

Slater brothers were tense and rechecked their revolvers by opening the guns' cylinders to verify all the slots contained a cartridge. Kyle looked happy as he checked the shotgun barrels were clear. He planned to use the double-barreled shotgun for the initial assault and then switch to his revolver.

"Kyle, take Andrew and deal with the sergeant and his men," Rex said. "Let's not wait on Dalporto. I don't trust that Ichneumon captain with the wounded. It's raining and that fastidious bastard has been out in it. Something's not right. Jeremy, come with me, we'll deal with the captain."

"That still leaves the corporal, what about him?" Kyle asked.

"The corporal we'll deal with when we find him," Rex said. They all heard the faint scream from the stern. "Go, get the sergeant. We'll deal with the captain."

They stopped to allow Kyle time to reach the upper deck. After hearing them on the upper deck, Rex jogged to the stern where he found two Ichneumon soldiers lifting a stretcher over the handrail and a man begging them to not. The captain was to one side watching. Two of the stretchers were missing.

"Halt, new orders," Rex screamed.

The soldiers stopped, holding the stretcher that was rocking on the handrail, balanced and posed to fall either way, into the dark river or back on the deck. Captain Bezel whipped around to see who had hollered. Shots from the upper deck caused the captain to look up. Rex shot him in the forehead. Then the Clovis Belle suddenly lurched as the port wheel reversed.

The stretcher balanced on the handrail sailed into the dark as several more gunshots rang out from the upper walkway. The two soldiers reached for their revolver as the turning boat made them stumble. Jeremy shot them multiple times, as Rex ran to the handrail to check on the stretcher and wounded man. The way the Clovis Belle had turned meant the boat's paddlewheel had probably run over the unlucky man. No sign remained of the stretcher or the man.

The rain and pitch-black night made a search futile. Even if Rex had seen a sign of the stretcher or the man, he doubted he could have marshaled the courage to jump in that freezing, dark, eel-infested river. He went to check on Kyle.

The Ichneumon sergeant had managed to snap off one shot that had hit Andrew in the leg before Kyle killed the sergeant. The other two Ichneumon soldiers were dead before they fully realized what was occurring.

"Kyle, go to the pilot house and tell Captain Dalporto to stop turning," Rex said. "Jeremy, help your brother and keep your guard up. I'm going after the corporal."

When Rex arrived, Tom Jarrell and Fritz were in the hallway outside the front hole with the missing corporal. The Ichneumon was on his knees with his hands tied behind his back. The Prussian prisoners still in the front hole were busy unlocking their slave collars when the Clovis Belle stopped going in circles.

"Fritz, organize some men to bring the surviving stretcher cases to the upper cabin room," Rex said. "Tom, the Ichneumon captain is back on the stern. Strip him and find someone his uniform will fit. I think the sergeant's uniform would fit you, but his's a mess. Look in their bags, I need several Ichneumon soldiers."

"What about him?" Tom asked, pointing at the trembling corporal.

"Chain him to an eyebolt. I might need him." Rex then jogged to the pilothouse.

Captain Dalporto was ecstatic. "My God, you saved my boat. Where are we headed, to Westport, some side cove to hide?"

"We're going to River Point. In fact, head back up the river."

"We can't, Hickory Ridge is between us," the captain said, alarmed. "No way can we sneak by the fort, not even in this rain and darkness."

"Do you know the Ichneumon flag semaphore code used between ships or ship to shore?" Rex asked.

"Of course I know. You can't get a rating on ocean going vessels without knowing the flags," Dalporto said.

"I figure we're about an hour below Hickory Ridge," Rex said. "In a half hour I want the Clovis Belle glowing, light all the lamps.

Kyle will run the pilothouse. You need to get the signal lamp. It's too dark for flags."

"You're crazy, they'll blow us out of the river," Dalporto said. He was getting red in the face. "Even at full power, the Clovis Belle needs four to five minutes to clear all those batteries."

"The message you'll send is from Captain Bezel, who will be standing with you, along with several armed Ichneumon soldiers. It'll read, 'In hot pursuit as per Saukko's Captain Chetan orders. Expect Saukko's arrival.'"

Dalporto, looking perplexed, asked Rex to repeat the message. He did and then asked the captain, "Can you send that?"

"Sure, but what does it mean, pursuit of who? Why would they believe it?"

"That's precisely the point. What does it mean? It'd take a bold gunnery sergeant to ignore a message from who he believes is an Ichneumon officer and fire."

"General Mehta will know it's nonsense," Dalporto countered.

"Maybe, but the fort is expecting the Saukko, it's late at night, and raining. Getting word to the general and his decision back will take time. We'll be clear the fort's field of fire before that happens, unless your boat breaks down."

The gall, the brazenness of that woman and those Wapiti warriors had astonished Benjamin Purnell. Maybe the bitch was his by-blow. Regardless he could not ignore the affront to his authority and that explained why the Orleans Boat Works manager, Herr Dunlap, was trembling in front of his desk.

"You're telling me she shot Razo and Jesse? Why the hell didn't they shoot her?" Purnell asked.

"I . . ., I don't know," Dunlap said.

"And you just allowed them to take all those machines, and pipe, and rivets, and steel plates, hell even the new steam engine that was still in its crate?"

"I didn't allow them, they stole that," the manager said.

"They stole all of it, you fool."

"They had purchase orders for everything. The paperwork looked correct. The captain was an Ichneumon. Who would ever expect him to be working with Wapiti pirates?"

Purnell had to agree. Using Captain Malik, as their front man, was a clever ploy. Still someone had to pay for this insult.

"Take this thief to the wharf and hang him," Purnell told the guards. The wailing old man was dragged way. "You stay," he told the sheriff.

Louis Stelzer, who was Orleans' sheriff, had been in Berlin with Levi Ottoman ensuring the archduke provided the alibi for the bogus navy orders.

"I want you to question all the boat works employees and weed out anyone whose loyalty is in doubt," Purnell said. "But first, replace the policemen who were on duty at the boat yard on the day of the raid."

"Just replace them?" Sheriff Stelzer asked.

"Good point, hang them with Dunlap."

The hammering on the locked bedroom door woke the businessman, and then enraged him. Such disrespectful conduct was unprecedented. The bastard pounding on his door would learn proper submissiveness at the whipping post.

"Stop that banging," Purnell shouted as he searched for his revolver in the nightstand.

Instead, another solid bang split the door and it flew open, allowing two large Prussian marines, holding double-barrel shotguns, and a Prussian colonel to rush into the bedroom.

"General Markel requires your attendance at the main wharf," the young infantry colonel said.

The gun forgotten, Purnell, stunned by the armed soldiers presence, just stared, prompting an angry "Now," from the Prussian officer. Something had gone terribly wrong and without further delay or comment, he quickly dressed.

By the early dawn light, Purnell could see the Prussian warship, Rhine Mar, at the wharf. The armored sidewheeler showed numerous holes and pockmarks from heavy gunfire. Most of the rear smokestack and all of the port paddlewheel cover were missing. Sheriff Stelzer and several grim-faced Prussian army and naval officers were in a group by the gallows where a bound Herr Dunlap waited on the platform with several bound policemen. More alarming, he could see several Prussian sailors on the Aruba.

"Herr Purnell, I'm declaring martial law in Orleans." the Prussian officer wearing the general's uniform said. There had been no introductions.

"And who might you be?" Purnell asked the officer.

"I'm General Markel. I'm also commandeering the Aruba while repairs are made to Rhine Mar."

"Emperor Schnabel will hear of this outrageous conduct. Orleans has always been a loyal Prussian port. I have always supported the Prussian navy. Martial law is uncalled for."

"Then how fortunate, you're going to Berlin," the general said. "Herr Hanson has requested your presence and I'm sure he could arrange a meeting for you with the emperor." The general then ordered a captain to release the prisoners on the scaffolding.

The Prussian's audacity left Purnell speechless. The general noticed he hadn't moved, and added. "The Aruba is embarking in two hours. I'd suggest you spend the time packing and arranging your affairs. Colonel, take several guards and assist him."

Purnell wondered if he should attempt escaping overland to Port Delta. The Ichneumons would protect him.

The news of the Wapiti convoy on the Erie River and steaming toward River Point brought every resident within several kilometers to the wharf area on the Southern River side. Several hundred Wapiti, Prussians, and Clovis, ranging from babies in their mother's arms to elderly people crowded the wintry waterfront. The commander of River Point, Matt Brewer had organized a corridor of soldiers to hold the crowd of spectators away from the wharf. Half the soldiers were Captain Beck's marines.

Colonel Leibinger went to Matt, who was standing on the wharf. Only one steamboat stopped. Leibinger recognized it was one of those small ThyssenKrupp boats made in Essen and used by harbor police everywhere. How one ended up in this wilderness, the colonel figured, would be quite a tale. The two other steamboats were loaded with what appeared to be heavy machine tools and barrels.

"Where are those boats going?" the colonel asked.

"We'll find out in a moment," Matt said as a wolf limped off the docking boat. "Hokee, you survived." The animal looked toward Matt, and after a moment, with its tail wagging, hobbled to his out stretched arms.

The injured wolf and Matt were old friends. He then watched a beautiful Island woman walking down the gangway. She paused to holler at the wolf who had discovered a cage of rabbits on the dock to behave, before walking over to them. The woman was Amy Caroom and she filled them in on Rex's perilous ruse to free the prisoners.

A steam whistle blast caused everyone to look down the Erie. Another steamboat was plowing up the river at a fast pace.

"That's the Clovis Belle," Amy yelled. "They made it by the fort." She was jumping and waving. Even dour Matt was waving.

Leibinger spotted Colonel Caprivi and Captain Beck among the passengers, many of whom looked like Prussian sailors and marines. He didn't see Captain Bromberg, the emperor's nephew. He learned later that Bromberg had been one of the wounded men the Ichneumons had thrown overboard before Rex and the Wapiti seized control of the Clovis Belle and stopped the slaughter.

That evening Rex and Amy went to her Smithtown home with the attached lab. Hokee spent the night in the lab by the stove while Rex spent his in Amy's delightful bed. That night a bitter cold front moved in, and by morning, the freeze had iced over the Southern River. In a few days, the cold weather would freeze a layer of solid ice on the Erie River, stopping all riverboat traffic above Hickory Ridge until spring. By the end of the month, the solid ice would reach Westport, putting any Ichneumon reprisals on hold until the spring thaw.

Caroom's Raid

Nitro Wild

Nitro Wild continues the chronicle of a modern man endeavoring to survive on an alternate earth of 19th century technology, slavery, and completing colonial empires. Rex Knight, an Afghan War veteran, has been mysteriously teleported from a peaceful surveying project in West Virginia to the semi-lawless Appalachia on Erden where the Prussian and Ichneumon Empires are vying for dominance. Endangered by the clashing empires are Rex's friends, the indigenous Wapiti and an escaped slave, Amy Caroom who is, among other things, his partner in a river steamboat and a machine shop.

The Ichneumon army is poised to ravage the Wapiti homeland when the winter ends. The Prussians are willing to help the Wapiti, but lack to means to stop the Ichneumon armored riverboats with their new exploding shells. Complicating matters for the Prussian army is the threat of rebellion by the slave owners in their territories over the emperor's edict outlawing slavery. Rumors of a coup d'état in Berlin are rampant. The Mongol Empire of Prussia's eastern border is mad over the stopping of the slave trade and threaten invasion. The Ichneumons sense opportunity to deal their rival a knockout blow. Their army will help the rebellious plantation owners seize control of the Prussian territories along with the Wapiti homeland.

Rex will need all his wits, shrewdness, audacity, and even duplicity to survive.